ALSO BY ISSY BROOKE

The Lady C Investigates Series
An Unmourned Man
Riots and Revelations
In The House of Secrets and Lies
Daughters of Disguise
The Continental Gentleman

The Investigations of Marianne Starr
The Willing Game
The Talking Board
The Murdering Ghose

MURDER AT MONDIAL CASTLE

The Discreet Investigations of Lord and Lady Calaway
Book One

ISSY BROOKE

ENGLAND, 1893

1

The servants, much like sensitive people or dogs before a thunderstorm, could tell when an explosion of emotion from the Earl of Calaway was imminent and they would melt away into the back corridors and distant rooms of Thringley House. It wasn't that they expected an outburst of violent fury or untrammelled rage directed at them; it was simply that any outpouring of passions from the usually cool Earl was so uncommon and unpredictable that no one wanted to be any part of it.

Only one small maid, new to service, hid behind a tall cabinet containing specimens of rare poisonous snails, and watched as the family solicitor inched into the breakfast room. He knew he was entering the scene of a storm which he himself would soon create. The maid, peeking around the snails, was so raw and green that she didn't even question the presence of natural history objects in the otherwise pleasant room. Starting her career in the strange surroundings of Thringley House was going to make her quite numb to any future eccentricities her next employers might have. If she made it that far; these snails,

Conus geographus, had killed at least two collectors.

But at least they were safely behind glass, unlike Lord Calaway.

The family solicitor came to a halt. Mr Postlethwaite's ancestors had all been in the legal profession. Their family tree was made up entirely of judges, magistrates, lawyers, commissioners and solicitors. Over the generations, these dusty, soft-spoken men of the bar had moved through life on a course parallel to the ancient Caxton family that held acres of land around the large village of Thringley. As the Caxtons had moved up in the world, gathering titles and status from the time of the Norman conquest and onwards, the Postlethwaites had been there too, alongside the great family, preparing the documents, arranging the deals, and offering quiet, careful advice.

But the Mr Postlethwaite that now quivered on the rucked-up rug of the breakfast room was the current patriarch's son, and he was twenty years younger than the Earl he faced.

And he brought very bad news.

The Earl of Calaway did not look at his wife. He knew that Adelia would be glaring at him. After all, she *had* warned him where things would end if he insisted on pursuing his so-called "ridiculous" dreams. He didn't want to see her pursed lips or face her silent righteousness so instead, he barked out, "Girl! Yes, you, behind the snails. Go and … do something in the kitchen."

He didn't need to look at the place where the maid was hiding. He knew she had been there all along; he always knew what was happening around him. He prided himself on his observational skills. And shouting at servants was probably better than shouting at the family solicitor. She was sturdier. Mr Postlethwaite would fall over if a strong draught came through a window.

"*Don't* shout. It's not like you. And anyway she's a housemaid, dear," Adelia said, turning to smile kindly at the maid who could not see her mistress's gentle expression as she was scurrying out with her eyes fixed on the floor. "She doesn't *do* the kitchen. I think she was only here on account of the rug."

The Earl flared his nostrils. He'd observed the maid but, as usual, had missed the wider point. No matter. He'd be tempted to send Adelia out, too, if he dared. But of course, he didn't dare. Thirty years of marriage to this remarkable woman had taught him many things, and self-preservation was one of them. She wasn't a tyrant. It was just that she was usually right about things – and he respected that.

Mr Postlethwaite the younger continued to tremble in front of them. He refused all of Adelia's invitations to join them for a restrained breakfast of eggs and toast. He clutched a thick yellow sheet of paper in his hands, folded so that the text could not be seen.

The Earl thought that he could guess what it said, at least roughly. It would be one more letter of complaint, or perhaps another of those scurrilous posters that had popped up in the local area. Maybe it was the third or fourth frankly libellous cartoon that the press delighted in printing. Last week, a woman had screamed at him in the street. Actually screamed. She had used words that would have upset the roughest of his farm labourers. The situation was becoming intolerable. Something had to be done.

He didn't know what.

But he was not a man to let uncertainty get in the way of a rash decision. He blinked. Why wasn't Mr Postlethwaite speaking?

Adelia sighed. "Mr Postlethwaite, please tell us what concerns you today."

Oh yes, that was it. The Earl hadn't invited him to speak, that was why the man stayed silent.

"My Lady, my Lord. Ah. I am sorry to report a potentially injurious development in the, ah ... the *matter*."

The Earl still would not look at Adelia. He thought, I'm in for it now. She warned me. She's not going to remind me that she warned me. She knows that I know. She'll be silently right, damn it. Why did I marry a clever woman?

"Injurious?" he said to the solicitor. "Has someone challenged me to a duel? That would be an amusing diversion." He tried to laugh.

"At which you'd lose," Adelia said. He could hear her soften the remark with a smile curving the words upwards. "Please, Mr Postlethwaite, speak plainly. You have known us for long enough."

Mr Postlethwaite unfolded the paper and slid it onto the table. "Mrs Duncan Cosslett is pressing charges. And unlike the ... the *others,* she has the money to do so, and the energy to do so, and the ..."

"Spite," finished the Earl. "She is a woman driven almost entirely by spite. I cannot imagine what else might be affecting her to cause her to take against me with such passion."

"Perhaps it was the loss of her husband?" Adelia put in. It wasn't that the Earl was an unfeeling man; it was just that he

10

sometimes lacked the capacity to understand that others might also feel things. So she had told him on many occasions, he reflected.

"Yes, well, as to that bereavement," Mr Postlethwaite continued, "she has sought the medical opinion of a certain doctor of Harley Street and he is convinced that you could have managed the case in a different way."

"You mean I could have stopped the chap from dying?" the Earl said. "Hardly. His liver had gone, his kidneys had gone; the poor fellow hadn't passed water in a week. He was either going to die or he was going to go pop. Nasty business, either way, don't you think?"

He risked a glance sideways and saw Adelia wince. "This is what we have talked about before," she said in a low tone. "Your bedside manner is what is lacking, not your medical skill."

"My medical knowledge is second to none. My bedside manner should have no part in the considerations."

He was sure that a look then passed between Mr Postlethwaite and his wife. He pursed his lips. But they didn't understand; he *knew* he was good at what he did. He spoke plainly to his patients and did not fudge the issues that they were facing. What would be the point of that? He had no truck with half-truths and empty platitudes, and yet here he was, the target for every malcontent in the area who had ever fallen ill and had recourse to the Earl's care.

It baffled him. He knew, as an Earl, he was the most unusual doctor most people had ever met. That was one reason that he spoke bluntly to them. He did not want to seem lofty or unapproachable. But Adelia often told him that he was not meant

11

to be a doctor, or at least, not the sort that people would turn to if they needed soothing.

She was wrong, he was sure of it. She wasn't usually wrong but about this, she was. She had to be. He couldn't bear the thought of the alternatives. And he *was* a feeling man, he thought fiercely. He *felt* he had to be a doctor. It was his only link to his father – his only real emotional link. The title? The earldom? That could go hang.

He was not meant to be an earl – now, that was a different matter. He had not been raised to inherit the lands or the main title. He had been content enough to go through life as mere Mr Theodore Caxton, and didn't even use the family's subsidiary titles to which he could lay claim, Viscount this, Viscount that, honourable the other. He let his older brother do the aristocratic thing in society while he happily sank into his studies. He quickly mastered all the main branches of science and mathematics and, to everyone's shock and horror, planned from a young age to become a doctor.

They told him that it was not appropriate, of course. Even without inheriting the Earldom, it was simply *not done*. Perhaps lower ranks could indulge themselves in such dalliances – if he had been a baron, perhaps – but the son of an earl, even the second son, ranked highly and had other, more serious duties.

But Theodore was a single-minded sort of man. He didn't want to become a doctor in order to rebel against his position and spite others, or to prove that he was better than anyone else, or anything else of that ilk. He simply saw the act of saving another's life as the very noblest thing that one could do.

To be a doctor was a *calling*.

As a small boy, he had watched his father grow ill. Nothing had helped ease the man's suffering. Every treatment and every innovation failed him. Then a young, jovial country doctor had been called in and whatever he did, he did it well. The young Theodore had listened at doors and watched from corners and had seen how the doctor had the very power of life and death over the man who was most dear to him.

His father recovered.

That young doctor had done something with science and knowledge that money and power could not do. He had given life to the old man. He had given Theodore his father back.

So Theodore had pursued his dream in spite of the naysayers and he had eventually qualified, scandalously, as a doctor.

But he had only been in practice for a very short time when everything had been destroyed. His father finally passed away of natural causes, and not long after that, Theodore's elder brother was killed in a carriage accident.

Theodore Caxton then found himself unexpectedly as the Earl of Calaway, with a frail young wife and a boisterous son, Bamfylde. He put his medical practise aside and shouldered all the duties of his title, a burden which grew even heavier when his wife died soon after the deaths of his father and his brother. For a while, life went very wrong. He made choices that were, in hindsight, ill ones. He made mistakes that he preferred to forget.

Those mistakes did not seem to want to forget him, however.

Still, nearly thirty years had passed since those dark times. The world had changed. His life had changed. A new wife, Adelia, and the births of seven daughters over a span of ten years had

13

turned everything upside down, in the very best of ways.

That was until six months ago, when he had found himself in a position to take up medicine once more. His youngest daughter had finally married and left, and the house was echoing and empty, and his life was his own once more. His duties and responsibilities had been passed on to his seven sons-in-law. He had seized the chance, dusted off his leather bag of medical implements and strode out of Thringley House and into the local area armed with all the largesse of his position and the zeal of a modern aristocrat who wanted to use his power for good, expecting to be feted and celebrated or at the very least, cordially welcomed.

Not slapped with potential lawsuits.

He suddenly sat up straight. Mr Postlethwaite and his wife were talking. She took the yellow paper from Mr Postlethwaite and he backed away, murmuring a litany of apologies and explanations and daring, in a few short words, to offer some suggestions, although the suggestions were mainly "Please stop trying to be a doctor" wrapped up in flowery obscure language.

The solicitor slipped out of the room before either the Earl or Adelia had chance to ring the bell for a footman. It didn't matter. Mr Postlethwaite knew his way out and if he was lucky, he'd be waylaid by the butler who would entice him to his cosy office on the ground floor. There, the butler would ply the solicitor with pilfered brandy to ease any juicy secrets out of him. It wasn't worth stopping that little play; sometimes those secrets found their way back to the ears of Adelia and many a potential scandal had been nipped in the bud by the understanding and machinations of his wife.

Theodore sat back in his chair and tapped his long fingers on the table, agitated. Adelia read the official letter and glanced up at him, a look from under her lowered lids that reminded him of the girl he'd met three decades previously. She had told him some hard home truths back then, and saved him from a steady slide into dissolution. In gratitude and genuine love, he'd married her. For fear of how his life would unravel without her, he had stayed loyal to her ever since.

He knew he had to listen to her now.

He pre-empted her advice by saying, "Yes, yes, I know. It is a difficult situation but one, I am sure, which can be resolved amicably."

She threw the paper down and shook her head, smiling ruefully. "You're simply going to have to pay them a great deal of money and stay out of sight for a while."

"Pay them to go away, do you mean?"

"Pay them to stop their silly campaign – and I mean for *you* to go away."

"You're sending me away from my own house?"

She laughed. "We ought to be in London anyway. We left far too early."

"We shouldn't have gone to London at all. We don't need to any more. You know how I feel about the season. It's a waste of money and time. All one does is parade oneself around like a prize cow being offered for sale at an auction."

"We are both far too old to be considered any kind of prize, livestock or otherwise. But I'll concede you did your bit when you were called upon – for our daughters' sakes." Every one of the seven was now well married to a range of significant men.

Theodore said, "In a few weeks' time I could go up to Scotland. That will get me away."

"You've never wanted to take part in the grouse hunting before."

"No, and I shan't do so this time. Far too flappy. And all that striding through wet heather. Dogs, everywhere, licking your hands when you least expect it. But there are always injuries to attend to. Whisky and guns do not mix."

"Theodore, my dear heart, my rock, my captain, my most well-beloved," Adelia said. "Listen to me. You *must* give up medicine, at least, in the manner in which you are currently trying to practise it. There is much to be done in the field of research. We have the space here to build laboratories! There are many advances you could make if you dedicated yourself to the study of diseases. Think of the lives you might save if you apply your intellect to rooting out the causes of illness!"

Theodore knew that she was trying to mollify him. "It is not the same," he protested. "To me, a real doctor is there at the patient's side, extending a hand in the very darkest of times." Like Doctor Hardy had done.

"But you don't extend a hand, dear heart. You sit there and you give them a list of the very worst things to expect, cheerfully outlining the details of their case, and they promptly expire in fright."

"No one can die of fright. It has been proven."

"Mrs Duncan Cosslett would disagree. As would the family of that young labouring lad, Jem Irving. As would Mr Benson the butcher. As would…"

"Adelia, please. No one likes to be reminded of their

16

failings. Although of course, these weren't exactly failings."

"What, do you think that it isn't your fault? You think that the patient is simply too silly to put their mind to a decent recovery?"

"I didn't mean that." But he was beaten and he knew it. "I shall go to Scotland," he said wearily. He thought about midges and rain and tweed, and grimaced. There would be enthusiastic Labradors. He would hate it.

Adelia smiled. She rang the bell and a smartly-dressed middle-aged maid appeared.

"Smith, arrange more tea, if you will. And my letters from the hallway."

"My lady."

Smith could move silently like an assassin and always gave Theodore the impression that she knew what was needed before anyone asked for it. The fresh, hot tea appeared far more quickly than could have been predicted. Tea was not generally a suitable breakfast drink but both Adelia and Theodore agreed that its potential harm was outweighed by its benefits. Smith presented a silver salver of correspondence to Adelia, who appeared to be hunting among the envelopes for something that she expected to find.

"Yes, here it is. Thank you, Smith. Advise Mrs Petty that I shall be down directly. I wish to discuss the matter of the disappointing herring."

"My lady." Smith virtually faded out of the room without appearing to move.

"Something you were expecting?" Theodore said, craning his head to look at the long, thin letter. It had been folded in the old-fashioned way, with no need for an envelope. The handwriting was looping and careful, each letter exactly the same height. "Is that from Harriet?" The bishop's wife was Adelia's best friend and general irritant in Theodore's life.

"No. Guess again." She teased him with the letter.

Of course. Harriet Hobson was no traditionalist and would not waste her time folding a letter in the old way. "Small, neat writing – a dark pen – a scent of roses. Our daughter Dido, perhaps?"

"Well done!" Adelia said proudly. She scanned the missive quickly. "She gives us the usual chatter. Our grandsons are faring well. Her husband is making even more improvements at Mondial Castle. They have constant streams of guests. They plan a garden party to mark the end of the season! She is happy and healthy. You know, my dear, do consider that it is nearly a year since we saw her last…"

"I am glad to hear she is happy." Theodore knew exactly where the conversation was now going. And much as he adored his second-eldest daughter, there was one fly in the ointment. A large fly, in the shape of her obnoxious husband, the Marquis of Mondial.

A marquis outranked an earl by one step, and were somewhat rarer in the British aristocracy. John, Lord Mondial would never have been as cEass as to point those things out in actual words. Oh no. He was far more subtle in his snobbery. Theodore could not quote a single instance when the Marquis had condescended to him – yet he came away from every meeting feeling like a small boy who'd been smacked.

"She is happy," Adelia said. "Dido is always happy. Yet she

would be happier still to see her father. And me. Here – why not read her letter yourself? She has actually invited us both to stay. They, too, have left London early. I should love to see what they've done with the indoor plumbing. She has a contraption around the bath that shoots water out at various angles, you know."

"Why?"

"To clean one's … crevices."

"I do not have crevices. I am a man of polite society."

"And a man of polite society does not reject a lady's invitation."

Theodore took the letter but he knew he'd already lost the battle.

They were heading for Mondial Castle by the end of the week.

2

"She may well be the wife of an earl *now*," said the cultured female voice with a sniff, "but some of us do *not* forget from whence she came."

The tortured, pseudo-correct grammar alone was enough to annoy Adelia. She couldn't help overhearing what Lady Montsalle was saying because that lady had ensured that Adelia would overhear it. Adelia had been subject to such tedious sniping and power games for the past thirty years and she didn't expect to ever quite leave them behind. While there were spiteful people in the world, there would be spiteful comments.

Adelia smiled at her companion, a sallow-faced dowager of impeccable breeding and absolutely no title whatsoever. Mrs Montagu Tott smiled back and rolled her heavily-lidded eyes like she was a mutinous girl of fifteen. They both knew exactly from *whence* Adelia came.

To hear people like Lady Montsalle snipe, you'd think Adelia had been raised in a coal mine and had seduced the Earl of Calaway with sinful charms, swaying hips and a dose of opium slipped into a drink. Such would have made for a romantic tale but the truth was a little more prosaic. Adelia had had a privileged upbringing as appropriate to any young woman of the upper middle classes. She had been tutored at home under a governess, and spent some time abroad perfecting her Italian, French and German. By the age of eighteen she knew how to dress, how to dance, how to waste a few hours completing passable needlework, and how to have an unremarkable conversation with anyone from a tailor's boy to a duke.

Those skills were essential in the family business – and here came the rub for those of Lady Montsalle's sensibilities.

Before Adelia took the Caxton name – the family surname of the Earls of Calaway – she was a Pegsworth. *Pegsworth's* had been one of the most prestigious galleries and art dealerships in central London, and had been so since the time of the Restoration. Indeed, a portrait of King Charles II hung in the lobby, reminding everyone of the generations of royal patronage that *Pegsworth's* had enjoyed.

Anyone who was someone was on good terms with the successions of the Pegsworth family who had inherited the business down the years. So the Pegsworth family were, technically, trade; but they were an acceptable side of business. Their lavish parties, gallery openings, private viewings and discreet deals were highly thought of, and invitations were sought after. The Pegsworths were good people to know and to be seen with.

So for someone like Theodore, who was happy to defy convention, the lack of an aristocratic background was no impediment when he asked Adelia to be his wife. Other men of his status had married maids and actresses; as far as he was

22

concerned, Adelia was perfect.

She had not been so sure, and had turned him down flat.

Lady Montsalle would have approved of that, Adelia thought, watching the woman glide away across the great hall. There was quite a little gathering of people at Mondial Castle this evening, milling around awaiting their fashionably late dinner.

Adelia and Theodore had arrived in the mid-afternoon and found that they were not the only guests expected. Dido had greeted her mother only briefly, looking harassed and careworn. "Oh, John throws these dinners every week, more or less," she said. "You know what he's like about his social standing. You would think I'd be used to it by now, but there's been a rush of people leaving London – the season, this year, you know? Quite dull. Not what it ought to be, they say – and we're quite overrun with folks fleeing town. And we have to do the dinner á la Russe and you wouldn't believe the work behind that. One footman per three guests, mama! Let me show you to your rooms. We can talk later."

"Are they all staying?" Adelia had asked, scurrying to keep up with her lean daughter. Dido almost ran, powering along the narrow carpets that were laid in almost every corridor. She had that efficient and don't-stop-me movement common to every overworked mother. And that was strange, because a woman of Dido's status shouldn't have needed to be involved with her children. Adelia wondered whether John was allowing her to employ the right sort of help. The choice of nurse and so on ought to have been Dido's domain and it was a foolish master indeed who meddled in that. Lord Mondial, however, expected to be in charge and Adelia wondered how far that expectation went.

"Some will stay tonight but most will not, thank goodness," Dido said. "There will be a little influx just before eight and you can all gather in the great hall because John likes people to admire the heraldry on the walls. You can barely see it all in the dark but you'll have to pretend and make the right noises. Then we'll eat, drink, play cards, and I shall have to play hostess to a tiresome late hour. Tomorrow, mama, we will be free to talk. Oh, I am so glad you are here!"

And with that, Adelia and Theodore had been abandoned in a suite of rooms.

"What did you make of that?" Adelia had said, turning to her husband.

He was more interested in the view of the lawns from the wide windows. "Those box hedges are exquisitely done! I wonder why ours have gone so yellow. I must speak to the gardeners here."

"I meant, what do you make of Dido?"

"She seems happy."

"What on earth makes you say that?"

He had turned to her with a look of bafflement on his face. "She smiled and she has a big dinner coming up tonight and lots of guests will be here, and we're here too. Why wouldn't she be happy? She did not say that she was unhappy in any way. You know she is our happiest daughter."

"Oh, for goodness' sake. Did you look at her? Where are your powers of observation? Does she need to carve it on a marble plaque?"

"I have no idea what you mean. I observed her smile. I

24

sometimes think you women approach every interaction like a romantic novel, hunting for hidden meanings and subtexts."

Adelia huffed. "At least the men in romantic novels are worth talking to."

Theodore had remained oblivious and Adelia had given up. She left him muttering about hedges while she had refreshed herself and dressed and gone down to join the throng, where she had heard Lady Montsalle's scathing assessment of her heritage.

She was still thinking about her infuriating husband – rather than Lady Montsalle, whose opinion meant nothing to her – when the announcement came that they were to go into the dining room. "At last," muttered Mrs Tott. "At my time of life, one doesn't want to go too long between meals. One never knows when one will be gathered into the arms of the Good Lord above, and one would be awfully disappointed to die hungry."

If the great hall had been designed to impress guests, the dining room was even more grand. While the great hall of Mondial Castle had been kept to a traditional style with high grey stone walls covered with animal heads, a huge fire and deep plush rugs, the dining room was the very epitome of modern style.

John Haveringham, as the Marquis of Mondial, welcomed the dozen or so guests into his home and stood proudly as they looked around in awe. Even people who had been in the room before gasped at the opulent decorations, the vast swathes of ferns and leaves on the table, the thick rich swags of ribbon that looped from corner to corner, and the silverware which glittered in the soft light from the hundreds of candles. Dido was next to the Marquis at the head of the table and she looked utterly dazzling. Adelia could have burst with pride. She looked so serene and beautiful, the very ideal of a marchioness. Dido was twenty-eight years old and had two sons and a rich, clever husband.

She had everything she could have ever dreamed of.

Although then Adelia remembered that the young Dido had mostly dreamed of owning horses and being able to eat whatever cakes she liked, whenever she liked. Those had been her aims for adulthood until she had been told to dream of marriage instead.

Still, it wasn't all bad. Adelia knew that John kept a fine stable of horses and she hoped that Dido still had the chance to ride them. She should have. The house was well-staffed and she should have had at least some free time even with her main duties of overseeing the staff and endless entertaining.

Adelia glanced around the room as the various courses were brought to the table from the sideboard by an absolute army of interchangeable servants. As well as the widowed Mrs Tott and the insufferable Lady Montsalle and her husband, who was a man distinguished only by his appalling halitosis, she recognised everyone else to some degree. Theodore had been placed next to a woman a little younger than Dido. Adelia caught the young woman's eye and smiled in greeting. She was Philippa Lamb, one of Dido's friends who was rapidly accelerating past the usual age for marriage. The pretty woman was still unwed in spite of a bevy of suitors. She was a vivacious socialite who had turned down every offer with a stock of now-dwindling excuses. It was something of a surprise to see an unmarried woman at an evening dinner party and Lord Mondial was known for his cleaving to what was considered to be "correct". Adelia thought that perhaps Dido had persuaded him to unbend a little, for her sake.

Adelia's immediate neighbours had been well-chosen by Dido. The gentleman to her right spoke to her of his travels in the Brazilian rainforests, and he was a witty and erudite man, ready to share a tale to entertain her even if it painted him in an unflattering light. And to her left was a restrained but pleasant middle-aged woman who always seemed to take in more than she offered in a conversation. That was a reassuring trait. She never gossiped, and Adelia respected that, even if it made her a somewhat dull companion over time.

The meal followed the usual pattern. Every course was exquisite and kept small so that no one felt over-faced by a vulgar amount of food in one sitting. After the soup, two boiled turbot were placed on the table, the brown side up at one end of the table and the white side up at the other. Then there was a joint of beef and the butler came in to serve some salad. Their palates were refreshed by a pineapple and rum sorbet so that the following roasts were fresh-tasting, though Adelia didn't care for the rather too lifelike rabbits. After a smattering of vegetables, including Jerusalem artichokes carved into wonderful shapes, there was a sweet course of jellies in elaborate moulds although Buckingham Palace was slightly listing to one side.

By the time the savouries came out, she could only manage a few braised chestnuts but she discovered she did have space for the ices. The butler reappeared with the dessert course of fruit and she was delighted by the gold grape scissors. But three grapes were enough for her. The extravagance finally concluded with the women retiring while the men smoked and drank. Once in private, the woman took their chance to drink unwatered claret and sherry; everyone had been rather restrained in public as it didn't do for a woman to appear to be fond of alcohol. They didn't stay parted for long. Some guests made their excuses and left but there was still a determined circle around the card tables even at midnight.

Dido slipped away from Mrs Tott and came to sit alongside her mother by the fire. "You are all alone, mama!"

"I am perfectly happy watching everyone else," Adelia told her. She was enjoying her glass of wine and felt pleasantly replete with food. She did rather fancy a nap now.

"You will be trying to guess everyone's secrets from afar."

"Will I? Is that what you think I do?"

"Is it not?"

"Well – perhaps. A little. But those secrets, once unearthed, will remain hidden in my mind, quite safe and private. I am more likely to be sitting here and admiring everyone's marvellous dresses. Except for that one over there. Grey is not her colour and the shape of her bodice makes her look like a pigeon who wants a fight. Now, dear Dido, is everything as well as can be, here?"

"Of course, mama!"

"But you asked me here for a reason."

Dido looked affronted. "Yes. I asked you here because you hinted, very strongly, that you had to get away. What *has* father been up to? I have heard rumours, you know. They say he is ... well, I cannot really repeat what they say."

"I can guess. They say he is the worst doctor in England."

"But mama, he is a genius!"

"And you are a loyal daughter. But they are correct in what they say. He is quite, quite terrible, and must be stopped before we are utterly ruined. Scandal beckons. Bankruptcy. *Jail.*" In truth, Adelia didn't think it could quite get that far, but who knew, these days? Being a wealthy aristocrat was not what it once was.

Dido's mouth opened and closed in shock. "No, mama, I cannot believe it. You are making a tasteless jest." She reached to take her mother's drink from her hand but Adelia evaded her deftly.

"I wish that I were jesting. And yes, we did need to get away from home though perhaps I overegg the pudding slightly. Anyway, I thank you for the invitation here. Your home is utterly lovely, as always. And yet the invitation came at the right time for you, too, though. Don't deny it. You did want me to be here."

"You have me," Dido conceded. She swirled her own glass of wine around, twisting it in her fingers. Hers was watered down. "But not, I think, for the reasons you suspect. John and I are perfectly happy – as happy as we can be. I'm under no illusions, of course, about him. You know. Him *as a man.*"

"What do you mean?" Adelia sat up straight, ready to leap to her feet, grab a candlestick or a poker and run the man through. She would do it without a second thought if her own daughter was in the least bit discontented.

"Oh, nothing terrible. It's only that after a few years of marriage, the flames die down somewhat. I knew that they would. But a smouldering fire is still a fire, and I am grateful for the warmth. No, I did not want you here because of any … marital issues. Everything is under control in that regard. I am afraid that it is a different matter. See over there – do you remember Miss

Lamb?"

"Of course I do. She would light up our summers when she came to stay with your other friends, that poor dear orphan. You were both once very close and I am pleased to see her here again; it has been many years. Yet she is as bright and brilliant as always. But is there yet any hope of a match for her? I had expected to see her married. I've expected it for nine or ten years."

"See, I knew that you would hit upon the matter!" Dido said, her face lighting up. "That is the reason I need you here, mama. As she is quite without a mother or father of her own to guide her, she has missed out on certain important things. Only her old grandfather the doctor remains and he is in poor health. She lacks guidance and will not hear advice from me or any of her contemporaries. Sometimes such advice need to come from an older person."

"Ha! When have the youth ever listened to their elders?"

"Mama, you know that we do. It is only that we pretend not to. Her time ticks on, mama, and I am dreadfully afraid that she will wake up as an old maid and it will be too late for her. She doesn't see herself as we do; she only knows parties and pleasure and she thinks it will last forever. But you have successfully married off all seven of us. You also aided Mrs Christie's daughter to wed and everyone thought her teeth would be the undoing of her. And what of cousin Mabel? You are celebrated for orchestrating her match and I am sure they will be very happy in British Columbia. After her scandal, that's probably for the best. So I was talking with Mrs Tott last week and we both agreed that you, of all people, would be ideal for the purpose."

30

"The purpose?"

"The purpose of arranging a match for Miss Lamb!"

"And what does Miss Lamb think about this plan?" Adelia asked. She watched the young woman from across the room. Philippa Lamb was in deep conversation with Lady Montsalle and another woman. Adelia scanned the rest of the room, hunting for eligible bachelors. There were none.

"Honestly, mama, I think she is secretly ready for it, but simply won't admit it. Sometimes I find her looking wistfully at me when I am sitting with John, and I fancy she envies the state of wedded bliss that we enjoy."

Adelia's suspicions were pricked up at that, but she pushed them aside. The notion of a dalliance between Lord Mondial and Philippa Lamb was a risible one. "Have you any ideas for possible suitors?"

"A few, but I need your help," Dido said. "I have made a very short list but you know people's families and their histories in far more depth. I won't be happy with any old husband for her, you know. He must be rich, handsome and clever."

"If I might give you one word of advice," Adelia said. "I think it is more important, above all, that he is kind."

"Is that how you chose John for me?"

"Is he not kind?" Adelia said, fixing her eyes on her daughter, ready once more to leap up and attack her son-in-law with household objects.

"Oh, he is kind. He does not argue with me and he would never raise his hand to me. He is a perfect gentleman, even in private. But mama, really, I would rather that Philippa marries a dull man with a fortune than a kind man in a cottage, and I know

31

that you agree."

"I do agree. Well, tomorrow morning, we shall look at this list of yours, and see about these dull, rich men."

"Thank you." Dido put her glass on a small side table, and grabbed her mother's hands. "Thank you! This means more to me than I can say."

"Why so?" Adelia asked with a small laugh.

But Dido was turning away as someone approached to top up her glass, and the moment was lost.

3

The house woke late the next day. Well, the servants were up and about before dawn, of course, but everyone else lingered in their rooms, feeling delicate and disinclined to encounter strong lights or smells.

Adelia didn't even bother to straggle down to breakfast which was laid out in the breakfast room from around nine and she certainly didn't attend the household prayers. She didn't get very hungry in the mornings these days, anyway. She wondered if that were another sign of aging, along with a decreased ability to handle alcohol. She sat at the dressing table and patted cream onto her face, working it into the wrinkles and sagging jawline. Theodore wandered through and sat on the edge of the bed, wrestling with his collar.

"We should have brought more of the household with us. I cannot believe Mondial hasn't assigned me a man," he muttered as his clothing fought back.

"He would if you asked him. He would be mortified if he thought he had lacked in his duty as a host. I can call for Smith, if you like."

"Leave her be. I can manage. And I'd rather not ask Mondial for a thing. He would use it as an excuse to sneer at my lack of a valet who dogs my every step, like his long-faced fellow does. How long must we stay?"

"Until we've arranged a match for Miss Lamb."

"Who? What's this, now?"

"Theodore! You were sitting next to her at dinner. I watched you have a conversation. She was our Dido's childhood friend. She spent almost every summer with us, Theodore!"

"Oh, *Philippa*. You ought to call her by her name. She is a sweet girl; of course I remember her. There were dozens of girls in our house every summer; I cannot distinguish between them all."

"She is a woman now, not girl. She is a fully grown woman who is in need of a husband and she will be Miss Lamb to you in public, Theodore."

"A husband? She also needs more meat in her diet. She is pale. She hides her pallor with rouge. I should like to examine her more closely in case she is ill."

From any other man, such a sentence could be misconstrued as an excuse to get close to a pretty young lady. From Theodore, however, it meant no more and no less than he said. Adelia smiled at her own reflection.

"What amuses you?" he asked, blissfully unaware of any secondary meanings his words could have had.

"Just that you are the most direct man I know, and I am grateful for it."

"Good. Then you shan't make a fuss when I tell Lord Montsalle that his back teeth are rotten and must be removed

34

before the infection spreads into his brain, then? It might already be too late."

"You will *not*."

"His brain might rot and he needs to know."

"No. Do not tell Lord Montsalle that his brain is rotting."

"What else am I supposed to do, then, while you gad about this place, matchmaking and scheming?"

"Lord Mondial has horses. Go and look at them."

Theodore wrestled one more time with his collar and gave up with a sigh. "Oh. Very well. Horses."

Adelia spent what remained of the morning with Dido, drawing up lists of potential suitors for Philippa. Dido looked tired but when Adelia brought up the issue, Dido waved her hand and began to talk about the children. "Of course I am tired," she said. "But it's a happy and fulfilled tiredness."

"But why don't you have staff to ease your burden? Why must you take on so much?" Adelia had insisted. "Most women of your class are simply dying from boredom."

"I refuse to be one of them. I have read many interesting books on childrearing. I spend the first few hours of every morning with my boys – I have already done so today. I oversee their education and their food and all aspects of their care. I know John should prefer to see them at morning prayers then have them paraded before bed once a day and otherwise for them to remain out of sight until they start school – and then they will be sent away and only return for the holidays."

"You will send them to school, though, won't you? You cannot allow them to miss out on a good education."

"Of course." But she looked sad at the thought, and Adelia let the subject drop. She turned to the list of suitors and they continued on their task.

Before luncheon, which was to be an informal affair, Dido had to attend to matters with the housekeeper. Adelia didn't bother changing out of her comfortable day dress. She took the chance to go around the house and gardens looking for Philippa but she could not find the young woman anywhere. Someone thought they'd seen her walking in the lower grounds by the ornamental ponds, but Adelia found the area deserted. Nor did Philippa appear at lunch, which was a collation of cold meats, fancy galatines and fruit. Most of the other guests had now left, and the room was oddly cold and echoing. There were no visitors that had called today although Dido said there were often guests invited from the local area; single women, the elderly and others generally unsuitable to be at the more formal late dinners.

"Don't worry," Lord Mondial had said jovially. "We'll soon fill this all up again!"

Adelia called at Philippa's rooms once more after the meal, and this time she was lucky. The door was opened by a stumpy ancient woman who had once been the Lamb family's nurse and was now the young lady's companion and chaperone. From the blinking way the woman thrust her head forward, almost into Adelia's bosom, it was obvious that the old lady was nearly blind. Her hearing was little better.

She was, therefore, the perfect chaperone for a lively young lady who wanted a measure of freedom.

"Lady Calaway!" Philippa caught sight of Adelia and almost elbowed the old nurse out of the way. "Come in, come in. Please excuse the mess."

"You're leaving, Miss Lamb?" Adelia said as she followed Philippa into the main room of the suite that had been assigned to her. It was a small but comfortable room with private bedchambers leading off to the right. A travelling trunk was standing by the table in the window, and a ballgown with a long train of rich pink was flung over the back of a sofa. In years gone by, *Miss Lamb* had been *Philippa* to Adelia, in private moments. But now she was a woman, as she had so sternly reminded Theodore.

"Oh! I thought that I might go home soon but – well, I was in an awful hurry and sometimes one does not think straight. I am sure you understand. Please, have a seat. I have not seen you properly for more than a year. Since Dido was married! I trust you are well?"

"Quite well, thank you," Adelia said, thinking that she did not understand about the packing in a hurry, not at all. "So you are *not* leaving?"

"Ah ... no. Not yet. I am simply, ah, reorganising."

"I see," Adelia said, though she did not. "Now, my dear, I shall not patronise you. You must be aware of the machinations and subterfuge that my daughter is indulging in? It involves you."

Philippa laughed. She sat down with a thump on a wide, armless chair, with no regard for the pleats and flounces at the back of her summery floral day-dress. "Of course I am aware. Dido never lets up. She is determined to see me married. I am a project to her, a pet project, you see! Once she gets an idea, she simply won't let go, will she?"

"In that regard, I fear she takes after her father."

"Ah, and how is my lord this morning?"

"He is well. He does not drink to excess so his head is quite clear."

"Unlike Lord Mondial," Philippa said, before fluttering a delicate hand over her mouth in an affected way. "Oh, hark at me, gossiping already – you must stop me, Lady Calaway, you simply must, I beg you. Since my own mother died I've had no one to instruct me to hold my tongue, as you know."

That made it sound as if the bereavement was recent but Philippa's mother had died when she was seven. Adelia and Theodore had often taken her in for the summer while she was a younger girl, and that was how she'd grown close to Dido. But since Dido had left the family home well over eight years ago, they had had little more to do with Philippa. She had become a young woman in those intervening years and sometimes it was as if she were a different person altogether.

"I will indeed stop you," Adelia said, "And let us return to the other matter. As you point out yourself, Dido is determined that she shall see you married to a suitable man. What do you say to that?"

"Oh – well, I suppose that I must."

"I know that you do not welcome such a change of circumstance."

"I do not. But grandpapa is old and ill and soon I shall be alone in the world, and I know that I must either make a match, or be consigned to the attic of a distant relative, wheeled out on high days and holidays so that they might feel magnanimous in being kind to me."

"Oh, that is not so," Adelia said. "If you were absolutely set against marriage in any form, then there are a few other options. You might become a schoolmistress, or better, a governess, for example. Perhaps you could consider nursing. I have even heard of women studying and embarking on careers in the law. You could apply to Miss Beale's new venture, her college at Oxford; it is to be for women only."

Philippa laughed. "St Hilda's? Oh, goodness me. You have known me since I was small. Have I ever led you to suspect I might be inclined to books and learning?"

"Well, no, you have not."

"And I am not against marriage." She sighed. "I am simply against all the men I've met so far. As husbands, I mean. They are all perfectly lovely people. And it just feels so awfully final, to be committed to one man for ever and ever. I love people in general. I adore meeting them and making new friends. It seems to me that when a woman marries, a door closes in front of her face and shuts her up in a house. It might be a very fine house – like Dido has – but it is a closed door nonetheless. Do you see? When we were younger, Dido and I planned so many adventures that we would embark upon when we were grown." She sighed in happy remembrance.

Adelia nodded.

Philippa continued, a wistful note in her voice. "We were to go to Italy and swim in the lakes under the light of the moon like Byron; we were to trek through Scottish highlands and wear tartan and learn to like porridge with salt in it. I spoke with her a few days ago and reminded her of these dreams and she just laughed and said they were foolish. I pressed her, saying, she could come with me to Milan for a month perhaps. There is no reason why she shouldn't. She could chaperone me. But she said, oh, the children." Philippa looked directly at Adelia. "It's always, *the children, the children.* I don't understand why she can't let them be in the care of nurses and tutors. Why does she feel so bound to them?"

Adelia had to repress her smile. "Because she is their mother."

"My mother was never so frivolous even before she died. She visited the nursery once a week. Sundays. I had to curtsey to her." Philippa frowned. "If it is the modern way to be more – more like Dido – then I should not bear it. I could not be like she is."

"I would not worry," Adelia said. "Motherhood is different for everyone. And it's a big leap indeed to be fretting about children when we haven't yet found you a man. The main thing is that you are amenable to the idea?"

"I am," she said heavily. "It must be done. I imagine you have already come up with a list?"

"Of course. You know me very well."

Philippa sprang to her feet and paced around the room, ending up by the window. She looked out over the lawns, with her hand resting on the thick curtains. Without facing Adelia, she said heavily, "And who is top of this list of eligible men?"

"I think you already know the gentleman. I believe Sir Henry Locksley would be utterly perfect for you." Adelia wished that she could see Philippa's face to gauge her reaction to the suggestion.

"Sir Henry Locksley," Philippa repeated. There didn't seem to be any outward disgust in her voice, at least. "Yes, I have met him at social events."

"I know he is not a peer, but he is a baronet and you would be Lady Locksley. And your children would inherit the title. That would be something, would it not?"

The subtle shrug of Philippa's shoulder indicated that she didn't give two hoots for an inheritable title. Dido remembered that she herself had not cared before she married the Earl. It wasn't until her children were born that she began to be more concerned with the future.

"It would be awfully strange to be Philippa Locksley."

"Why so?"

"It is not me. I have a sense of myself and a different name means I would be a different person."

"You worry about the strangest things," Adelia said. "He is young, handsome and principled. He has no major vices that anyone gossips about. No scandal has attached to him, at least, not since he was a student and all of that may be forgiven. How well do you know him?"

"Barely. As I say, we have been introduced in public and nothing more. Dido knows him rather better."

"And is there anyone else you would rather have at the top of the list? You may speak freely, dear," Adelia said. "I have only your best interests at heart. If someone else has stolen your affections and they are a suitable candidate then I promise to do everything I can to arrange things between you both."

There was a hesitation before Philippa spoke. "No, there is

no one else."

Adelia could not ignore that pause. She went over and stood at Philippa's side. "Miss Lamb, it is vital that you speak honestly to me. Who are you thinking of, right now?"

"No one," Philippa replied forcefully. "I swear upon – upon anything that you care to name – that there is no one in my heart." But she looked away and her cheeks coloured. "It is not my fault if I am in someone else's heart, though, is it?"

"An admirer?"

"Yes. But he is *not* suitable in any way and I have *never* encouraged him."

"Well, then, it is settled. And a marriage to another is the clearest possible signal that you can send to this other person, is it not?"

"Yes, I suppose so. How will you manage this match? The season is almost over and everyone will be returning to their houses now, or heading away. Dido might let you invite him here. He can be added to the list for the garden party."

Adelia could not help herself. "Don't be angry at me, dear one, but you know how efficient I am. I have already arranged it. Sir Henry Locksley arrives tomorrow."

4

It was one of those intolerably hot and stuffy days that made
the end of summer so unbearable. Sir Henry had arrived two
days previously and had been stiffly welcomed by Lord Mondial,
with all the courtesy and none of the warmth the peer could
muster. Dido and Adelia had conspired to invite a few other
potential suitors, but the next man on their list was unavailable
and as soon as it appeared that Philippa was at least amenable to
the idea of marrying Sir Henry, Adelia counselled that perhaps
they ought to give the man the best chance by not introducing
any competition. At least not for the time being. Dido had agreed
and Philippa had not appeared to care either way. Of course, it
would not have done for Philippa to show too much enthusiasm
but her utter passivity was of some concern.

Dido told Adelia not to worry.

So Adelia and Dido took it in turns to supervise some
informal meetings between Sir Henry and Philippa, usually in the
company of other people from the local area too. There were
enough of the right sort of folk around to make such socialising
something of a pleasure. Having less fun, unfortunately, was

Theodore, who was growing more discontented by the hour. He was itching to find out what was happening at home but Adelia had banned all correspondence with the Postlethwaite firm. She trusted them to make everything right.

And they would have an easier job of it without Theodore's interference.

"I am rather afraid that your father is going to sneak off home in the night," Adelia told Dido as they sat in an upstairs room on the shady side of the castle, just after a late and casual luncheon. "Then he will take up his medical practice once more, and find himself brought up in the courts."

"I don't understand why he is so set on such a strange career. He does not need to work."

"Not for the money, no; and anyway, he does not charge for his services. He considers himself a philanthropist using his God-given gifts and station. I think that might be part of the problem," Adelia said. "People don't value what they get for free and are more vocal in expressing displeasure. But the main problem is his bluntness of manner. He cannot see the point of expressing sympathy. Yet for some people who are unwell, sympathy is the very best medicine."

Dido smiled. "He was terrifying to us when we were small."

"No! You were never scared of him, were you?"

"Well, perhaps only a little, when he talked very seriously and looked so stern. Once I grew older, I was not so very scared, except for that time I climbed a tree and fell and he was scathing about how I had misjudged the strength of the branches and my own weight, suggesting I was far heavier than I had thought. I was upset for a little while about that. And Mary was never scared

44

of him but she was his favourite. I imagine that she still is. How is she? I have letters from her, but you know how tight-lipped she can be about her travails. She will always pretend that nothing is wrong."

"The summer has been good to her and her lungs are better than they've ever been. Her husband treats her like a queen. She is well," Adelia said.

"I'm glad to hear it. She is so sweet that she deserves to be treated properly. Now, Felicia was *always* scared of father. And she definitely still is."

Adelia shook her head. Of her seven daughters, Felicia had been born fourth and was the silliest, sweetest thing she'd ever encountered. Her head was nothing more than the fairy-like fluff of dandelion clocks. No wonder she was troubled by Theodore's forthright manner. She was scared of unseen things, ghosts, gossip, creaks in the night, sideways looks from strangers and the passing of a black cat. But it was a shame. No child should be scared of their parents. "We could invite all of your sisters to this garden party," she said, tapping the paper on the table in front of them. "Although Felicia might not come." As she spoke, Philippa slipped into the room, looking flushed.

Dido clapped her hands. "Have you been meeting with Sir Henry?"

"I? No – I have been walking in the garden but it grew too hot." She pulled at her tweed walking dress in annoyance. "I should dress like a lady golfer. They have much better ideas about clothes."

"Oh, please don't be so common. You should go to the fishpond. It is always cool there."

"I don't like the yew trees. They loom over me."

"I agree with you there," Adelia said. "They can be nasty things, all dark and deathlike."

"Mama, please don't!" Dido said hastily. "You are as bad as father with your speaking sometimes. Don't plant nightmares into my head. It is a good job Felicia isn't here. She would not sleep for days after hearing you say that. Let us finish this additional guest list. Philippa, do sit down and help us."

Lord Mondial had decreed that they were to hold a lavish garden party before many people headed north to Scotland for the start of the grouse hunting season. And he had given his wife barely a scant three weeks to prepare everything. He simply assumed that it would be done as soon as he commanded it; he seemed to have no concept of the work that would go on behind the scenes. The main invitations had all been sent out, but they were double-checking the list and the subsequent replies and adding a few extra guests as they saw fit.

They bent to the task in hand for a little while before Philippa sat back and said, out of nowhere, "Oh, Dido, did they tell you about the man?"

"What? What man is this?"

Adelia laughed. Philippa had been an impetuous child and clearly some things had not changed. She sometimes started conversations in the middle, forgetting that she had engaged in the first half of the conversation in her own head and not out loud.

Philippa explained, "There was a man caught lurking in the garden earlier."

"Where, and when? No, no one has told me this." Dido

46

sounded angry.

But as the explanation unfolded, Adelia began to feel annoyed rather than alarmed, although she held her tongue about her suspicions. She thought she knew who the man might have been, particularly when Philippa said, "One of the gardeners chased him off with a spade. The man said he was here to visit someone but wouldn't say who that was; he said 'she', though. He was not old, not young, and very well-spoken but dressed like he'd been sleeping on the floor of a tavern."

"Goodness," said Dido. "I do not know whether to be horrified or sympathetic. Perhaps he is a rich man down on his luck."

"No doubt there will be a reason for that," Adelia said. "I am relieved that the staff are aware of this trespasser and I am sure we will all be perfectly safe." If it was who she thought it was, he was an annoyance but nothing dangerous. He plagued her in ever inventive ways but he was harmless. "Now, about this garden party. Should we not invite the local vicar? I notice he has been omitted from the list. Is that accidental or is there something I should know about the man?"

Dido did not seem to notice the swerve in topic and for that Adelia was grateful. Adelia did not want to explain to her daughter that the strange man lingering in the bushes was almost certainly Dido's Uncle Alfred.

The guest list was finally agreed upon and talk turned to Sir

Henry, but before Philippa could be persuaded to spill her feelings on the matter, someone tapped at the door and entered before anyone could call out. Of course, Lord Mondial would not wait for permission to enter any room in his own home. He cast a glance over the three women. A lesser man – or a more amusing one – might have made a joke about the opening scene of Macbeth. However, Lord Mondial had never made a joke in his life. He nodded briefly to Adelia, even more briefly to Philippa, and then turned to his wife.

"My lady," he said formally, as if they were in a public gathering, "I should be grateful for your attention to a personal matter."

"Is it the children? Is everything all right?" Dido was already getting to her feet.

He blinked as if he had forgotten they had two boys. "I imagine that they are fine. They usually are. No, I need you to walk with me in the gardens. There is something we must discuss. Don't look so worried; it is a minor matter and wrinkles will ruin your face."

He turned away and left the room abruptly, secure in the knowledge that his wife would jump immediately to do his bidding. Adelia tried to catch her daughter's eye as she went, but Dido studiously avoided Adelia's gaze as she left.

Adelia made a neat pile of the paperwork. If Theodore ordered me about like that, she thought, the man would find himself starving in a ditch before the day was out. She kept her feelings to herself and said, "Well, that is that, for the moment. Miss Lamb, I must say, we have quite a history together…"

"We have, and I shall be forever grateful to your care when

48

I was a girl. You can still call me Philippa, you know. It would remind me of happy times."

Adelia smiled. "You know I care little for false ceremony but I want to give you the respect that you deserve. And it is of happy times now that I want to speak. This is a somewhat delicate question and I am talking with you as a woman speaks to another woman, as equals. I am only Dido's mother, but you are her close friend. Tell me: is she truly happy in her marriage with Lord Mondial?"

Philippa said, quickly, "Oh yes, of course she is!" Then she turned her face away and sighed.

"Go on," Adelia said.

"It is nothing." Philippa stood up and shook out the folds of her skirts. "I feel restless. My walk was short and unsatisfactory. I wish this weather would break."

"Go down to the fishponds, perhaps? Ignore our nonsense about the yew trees. I meant no harm by it."

"I think that I might. Thank you, my lady, and please do not fret about Dido. You have nothing at all to worry about. He is a most excellent man. Everyone says so, especially he himself."

"I shall try not to worry. But it is a mother's lot to fret endlessly, and I have seven of these worries to carry with me. They marry and leave my house but they never leave my heart."

Philippa smiled weakly and slipped away.

Adelia tidied up the rest of the writing paraphernalia. She paced the room and glanced out of the window. The air was shimmering with the heat and nothing stirred in the gardens. She stood in the shade looking north, and wondered if she ought to return to her own home. She didn't care much for the idea of the garden party and the house was soon to be filling with more and more people. It would be exhausting.

In a way, she knew that she was running away from the problem of her husband's idiotic medical practice and it wasn't going to solve itself. Their absence would let the current scandals die down a little but as soon as they returned, Theodore would take up his crusade again, and the problems would resume as before.

If only he could accept that he lacked the bedside manner that a good doctor needed! Perhaps if he had been able to pursue his career when he had been a young man he might have learned the necessary skills – though she doubted that. His blunt rationality ran deep in his nature. It went right back to the relationship he had had with his own father, and the country doctor who had saved his father's life.

Adelia had to come up with something else to give Theodore's life meaning. But now that all of his daughters had grown up and were married, what else could a wealthy Earl do? He was not one for dalliances and affairs; he did not gamble; he had little interest in sport, literature or the theatre. He travelled from time to time, and collected things that he carefully arranged in cabinets around the house, but one could not spend one's life on the move, gathering up the objects of the world. That would not satisfy his need to be *essential*. Essential in a way that his dead father would recognise.

She left the room and walked slowly back to their assigned suite, which was on the floor above. Mondial Castle was large and rambling, and the interior corridors were blissfully cool by virtue of the thick stone walls. She wanted to loosen her stays, perhaps throw off her day dress altogether, and cast a loose silk robe around her shoulders like a dissolute actress. It was exactly the kind of weather for lounging on a couch and drinking something cool and faintly alcoholic. Maybe I should, she thought with a secret grin. Goodness knows, I am old enough to be able to do as I please.

But the matter of her background – which was never quite good *enough* – meant that she was forever doomed to be judged against higher standards than those born into the aristocracy. It was the curse of the middle classes, she thought. A woman born into the peerage could run naked through Covent Garden if she pleased, and the scandal would light the papers for a little while but soon fade. Only if the woman continued to act in such a manner would questions be asked. But a woman of the gentry had to do everything so correctly at all times that it was a wonder they managed to function at all.

She was doomed to be always climbing higher simply to stay still, and to be despised for that climb nevertheless.

Well, despised by old-fashioned sorts like Lady Montsalle, perhaps. Others were more kindly and generous, and for that she was grateful. Life would have been intolerable otherwise. She spotted one of those kindly others on the floor below, and she leaned over the bannisters to call out a greeting. It was Sir Henry. But before she could speak, he had already moved out of sight.

She turned around and headed back down the stairs that she had come up. His ochre-coloured coat slipped around a corner and she tried to catch him up without exerting her old bones too much; but it was no use. By the time she reached the ground floor, he was gone. She carried on to the wide front doors, where a manservant in formal livery was just closing them. He spun and began to open the door once more to allow her to leave.

"No, thank you; but tell me, did Sir Henry pass this way?" she said to him.

"Yes, my lady, a moment before you. Shall I call him?"

"No, thank you. It is too hot to be walking, calling or any other such thing." Then she remembered that Philippa had gone out for a walk, too.

She smiled.

"My lady?"

"Oh – no, thank you, that will be all." She headed back upstairs again, and couldn't repress her smiles. So the match between Sir Henry and Philippa Lamb looked more likely than ever. For surely he was following her – perhaps on an arranged assignation! Adelia ought to have disapproved of it but this was exactly what they had all planned. She had no doubts as to Sir Henry's honour. Even a secret tryst among the yew trees offered no hint of danger to Philippa's chastity. And if a little gossip emerged, it would not matter if they were soon to be wed anyway.

Adelia could have clapped her hands in joy. Her prowess as a match-maker was indeed great.

5

Lord Calaway loitered grumpily in the stable-yard. On the previous day, he'd loitered grumpily in Lord Mondial's extensive library and he had actually had fun in between bouts of grumpiness though he wasn't going to admit that openly. He had lost himself in books for many hours and made copious notes about scientific developments that he had missed. At home, of course, he took all of the most important London journals, and made pains to attend lectures at the Royal Institution where he was well-known as a significant patron, yet there always seemed to be something new happening that he didn't know about. It was both infuriating and exciting. The miserable lot of the majority of humankind was improving on an almost daily basis. He had little to do with the truly poor folk in his everyday life but that did not mean he wasn't sensitive to their plight on a very abstract level. He might not have noticed if someone in front of him was worried about their children, but he would have noticed their malnutrition and if the person was an estate worker of his own, he would have taken that matter very seriously – almost as a personal slight against his own management of his lands.

The previous evening had brought on a headache which he self-diagnosed as an excess of close study and bad lighting, and he had prescribed himself a dose of fresh air. He had hoped to take a bracing walk on the hills but the oppressive heat had made his head feel as if it were in a vice. He wanted to avoid any laudanum-containing cure, as he tended to suffer sweaty after-effects once the opium wore off. He envied his wife, who could retire to her chambers with a moderate dose of silver-coated opium pills and emerge the next morning as fresh as a daisy.

Thinking of his wife made him sigh in exasperation. She was right, of course, to drag him away from home so that Mr Postlethwaite could do whatever it was that he did and make all the problems relating to the potential lawsuit go away. And she was an absolute marvel, of that he was certain, when it came to arranging marriages. She seemed to know how people would fit together with the skill of a cabinetmaker carving out a mortise and tenon joint. She had spoken lately of a slight ill-ease about Lord Mondial and their daughter, but as far as Theodore could see, Dido could not possibly have been any happier. Theodore did not doubt Adelia's talents as a match-maker in any way. If Adelia had once thought Lord Mondial was the best husband for Dido, then he was, and that was that. The case was closed.

Theodore wandered past the loose boxes that ranged around the courtyard of the stable area. The horses stayed well back in the shade, not even caring to let their curiosity override their desire to stay cool. Only one big rangy hunter came forward briefly to eye Theodore sideways in the hope of treats. Theodore put his hands behind his back and the big bay horse retreated, swishing his short tail in annoyance.

A shot rang out.

Both Theodore and the hunter had the same startled reaction: a tensing of the body, a stiffening of the legs, a freezing of the head while the eyes rolled in the direction of the sound.

A second gunshot echoed off the stone walls of the castle and the courtyard, but Theodore had just begun to tilt his head and he got a sense of the origin of the sound. It didn't come from the castle itself, but from the lower grounds though it was distorted and possibly deflected by the walls.

He ran. And he ran towards the shots, of course. He tried to shout as he went but he was in his late fifties and he had to make the choice to breathe well and run silently. He hurtled over the hard parched lawns and headed down towards the walled area that enclosed the ornamental fishponds. Alongside this area was a dark path lined with gloomy yew trees and he could see a pale shape deep in the shadows.

And he could hear groaning and it wasn't coming from his own tired lungs.

Theodore slowed down, thinking now of his own safety. "Who's there?" he called out as strongly as he could manage. "There is an army of us, you know, behind me – so show yourself and throw down your weapon!"

"Calaway, for God's sake, get over here," replied Lord Mondial in a broken voice thick with something strange.

Tears.

To hear another man cry seemed to plunge a cold knife into Theodore's heart. He leaped forward into the darkness of the yew tree walk. His eyes adjusted slowly but there was enough light to make out a scene of horror.

Philippa Lamb, the dear sweet girl who had been Dido's friend in childhood, and who was now being courted – at his wife's management – by Sir Henry Locksley, lay on the floor, her upper body supported by Lord Mondial who was kneeling in the yew needles and dusty dark earth. Philippa's pale dress was shockingly marred by a huge red circle in the centre of her torso. Her head hung down and she made no sound.

"Help us!" Lord Mondial said, trying to hold her up. Theodore fell to his own knees and reached out for Philippa. As she slumped forward, becoming a sudden dead weight in his arms, he noticed that Lord Mondial was also injured.

"Your arm, Mondial," he said urgently.

"It will heal – see to her, see to her, damn it! You're a doctor! What's the bloody point of you if you can't save her? Oh God – no…"

All Theodore could do was lay her flat on the ground and arrange her clothing to make her decent in death. "The internal organs have been ripped apart," Theodore said, assessing the situation quickly. The poor girl. He clung to rationality, using his training to stave off the clawing and cloying emotion of impending grief. "She is not breathing and her pulse is quite gone. Even if the bullet had not lodged so deep inside her, causing such massive bleeding, no doubt the shock would have killed her. Her lungs might have been punctured. Also…"

"God's sake! Shut up, will you? Shut up!"

"Ah. The pain is affecting you."

"*I'll* bloody well affect you. Save her. *Save her.*" Lord Mondial was sobbing now, his right arm hanging down, blood spreading through his sleeve and even dripping from his fingertips. Others were arriving, and they were surrounded by men and shouting and cursing and very little effective direction. The lord of the estate sat uselessly crying and no one dared look at him; certainly no one would approach him. It was one of those situations which would never be mentioned again.

So Theodore got to his feet and took charge, assuming his most lordly air. He could not save Philippa; she was already dead. But he could preserve the crime scene, he thought. He could always find a way to be useful, he reminded himself. His father had taught him that.

He ordered the most capable-looking gardener to organise a search of the entire area. "But you must go carefully and look before you place your feet anywhere; take the utmost care to not walk over tracks or trails that might indicate which way the miscreant went. Do not allow your lads to blunder mindlessly. Be like trackers. Be like poachers in the night; and I know that you know how to do that."

As the gardeners spread out on their task, he turned then to the injured Lord Mondial who was growing pale. The Marquis spat out some curses but Theodore shrugged them off. He knew that Lord Mondial was not going to die. He ordered two strong men in livery – the Marquis could afford to keep a bevy of male servants – to help the injured man to his feet.

"What about her?" Lord Mondial said. "What about Miss Lamb?" His sobbing had stopped and been replaced by anger and pain. "She was here under my protection."

"That is why we must find the person who did it. Can you tell me exactly what happened? Speak now while it is fresh in your mind. It is of the utmost importance."

"What? Here, now? God's sake, man, I need a drink. What's done is done. Get me inside. Get her … let her … what does one do now?" he finished, weakly.

They were now surrounded by all the staff of the house, though Theodore could see the housekeeper preventing Dido, Adelia and the other women from coming too close and seeing the horror. He said to a nearby lingering boy, "Go directly into town and ask for a policeman to come here immediately," he said. "Can you ride?"

He looked startled. One of the footmen holding Lord Mondial said, "I'll go, my lord."

"No," Lord Mondial said. "I'll have no police here. Boy, you stay here."

"With respect, Mondial…"

"This is my house!" the Marquis thundered. "No police!" And the effort of shouting and the blood loss made him finally pass out.

Lord Mondial came back to consciousness in his own bedroom, attended to by Dido and Lord Calaway. Lord Mondial's own valet, Tobias Taylor, had seen to his master's clothing, whisking the worst of the soiled stuff away out of sight. He returned and helped Lord Mondial to be patched up. A doctor arrived with the police, within the hour, and was sent away immediately by Theodore who took umbrage at the idea that anyone else was needed. "The shot has gone clean through Lord

Mondial's upper arm," he told the doctor, in plain earshot of everyone else including the Marquis himself. "It has ripped through tissue and muscle but it has missed the bone. Therefore all we need do is keep the wound clean and as long as infection does not set in, he will recover. His arm, however, will always remain weak."

The policeman that came with the doctor was an Inspector, a man of rough accent and carefully learned manners; like most of the police he was of a far lower class than the residents of the castle. He spoke with a confidence lent to him by his uniform not his birth. And Lord Mondial was having no truck with it at all.

"Get him out of here. I told you all, no police. He's trespassing. You, man. You're trespassing. You're not needed."

"A crime has been committed, sir."

"You may address me as my lord!"

"As you wish, my lord," said the Inspector, managing to make it sound as if he had just called Lord Mondial "Jack". "There has been a murder. Thanks to this gentleman's quick thinking, a thorough search has been undertaken of the grounds."

"And have you found anything?"

"No."

"Then what was the point? I knew you were useless. Get out, I tell you."

"Mondial, listen," Theodore said, coming to the bedside. "There's a dangerous man about the place. He might strike again. You might not care you've been shot but what about justice for Miss Lamb? What about the safety of the other ladies here?"

"Dangerous man? It was a chance robbery by a passing

footpad that has gone terribly badly. Could have happened anywhere and he will be long gone."

"It was a murder."

The Inspector said, "Was anything taken, sir?" and at that, Lord Mondial hurled a jug of water towards him, wrenched with his uninjured left hand from the chair by the head of the bed. The Inspector took two quick steps backwards and it bounced harmlessly on the carpet, spilling the contents. The Inspector turned to Lord Calaway.

"I'll come back when he is more settled," he said mildly. He let himself out of the bedroom. Dido sat on a chair by the other side of the bed and she had not moved even when her husband had thrown the jug. She bent her head and wrapped her arms around herself, and Adelia stood by her side, her hand on her shoulder.

Outside, the careful, quiet men from the funeral parlour would be doing what they needed to do.

Theodore picked up the jug from the floor and placed it carefully back on the chair. Taylor the valet came back in with a mop and began to tidy up silently. Lord Mondial sagged back on the pillows. His face was as pale as the bandages around his upper arm. "Where's my damn brandy?" he snarled.

Theodore nodded at Taylor who disappeared with his mop and bucket. While the valet was gone, Theodore said, "Do you really believe it was a chance robbery? Here on your grounds? Has this happened before?"

"No."

Theodore said, "Has anyone been seen lingering in the gardens? Have there been reports of strangers acting oddly in the area?"

"Again, no."

Dido raised her head and looked up at Adelia, who shushed her. Theodore thought that his wife looked very pale and made a mental note to administer her a tonic.

Theodore carried on with his questions. "Was anything taken? If it were really a robbery, something must have been taken?"

"Of course it was really a robbery! He shot my arm not my head. I'm not stupid. Yes, my pocket-watch has gone. He forced me to hand it over."

"And what did he look like?"

"I don't know. It all happened so fast."

But slowly enough to demand a watch, Theodore thought. "So he was a stranger to you?"

"I suppose that he must have been."

"You would have recognised a friend at such close quarters."

"My arm is on fire. You have no idea how that feels. My wife's friend is dead – shot in front of my very face – at the moment, I would not recognise my own father."

Taylor returned with a generous glass of brandy which Lord Mondial knocked back in one swift movement. He shoved the glass back at Taylor who was sent off again, this time to return with the bottle.

"My lord…" said Dido warningly but he growled and she did not continue.

"I don't want that Inspector to come back," he told Theodore. "The rural police can't catch a pig thief and I won't have them tramping all through my house. I'll tell you what, if it

61

makes you any happier, I'll pay for some detectives of my own. I'll send for someone from London. Someone who knows what they are doing. I know enough judges and magistrates to have the very best recommended to me. How about that? Will that shut you up?"

Theodore nodded. "Yes. It would be for the best. I understand."

"There's no guarantee anyone can come up. Or when. It doesn't matter. What's more important is that she must have the best of funerals."

Adelia spoke up. "My lord, with respect, she'll return to her family…"

"Her doddery old grandfather, Hardy? If she must. Whatever must be done, let it be done. I shall pay, of course. No one will say I shirked any of my duty. Now, get out, the lot of you. Taylor; well done, today. Thank you. Leave me the bottle. I shall *not* be coming down to dinner. Dismiss all the guests."

Theodore glanced at Adelia, who shook her head. "I shall stay here with my daughter who needs me," she said firmly.

Theodore said, "Mondial, you're right to agree to summon a detective but think on this: they will surely want everything to stay exactly as it is right now. You cannot dismiss anyone. The detective will need to speak to everyone. The guests must stay here."

Lord Mondial had knocked back his second glass of brandy. "Very well. This is all a damned inconvenience for the sake of a passing footpad." He turned his head away, and they all shuffled out.

6

Adelia felt as if she were going to explode with a mish-mash of boiling emotions. She was devastated, utterly destroyed with the death of Philippa Lamb. An inconvenience? She could have slammed the jug onto Lord Mondial's head when he'd said that. She'd known the girl for so long, and she was so pretty, and popular, and full of life. She had done no harm to anyone. To meet her death in such a violent and senseless way was sickening. She imagined how it would be if one of her own daughters had died in such a way, and she felt ill. That illness turned to anger. Who could have done such a thing? Passing robbers attacked in the street, in alleys, in dark country lanes – not the serene gardens of an estate around a castle.

And all mixed up in her anger and her grief was, strangely and almost unseemly, a flicker of pride at how well Theodore had managed the terrible situation. She sat in their suite that evening, dining off a tray on the table by the window, while her husband sat opposite her and tucked heartily into the food that she was only able to pick at.

Of course, a large formal dinner was not going to happen

on the same day as a brutal murder. Everyone who was still present was eating quietly in their rooms. Adelia had spoken to Miss Lamb's companion and invited her to spend a few hours with them, but the distraught old nurse had been taken under the wing of the housekeeper.

"You were marvellous today," Adelia said eventually, unable to suppress her slightly tasteless pride in her husband. "You really were. You took charge in the most magnificent way."

Theodore looked up from the cold boiled beef. "I did what needed to be done, no more and no less."

"But you were so efficient. Lord Mondial doesn't need to summon a detective from London. He really didn't want one. You needn't have persuaded him. He doesn't need one while you're here! I expect you can easily change his mind and he would be happier if he knew you were looking into things. It keeps it in the family."

"I am a doctor," he said with a puff of a laugh.

"You are an earl; it doesn't stop you being other things too. That medical eye of yours might be very helpful."

"Medicine can help Mondial but it won't do a thing for the girl."

"Poor Philippa."

"She wouldn't have suffered," he told her bluntly. "So that's a good thing to remember."

"Thank you," Adelia said, trying not to remember anything at all. "No, I simply mean that you have a good eye for details and you notice the connections between things. Those skills certainly make you a good doctor in many ways but they might also make you a good detective."

He tapped his fork idly on the edge of his plate. "Perhaps. But I have no stomach for that sort of thing. No drive for it, I mean. No desire to be a fancily-dressed titled version of a Bow Street Runner."

"No, not generally," she agreed. "But in this particular matter, there is no one who is better placed. I wonder if her family has been told yet? Dido might have seen to it but she might have been too overwrought."

"It's just the old grandfather, isn't it? I never did meet him."

"Yes, you did."

"Oh, did I? He made no impression on me, then. And wasn't he away for most of the girl's childhood?"

"He was. He had gone to the colonies to work as a doctor and did not return while we had his granddaughter for those long holidays. Yet you do know him; and he has made every impression on you, my dear." Adelia shook her head in exasperation. "You met him when you were a small boy. Was it not Doctor Hardy, as a young man, who had saved your own father's life?"

She watched him as the blood drained from his face. He went as white as Lord Mondial had been. He frowned as he struggled to make sense of what she'd said. "But he was not a grandfather when…"

"Of course he wasn't. He had just begun his practice and been wed to a nice young lady from Sussex. Their daughter was our dear Philippa's mother. You are no longer young yourself, dear; the years have passed. You must have known this. I will have told you." She told him many things about people and their connections. She knew he faded her out. But this?

He blinked. "I did know it; I must have known it. But as you say, the years have passed. Other things have filled my head."

She was still sceptical. He looked like he was hearing the information for the first time. But then, he had lost some memories during the few years after the death of his first wife, when he had been left alone with a young son and nothing but endless money and fake friends for company. The excesses and indulgences of that time had eaten away some of his recollections. She wondered if it had also affected Bamfylde in ways they did not see clearly; it would explain Theodore's son's current situation.

She pushed that out of her mind. Bamfylde was now in his thirties and he hated his stepmother with a passion usually reserved only for those characters in fairy tales.

"Well, no matter," she said mildly. "I will speak to Dido later and ensure that word has been sent to him. He is in poor health now, I understand."

"It does matter," Theodore said suddenly and with an alarming fierceness. "I should go and see him and break the news to him in person. He deserves no less."

"My dear, that is very noble of you, but when was the last time you saw him?"

"As you say, I must have been a child."

"Quite. It is well over fifty years ago, I'll wager. Your father was but one of the thousands of men and women he will have treated over the years."

"Are you saying he won't remember me?" Theodore said with a hurt and incredulous look on his face.

"I am sorry, my dear, but he most likely won't."

"He was the most important man to me, beside my father."

"I know."

"I ... don't know what to do." He sounded broken and helpless.

"Stay here and use your powers to assist in solving this case."

"I have no powers and I know nothing. I suppose I could ask the staff some questions. Ask them what they saw and so on."

Adelia saw her mistake immediately. But it was too late.

"Ah! No. No! Do not do anything like that to prejudice the case," she said in a rush. If Theodore's bedside manner was appalling, his personal investigative skills were going to be even worse. "No, I mean, you should look for clues and think about how they might fit together. Use your rational mind *from a distance.*"

"That's all meaningless without information. Information that comes from people."

She pushed her plate to one side. "Well, as to that," she said. "You may leave the gathering of that information to me."

"To you?"

"I know people, do I not? I am the best match-maker in the county. I know everyone and I know their secrets. I can speak to a maid as well as I can to a duchess. Let me winkle out the information and pass it on to you; you can put the puzzle together."

Theodore leaned over and took her half-empty plate. The sight of death clearly hadn't affected his appetite at all. He polished off the remains of Adelia's food while she politely looked out of the window. When he was done, he piled up the crockery on the tray and dabbed his mouth elegantly. He looked around as if he expected a servant to dive forward and remove the tray but of course they were alone. Smith was elsewhere, possibly eating in the servants' hall or more likely in the place just called The Room where the upper servants dined, waited upon by the more junior staff. Theodore stared at the plates as if he weren't sure what would happen to them now.

Adelia smiled to herself. He might have been clever, but sometimes he wasn't very bright. She said, "Let us go over what we already know." She wanted to be active and do something. It wasn't just that she thought Theodore would be good at putting the clues together; she herself could not stand the thought of sitting in her room while a murderer roamed around the area. She didn't want to think about poor dead Philippa. So to stave off those feelings of loss, she resolved to be as busy as possible.

"What do we know?" Theodore said. "It was a robbery but in the event, the robber discharged his weapon twice and ... no, wait a moment."

"What?"

"Was the attacker one person, or two? I heard both the shots as they were fired. Either he was able to reload in ... let me see ... a matter of seconds, or he had two weapons, both ready loaded, or there were two people involved. One of those people shot Miss Lamb and the other shot Mondial."

"But Lord Mondial did not mention two people."

"He did not, but he himself admitted his judgement has been clouded. Still, I find it hard to believe that two robbers have set upon them; he would have noticed that unless one was hiding in the trees and shot at a distance." He clicked his fingers. "Paper!"

Adelia jumped up and fetched him some sheets of foolscap and a pencil that he swiftly sharpened with his pocket knife. He dropped the tray to the floor with a clatter and began to make notes.

"I need to examine the clothing of Miss Lamb and Mondial. How close were these shots fired from? If there is powder on them, then the robber – or robbers – were very close, and Mondial *must* have known if there were one or two."

"Indeed. Let me speak to the funeral directors to make the initial introduction," Adelia said hastily.

"Yes, yes. Now, if there were only one assailant as Mondial suggests, then that raises other questions. I cannot believe the pistol was reloaded so quickly. Even the best shot cannot do that. Therefore the robber had two weapons. A pair of pistols. That would seem unusual. I do not have a great deal of experience with highwaymen or street robbers but while carrying one weapon is par for the course, two seems both excessive and generally unnecessary unless one knew in advance that one would need to fire two shots in quick succession."

"That makes sense."

Theodore tapped the pencil on his teeth. It made Adelia want to scream but she didn't want to upset his thought process so she stared out of the window again. Dusk was not yet coming on, and the air continued to be hot and oppressive. "Dido!" she said with a jolt.

"What of her? Is she outside?" he said, glancing to the window.

"No – but she should have been. Listen. I was in the upstairs room at the back of the castle with Dido and Miss Lamb. We were making plans for the garden party. Then Lord Mondial came in and asked Dido to walk with him in the garden. He insisted that he had some information to share with her. She left with him. When the shots rang out, I had assumed she was still with him, but she clearly was not. So where did she go?"

"That makes our daughter a suspect," Theodore said.

"No, she is not. She could never be! Dido, firing weapons?" Of all their daughters, she was not the one to do that. Margaret, maybe; she was impossible to work out. And Anne had once threatened violence with a pistol, but it had been her own life she had wanted to take. Adelia shuddered at the memory. Troubled Anne seemed more settled now. Adelia returned to the problem of Dido and said, "Let us speak with her first, and also the servants, as they will have noticed who goes where; they always do."

"Do they? They seem remarkably stupid to me."

"They have more brains in their heads than many a dinner party guest we've had to endure," Adelia snapped. "I am not saying she is a suspect but she must tell us where she went after going out of the castle with Lord Mondial."

"And how did Miss Lamb come to be in his company?"

Adelia winced. "As to that, I have some suspicions." She didn't want to think about them. But she had to.

"Out with them. Oh – no, not that. Criminal conversation, as they say?" Theodore was shaking his head in a disbelief that matched Adelia's own feelings exactly. "Miss Lamb and Mondial?"

"I can scarcely believe it." Adelia remembered her talks with Philippa. "In all honesty, no. No! She assured me that there was no man in her affections and I believed her. However, she alluded to the fact that she thought she was the object of another's affections which she did not reciprocate. Could that have been

70

Lord Mondial?"

"He is married."

"Yes, but that does not stop a man from lusting after another woman not his wife."

"He is a man of honour! And he is our son-in-law."

"*And* he is a man accustomed to have whatever he pleases. It would be not so unusual for a man of his status to take a mistress or two though he ought to, for decency's sake, install them somewhere in London and not parade them around his own household." She sighed heavily. "I fancy now that he might have been pursuing Miss Lamb and perhaps she did not care for it. In fact … I must speak once more to her companion, for I am sure that Miss Lamb intended to leave this place a few days ago, and I caught her packing to go. Something stopped her. I wonder what it was? Oh, if only she had gone!"

"I have begun a list for you, my dear," Theodore said, ignoring his wife's sudden flood of grief. "You will speak to the funeral directors, and you will speak to Dido and the servants, and also Miss Lamb's companion. Are you sure I cannot do any of this? It is a burden on you at this time."

"Quite sure. I need to be active. Trust me, if you love me."

"You know that I do."

"Don't look so hurt."

"I was merely adjusting my face." He began to draw small squares on the paper, doodling idly while his brain worked, which was preferable to tapping the pencil on his teeth. "As well as the companion of Miss Lamb, who else remains in the house?"

"A multitude of servants."

"None of whom will own pistols, surely?"

"They might, in secret, though it is unlikely. I will get a list from Dido. There is also Sir Henry Locksley…"

"Ah, yes, the intended groom. Well, he shall have to look elsewhere for his marriage now. Good job for him that proceedings hadn't got any further, hey?"

"Theodore! And that is *precisely* the sort of tasteless comment which reinforces why you must *not* speak to anyone so bluntly and plainly."

"I was simply thinking practically."

"Murder is a matter of emotion." Adelia glared at him until he looked down. Then she said, "Although there is something you must know about Sir Henry … I saw him go out after Miss Lamb."

"When?"

"Just after Dido had left with Lord Mondial."

"So he was in the gardens at the time of the murder?"

"I believe so."

"Anyone else?"

And Adelia hesitated.

There had been someone else seen in the gardens over the past few days. Someone who shouldn't have been there at all. Someone she didn't want to think about.

From the description, and the fact that he constantly turned up to plague her, she felt sure that it was her brother Alfred Pegsworth. She was going to have to deal with him now, too.

"No," she said firmly. "As far as I know there was no one else."

7

It was a strange, sombre and quiet castle which awoke the next day. Even Theodore picked up on it. He took an early morning walk around the misty grounds and allowed himself to remember how Philippa Lamb had been when she was a girl; full of laughter, full of joy. A tear moistened his eye and he felt no need to wipe it away in haste. She had been an innocent young woman and her death was senseless. He felt for her, and for everyone close to him who had been touched by this loss.

The heat of the sun had hit the cooling earth and brought up an ethereal fog which made the gardens seem large and unfamiliar. There was no hope of stumbling across any clues in such disorientating surroundings. He wondered about the detective that Mondial would reluctantly send for, and an odd flash of something very like resentment rose in him. Adelia could be right, he thought. She often was. This was something that *he* could solve with no need of an expensive London detective. He didn't doubt his own intelligence.

The idea of it tickled him.

He batted the bubble of pleasure back down instantly with

a feeling of disgust that he could experience such contrary emotions like that. No. Be dignified and show some respect, he ordered himself; a dear sweet girl is dead and this should not be a reason to be happy. But the mystery of the thing – that is something else. The mystery calls to me.

Solving it would be a good thing to do.

Perhaps even an *honourable* thing.

If he could rise to Adelia's high opinion of him, that was.

He trudged back up the slope to the castle, his boots leaving dark steps in the silver dew-soaked grass. He popped his head into the breakfast room, where a white-faced girl with red eyes was laying out the plates for the morning meal. He was about to tell her she had conjunctivitis when it occurred to him that she might have been crying. She was startled to see anyone the place about so early.

"Everything is to go on as normal. Lord Mondial has ordered it," she said to his enquiry. "We are not to mention the … unfortunate matter."

"No doubt appearances must be maintained and I suppose that after all, she was not a member of the family," Theodore replied.

"But who did it, my lord? They say there is a murderer on the loose. They say a man was creeping about the gardens a few days ago. Will he come back? They say we are not safe here now. Maud has already run away."

"You're perfectly safe," he told her, hoping to reassure her. "It was a robbery, after all. You're only a servant and have nothing worth stealing."

She blinked at him as if his words didn't help at all.

74

"And worrying can hardly prevent anything bad from happening, so you may as well just get on with your duties," he added, expecting that would cheer her up.

It didn't seem to.

He shrugged and headed back to his rooms to let Adelia know they would be able to get breakfast as usual. He was hoping for a nicely boiled egg.

They were the only ones present in the breakfast room so they conversed in low voices as the handful of servants – who didn't count as people being present – flurried around them. Adelia planned to go directly to Dido and to make a complete list of everyone in the house. That *did* include the servants, of course. Theodore was already looking sideways at all of them, wondering which of them could possibly handle a pair of pistols. Then Adelia planned to approach the funeral director and to try to persuade him to let Theodore in – perhaps they would visit the funeral parlour together. Theodore himself wanted to examine Mondial's own clothing and he thought he'd be best speaking to Mondial's valet first about that.

Thus fortified by a plan of action and a great deal of scrambled eggs, as the boiled ones were "not done right", they went their separate ways. Adelia slipped along the corridors to see if her daughter was in the morning room and Theodore headed upstairs to waylay the valet, Tobias Taylor.

Halfway up the stairs he stopped. Sir Henry was coming

down. The younger man looked strained and had circles under his eyes. He greeted Theodore with a glum, unsmiling face. "Dashed bad business," he muttered in a low voice. "Makes you wonder, doesn't it?"

"Makes you wonder what?"

"Just – I don't know. About life. Death. The point of it all."

"Now, you mustn't let yourself sink into such speculations. That's how people go insane, you know."

"Do the mad know that they are mad? For if not, I suspect it's a preferable state to this horrible everyday *knowing*."

"If you think that you are mad, then you are not mad," Theodore said. "Look here, Locksley. I don't know you awfully well but you seem to be a decent chap, if a little melancholic. Take my advice, as a doctor and as a man, and move on as quickly as you can from this affair. Things had not progressed very far with the girl, after all, so you cannot sink into an unseemly grief when you were not even officially – you know – *connected*."

"Thank you, my lord. I shall heed your advice as much as I am able. But does it not affect you, even so, just the mere thought of death? It does me. I find myself looking at quite beautiful things like flowers and thinking, *what's the point when it will all soon be gone?*"

Theodore leaned on the solid bannister and regarded Sir Henry with a growing suspicion. The man was in his late twenties, maybe his early thirties. He looked careworn and far more upset than he should have been, at least to Theodore's mind. Yet they'd not even been engaged. No understanding between the pair, as far as he knew, had yet been arranged. Perhaps, Theodore thought, there was more to this than met his eyes. After all, hadn't

Adelia told him that she had seen Sir Henry leave the house after Miss Lamb? He must have been in the gardens when the terrible event had occurred.

"I say," Theodore said, attempting to sound conversational. He rested one foot on the stair above the one he was standing on, thinking it would make him look casual and approachable. He felt awkward. Sir Henry moved to one side, obviously thinking that Theodore was about to carry on up the stairs. Theodore remained where he was, stuck now in a strange pose. "I say," he said again, "You are right. Terrible business. I was the first to find them, you know. Where were you?"

Sir Henry's eyes opened a little wider. "I was – I was down in the gardens."

"Walking?"

"Yes. Strolling, I should say. I dead-headed a few roses. I can show you because I left them dumped in a pile when I heard the commotion. Are you a detective now? I thought Lord Mondial was sending for someone. They need to get a wriggle on if they hope to be here before the rains."

The rush of garrulous over-information interested Theodore. He stored away each of Sir Henry's sentences in his memory. "I am not a detective in spite of my wife's fantasies," he said.

Sir Henry coughed as if he had said something unintentionally amusing.

Childish reaction, Theodore thought. "As for the man from London, yes, Mondial intends to send for him as soon as he is able to. He might have already done so. Rain, you say?"

"Thunder is coming – can't you feel it? Storms, I should

say. The road below the house always gets impassable when the river floods."

"You've been here before, then?"

"I – yes, I am relatively local."

"I see." Theodore didn't quite see, not yet, but he thought it was significant. "So you were dead-heading roses. I didn't have you down as a gardener."

"I am always happier out of doors. Less confining. But don't look to me as a murderer, sir! I was at breakfast, as usual, as anyone can vouch for, and then I returned to my rooms. I read a little of a book and then engaged in some correspondence in the library. After lunch, which was rather late I seem to remember, I decided to go for a walk."

"It was a hot day."

"Stifling," Sir Henry agreed. "But I need to be active. I am a man who needs to move. I headed out through the rose gardens."

"Did you see anyone?"

There was a momentary hesitation. "I – I will speak my mind to the detective when he comes."

"I ask only as a friend. And, as you know, I was almost as a father to Miss Lamb." Well, Adelia had been like a mother to her, so that made him father-like even if he had been distant and mostly unconscious of her presence.

"I don't like the insinuation that I might be in any way involved in this heinous crime," Sir Henry said, turning his face away and tipping up his chin. "I don't see that I have to justify my movements to you or to anyone, quite frankly! I say, if you want to point the finger at anyone, you need to look to Lord Mondial's valet; that Taylor chap. Yes, ask him what *he* was doing

78

yesterday afternoon, coming from the stables?"

"The stables? I had been there, just before the shots were fired."

"No, this was afterwards. I heard the shots from where I was but the rose garden is the opposite side of the house to the yew trees and that pond. I wasn't sure what I'd heard and I didn't run. I dumped the clippings and headed towards the sound. I was curious, nothing more, so I walked steadily. It was too hot to be running for no reason. I came around the back of the house and across the patios, along the top of the lawn, and then I heard some shouting from the pond but I couldn't see anything. So instead of sticking to the paths, I risked the wrath of the gardeners and turned right, cutting across the lawns to go more directly towards the sound of the hullabaloo. And that's when I saw Taylor but he was going *away* from the noise, you see. He was coming from the stables and heading back to the house. So you should ask *him* what he was doing. Good day to you, sir!"

Sir Henry pushed past Theodore. Theodore didn't mind the slight at all. He was bubbling with excitement. He rushed back to his rooms and grabbed a sheet of paper, and began to sketch out exactly what Sir Henry had described to him.

The way that Sir Henry had described his movements did make perfect sense, as long as he was not lying. What didn't make sense was the suggestion that Tobias Taylor the valet was seen coming from the stable area. Theodore had been there before the murder and he was sure that he had been alone. The horses had been curious about him; they would surely have indicated if someone else had been there? He hadn't even seen any staff – no grooms, no stable-hands, no coach-boys, no one at all.

However, if Sir Henry was not lying, he might yet be mistaken. He could have seen another man, not Tobias Taylor. Although Theodore had promised Adelia that he would leave the detailed questioning to her, he could not resist following this particular snippet. Anyway, he thought, Mondial's valet was far more likely to open up to Theodore, man to man, than to his wife, however clever she was.

It didn't take much to convince himself it was the right thing to do, and anyway, he wanted to examine the clothes that Mondial had been wearing when he had been shot. Two birds, one stone, he told himself cheerfully and headed off to Mondial's private suite of rooms in a far wing of the castle.

He tapped on the door and was greeted by Taylor himself. He was a tall man, with narrow shoulders and a long, thin neck that made him look like a heron. He had heavily-lidded eyes and a sardonic smile, and nothing at all between the ears, as far as Theodore could tell.

"How is my lord today?" Theodore asking, trying to peer past Taylor. The room behind the valet was a day room, a pleasant private space where Mondial would read or sit or entertain very personal guests. His bedroom lay even further inside the suite, not directly accessible from the corridor.

"My Lord Mondial is much better, thank you," Taylor said. "I shall inform him of your solicitations."

"Please do. Or might I see him? You know I am a medical

80

man."

Taylor opened the door wider to show Theodore the empty room beyond. "I am afraid not. He has ridden into town early this morning."

"Ridden!"

"Exactly so. His arm is bound up and he is an able horseman. I believe there is business to which he must attend."

"Of course, of course." Summoning a detective, informing Miss Lamb's relatives – it all made sense. Lord Mondial knew his responsibilities. It didn't matter to Theodore however; the Marquis's abscence was to Theodore's advantage. He smiled and said, "I am gathering information to pass on to the detective when he arrives. It seems the best thing to do, you know, while it's all fresh in peoples' minds. I wonder if you could tell me where you were when it happened yesterday?"

Taylor's thin lip curled in distaste. "I was here," he said curtly. "I was in my lord's rooms all day, and when I heard there had been a disturbance I was in the dressing room, brushing my lord's tweeds, ready for his trip to Scotland."

"You did not leave the house for any reason?"

"What reason?"

"This is what I am asking you," Theodore pressed. Why could people not simply answer the question directly? Perhaps this *was* something better left to Adelia.

"I had no reason to leave the rooms until I heard the crisis occur. I know my duties and my place," he added, as if he were suggesting that Theodore did not know his own place.

"I see. Of course. I understand," Theodore replied. "One last thing, if I may. Lord Mondial's clothes? I should like to examine them."

Taylor stared at him, utter incomprehension on his face. He did not reply.

Theodore tried again. "I wish to look at the shirt, jacket and waistcoat that he was wearing. His cravat, too."

"They have been destroyed. They were utterly beyond repair." Taylor's incredulity overrode his place as a servant. He said, "What could you possibly want with my lord's clothing?"

"I am interested in the marks left by the firing of the pistol."

Taylor was still shaking his head. "No, sir. No, my lord. It is impossible." He began to close the door.

Theodore retreated to the corridor and stood for a moment in silent contemplation. When he turned to walk away, he came face to face with Lord Mondial, dusty and red-faced from his ride into town.

8

Adelia was pleased to find her husband waiting for her in their rooms when she returned from talking with Dido. It was just before luncheon was due to be served, and she needed to change out of her day dress into a more elaborate and colourful get-up suitable for meeting people. She also needed to freshen up after a grief-filled morning of tears and confusion. She felt worn out, hollowed from within like an empty vessel. She mourned the loss of Miss Lamb, of course. But her grief was layered. She also mourned for her daughter's sadness, and wondered how many of Dido's tears were for Philippa and how many were Dido's own secret troubles given free outlet under the mask of mourning her friend.

"Oh, our poor daughter," she said, flopping into a wide easy chair by the windows. She picked up a sheet of paper and fanned herself with it. "She is utterly devastated and Lord Mondial is of no use whatsoever. That man! I fear I may have made a mistake in arranging this match. He needs a good shaking. It reminds me of the wedding itself – I should have taken what happened then as a warning sign."

"What do you mean? It was a glorious day," Theodore said.

She was sceptical as to whether he could distinguish between all seven of the weddings that his daughters had had. She said, "Not the wedding day itself. But do you remember how they had planned a three-week tour of Italy to commence a few days later, but then his mother was taken ill?"

"She was not seriously ill. They still went."

"They still went *and then she died* so actually, I would say that she was seriously ill. But I remember speaking to Dido beforehand and she said that because it was arranged, he must carry on. He was so much a man of his word. And he's playing the same trick now. I can't work out if he's callous or simply so, so concerned with sticking to what he's said he will do. It's some point of pride with him. I wonder what has made him so rigid." She stopped and looked more closely at the paper in her hand. "What is this? Are you an artist now?"

"Ah, no! You will be very impressed," he said, dragging up a chair to sit alongside her. "These are the movements of Sir Henry Locksley during yesterday's terrible situation."

"Impressed? I am alarmed. To know this, you must have spoken to him and I thought that we had agreed to leave the more delicate matters of actually speaking to people to me."

"Of course, but don't worry. It all happened quite naturally and I don't think I've upset anyone. Look…" He picked up a pencil and used it to indicate Sir Henry's path through the grounds, and who he claimed to have seen.

"Tobias Taylor?" Adelia repeated. "He came down from the house with everyone else when the alarm was raised. I was in front of him. He was holding a clothes brush."

84

"Oh, but that corroborates his story," Theodore said, his face falling.

"It does not. A brush is the easiest thing to let drop when something calls your attention; why would he bring it with him unless he meant for it be seen? It makes him look more suspicious. And I don't like that valet; he fancies himself to be one for the ladies. But more to the point – what do you mean, *his story?* Who else have you spoken to?"

"Well, I did as we agreed and went to Mondial's rooms in order to investigate his clothing," he said.

She pressed her lips together and nodded slightly. She wanted to be angry at him but he was correct. They had agreed for him to do that. So she had to be silent and let him continue.

"Taylor was most unhelpful. He seemed to think that it was not my place to be asking him anything. The man might be a valet to a Marquis but he has entirely the wrong sort of attitude."

"Yes, dear, he's a complete cad, but what did he say?" she asked through gritted teeth.

"He told me that the clothing had been destroyed as it was beyond repair. No doubt that is true. It would have been soaked with blood; indeed I saw that with my own eyes. Damn it! I wish I had thought to look more closely at the powder marks around the place where the bullet had entered his arm."

Adelia, in spite of her annoyance, smiled. It was heartening to see her husband passionate about something.

Theodore drew an idle doodle on the paper as he continued. "He also utterly denied Locksley's assertion that he had been out of the house at any point. He claimed to have been in Mondial's rooms all day, brushing his tweeds."

"Hence carrying the clothes brush," Adelia said. "I do not like the sound of this man. Everything I hear makes me suspect him."

"Yet Mondial holds him in the highest regard. Should we warn him, do we think? He needs to know if he has a duplicitous servant." Theodore said. Then he stopped and jabbed the pencil hard into the paper. The lead snapped. "The man is of singular appearance. Tall, thin, like he'd snap in a wind. Even at a distance, he is remarkable. I don't understand why he could be a ladies' man. What is the appeal of a man like a stick?"

"It is the way that he looks at a young woman and speaks with them as if they are the most amazing person he has ever met," Adelia said. "I have watched him at work."

Theodore shook his head, the concept quite alien to him. He continued. "And he has been in Mondial's employment, I understand, for many years. Mondial *would* have recognised him, had he been the assailant. Even masked and disguised, surely the master would know the servant – such a personal servant, one who has been so close for so long."

"I agree," said Adelia, impressed all over again by her husband's perspicacity, at least in certain matters. "Taylor may be lying but it could be for any number of reasons. Sir Henry, likewise, could lie for innocent reasons – well, innocent of murder, at any rate. Oh, I don't like to think of Sir Henry being involved!" She knew she was letting her feelings influence matters. She liked Sir Henry, so he couldn't be a murderer. She didn't like Taylor, so he could be any kind of villain she cared to consider.

"*Someone* must be involved."

"Not necessarily. It could yet be the work of a passing robber, as Lord Mondial suspects." She said it with reluctance. They would never solve that kind of murder.

"If that is really the case, then I suppose that he *must* turn it over to the local police," Theodore said. "But he is stubborn and private. And I think it must be someone in this household."

"Why?"

He tapped the broken pencil on the paper with each point that he made. "Two pistols. Private land. Not a typical robbery. The house untouched. No precedent. The odd movements of Mondial, Taylor, Miss Lamb, Locksley, even our Dido. Oh – and I encountered Mondial as I was leaving his rooms. He had just got back from a visit to town. He rode!"

"With his arm as it is?"

"Yes, with his arm all strapped up. He is made of stern stuff. Do you know, he told me that he has arranged for Miss Lamb's body to return to the town in which her grandfather resides, and of course he intends to continue on here as normal, as if nothing has happened."

Adelia nodded sadly. It had been the cause of much grief this morning. "Just as with the honeymoon trip around Italy, he actually still intends on going ahead with the garden party, as the invitations have almost all been sent out. We had barely finished the additional list! There was no need to continue. We could send out cancellations – we could do so today. Yet he said no. He said he had told people and they might have already made arrangements to attend."

"Good heavens. The man is heartless. Callous, as you say. This is supposed to be a house of mourning."

"It is not a house of mourning, though. Not officially. No one is covering the mirrors here. She was not a relative of the family and he claims it was merely a robbery that happened outside the house – and therefore nothing can attach to him or his name. There is no expectation that he will behave as if he is in mourning."

Theodore frowned. "He is logical and I admire that. But you know more about matters of etiquette than I do. What will the *set* say?"

Adelia sniffed. The London set were fickle and flighty. "The fashionable people will be simply *delighted* to come here for the party. It will be the most well-attended event in the county for years, because this is a scene of gossip now. And while everyone will agree that it is in poor taste to hold the party, no one will dare to be left out. They will all come while swearing that they ought not to be here."

"Then the blame rests on Mondial for going ahead with it."

"And he says he will be blamed for cancelling it. He is a man of his word. He and our dear Dido have had strong words about it, this morning, and she is very upset. Yet even her distress seems not to move him," Adelia explained. "He had decided a party was to be held, and he will not be swayed. In fact…"

"What?"

"I do not wish to be the cause of gossip so you must keep this to yourself, but Dido seemed to hint that he was concerned that if he cancelled the party on account of 'a mere house-guest to whom he had no connection' then people would read some scandal into that, and assume that there was more of a connection. In his strange way, he believes that less scandal will attach to him this way. It is nonsense, of course. Yet I cannot help wondering if there is no smoke without fire. For, after all, why *was* he alone with Miss Lamb?"

"Why indeed," said Theodore. "What did Dido tell you about her own movements yesterday?"

"This is complicated," Adelia said. "Let me copy you, and draw a map of it all." He sharpened the pencil for her and passed it over. She drew a small square. "To begin; we were here, and Lord Mondial came to the room where we were planning the garden party and asked Dido to walk with him. This much I know to be absolutely true."

Theodore nodded.

"They left together." The pencil scraped across the paper. "Now, in Dido's account, she left the house with her husband by the rear doors and stepped onto the patio. She told him she thought that it was too hot to walk, and asked that he converse with her there in the shade on the patio. But he insisted that they proceed through the gardens. He told her that she was pale and wan, not pale and interesting."

"And she agreed?"

"She is not accustomed to disagree with her husband even though any decent lady would wish to remain pale and not step out into the sun at all. But she obeyed."

"Obeyed! Yet she is your daughter," Theodore said with a smile.

"And yours; yet she is her own person too, and she wants only to please and to do her duty as a wife and make him happy. Don't start – yes, it is a duty I might sometimes fail at." She allowed a small smile to cross her face before returning to the serious matter at hand. "So Dido went with him onto the lawns, reluctantly, and a window in the upper floor was flung open and the children's nurse called out."

"A window in the nursey?"

"No, they are barred and the nursery itself is on the very top floor. This was from the schoolroom, and the nurse called out that one of the boys was ill, and what was she to do about it?"

"I can't imagine that pleased Mondial," Theodore said.

"Oh, of course, he was utterly livid. He was angry that they were being interrupted, and furious that the servant had actually shouted across the lawn. She went red when he turned around; Dido says that the nurse hadn't stopped to think. She'd seen Dido, and knew that Dido would want to be informed. She called out before she could stop herself. She has offered her resignation but Lord Mondial has already sacked her without any character."

"The cad. This is his home to run as he sees fit, but surely as the child was ill – oh, my grandchild! Tell me, what is wrong, and which one is it?" He was almost getting to his feet.

"Sit down. It was a passing stomach ailment and affected both boys in but a mild way. They have been dosed with chamomile tea and mulled eggs and remain in bed. It is a blessing, as all the alarums of the day have passed them by."

"Marrow toast. They must have marrow toast," Theodore said urgently.

Adelia smiled at her husband. He adored his grandchildren even if he seemed unable to remember their names or tell them apart. He was quite happy to get down on his hands and knees on the rug by the fire and let them crawl all over him. Adelia looked forward to the time that the boys were older and could hold better conversations with their grandfather. Dido had been the first of their daughters to have children although she didn't doubt the rest would be far behind – except Mary, perhaps. As for Theodore's son and heir, Bamfylde, there were probably dozens of his children, unacknowledged, scattered about the country.

Theodore was deep in thought. He jerked himself out of his reverie and said, "So, what happened next?"

"Dido returned to the house of course. She didn't know, at that time, how serious or not the illness was. All she knew was that the nurse had called her, and even the wrath of her husband could not prevent her from going to her boys. She is, above all, a devoted mother."

"And Mondial followed?"

"No." He is not a devoted father, she thought. "He stormed off, so she said, raging and muttering. She assumed that he wanted to walk off his anger and she let him go; she had no interest in anything but getting to her children by that point. She didn't see why he could not speak to her later about whatever the matter was. But as you have seen, he is a man of stubborn character and fixed ideas. If he decides something is to happen then that must happen when he decrees it."

"So he went to the yew tree walk?" Theodore said.

"Yes, and there he must have encountered Miss Lamb, who was also walking."

"And there she was shot. What does Dido think about the whole affair? Does she believe that a robber could have wandered into the grounds? If I were a highwayman, I would not prey upon people in their own gardens. For anyone walking in the gardens here is not carrying money or jewellery. A good robber would either come to the house to raid it, or he would prey upon people who are travelling or enjoying time in town."

"I agree with your logic. And not to mention that these attacks surely happen at night, not during the day. Do you think there is a chance that Miss Lamb and Lord Mondial were deliberately attacked? That it could have been planned in some way?"

"Yes, I do," said Theodore. "And that leads to another thought. If planned, then there is someone out there who wants to do harm to Mondial. He must be upon his guard." He shook his head. "Yet he wants to ignore the whole thing and carry on as usual."

"The garden party will be the event of the month, now," Adelia said.

"No, I mean there is more. I met him, as I told you, on his return from town. He has sent word to Doctor Hardy, Miss Lamb's grandfather." Theodore curled his lip. "By post. Can you imagine? You criticise me for my lack of tact, my dear, but even I can see this is news that ought to be broken in person. But here we are and it is done. He has made arrangements with the funeral directors. Even now she is probably on her final journey."

"I am sorry," Adelia said, seeing that he was frowning.

"I am, too. I will not get the chance to examine the body."

"No, I meant … never mind."

"Furthermore," he blundered on in his oblivion, "Mondial has changed his mind about engaging a detective. He was never very keen and claims he agreed to my suggestion in the heat of the moment while pain addled his mind. No detective will be coming from London or anywhere at all."

"Oh! So you are to investigate?"

"No," he told her. "He has actually asked us to leave."

"But the party ... and Dido ..."

"Yes. I reminded him of these things, and reminded him also that if he believes a robber is on the loose in the local area, the police *will* override his wishes."

"I imagine he did not take that lightly." Adelia wondered how forceful Theodore had been in his conversation.

"He did not. He claims that he thinks the robber has fled; he does not believe the murder was intentional, and now he has gone before he can be found and hanged for it. That makes sense. He feels there is no point in keeping the matter open. He also reminded me he knows all the local judiciary and his connections can overrule any petty policeman."

"Why did he ask us to leave?"

"I think he spoke in anger. I cannot imagine that he meant it. But I am not sure. I pressed him pretty harshly on his reasons."

Adelia paused in thought for a little while. There would have been some reason, she was certain of it; Theodore wouldn't have noticed the undercurrents in Lord Mondial's speech but there will have been a subtext, she knew it. And if Theodore had 'pressed him harshly' then Lord Mondial had quite possibly been roused to anger. She recognised that the Marquis would not want police swarming over his house, and she could understand why he was simply forging ahead with plans in spite of what had happened. It was the kind of man that he was. His determination and unswerving nature had often been cited as his best points.

Now she was seeing that those character traits were double-edged swords.

"So what do we do now?" she asked at last.

"We stay, regardless," Theodore told her. "He will come around to it. You can persuade him to let us stay, I am sure. We will stay for as long as our daughter needs us here."

9

It was a silent and stilted dinner that evening in Mondial Castle. Dido presided alongside her husband, whose arm was strapped up out of the way and hidden under a coat that was unbuttoned. As no bones had been broken, it was merely a case of keeping things held fast while the flesh knitted itself together. He seemed fairly able to manage well enough with his left hand.

"You must begin to move it as soon as you can bear the pain," Theodore told Mondial as they took their seats.

"Excuse me?"

"Your arm, Mondial. Early exercise will be key to your full recovery."

"I see. Thank you."

Theodore beamed at Adelia who, for some reason, was glaring at him.

Sir Henry was also present and he looked excruciatingly awkward. The chair where Miss Lamb would have sat was now removed, as was the seat previously occupied by her chaperone. She was remaining in her rooms until someone from Miss Lamb's household arrived to collect their belongings and escort her home. Her lack of full vision and her doddery state rendered independent travel impossible. She was also, of course, sunk deeply into grief and mourning.

The rest of the long table was empty. It was an unusual state of affairs for the usually bustling castle. No doubt Mondial would soon fill it up again.

Theodore looked at Sir Henry and wondered if he was looking at a murderer.

But why?

Unless Miss Lamb had not been the target; unless it was Mondial that Sir Henry wished to murder.

Then why did Sir Henry remain here after his failed attempt to take another's life?

Perhaps to convince everyone of his innocence.

But what could have possibly motivated Sir Henry to even try to kill Mondial?

As Theodore let his thoughts trundle along these logical paths, he became aware of a silence that seemed to be aimed directly at him. He dabbed at his chin, expecting that he was covered in soup or something equally obnoxious until Adelia said, in a tone that suggested she was repeating a question, "It would be lovely to see your mother again, would it not? And she would be pleased to come to the garden party."

"I – what? Oh. Yes, she loves a party." The Dowager Countess of Calaway was a cheerful and social woman, who seemed to get on remarkably well with Adelia. "But look here, Mondial, about this party you intend to hold. You have plenty of time still to cancel it. The invitations have only just been sent out. I am sure that no one has cancelled important plans, yet, to attend, and even if they had, they'd understand why you'd call it off. Have a thought, man. It's a question of decency, don't you think?"

Adelia was almost hissing at him but Theodore ignored her. She had tried to be tactful, no doubt, and Dido would have used her wifely charms, but now it was time to speak plainly, man to man. Surely Mondial would respect that.

Mondial did not look very happy about it at all. He flared his nostrils. "If the poor dead girl had been a relative of mine, then I completely agree with you. However, she was not. I see nothing in the manuals of etiquette that suggest I ought to cancel *my* plans because some girl has been attacked by a passing footpad and not even in my own home. Do you not recognise that such a course of action could, in fact, be misinterpreted?"

"Who would misinterpret it, damn it? Why would anyone misconstrue this? Cancel the party, if not for the sake of politeness, then for your wife's sake. She has lost a close friend."

"Calaway! Once more you overstep the bounds of decency. I tell you, sir, that I will not be spoken to like this in my house."

"That's the problem, isn't it? No one speaks to you in a way that you need to be spoken to."

"I shall have you ejected, and you shall not return!"

Theodore threw down his napkin and tipped up his head. "It would be your right to do that. But would it *be right* to do that?"

Dido sniffed and Adelia coughed very meaningfully. The men were reminded of the women's presence. Propriety settled on them like a thick and stifling blanket.

Lord Mondial picked up his spoon and continued to eat.

Even that act annoyed Theodore as he realised that the Marquis was positioning himself as the bigger man by dropping the argument first.

The meal resumed in utter silence.

The ladies withdrew. Sir Henry took one look at Mondial's thunderous face and fled too, citing a sudden bilious attack. Theodore trimmed a cigar and accepted a glass of brandy from Mondial, who began to pace around the room. Theodore thought, this man is seriously agitated. I shall ignore his previous outburst. He didn't mean it, I am sure, and I can forgive him his emotions.

"Are you in pain?" he asked. "It makes a man speak out without considering his words first. I hold no grudge, you know." I can also be a decent man, he thought proudly.

Mondial stopped by the fireplace. There was a display of pinecones in the empty grate. "You are impossible, Calaway. Utterly impossible. Yes. I cannot say this in front of my wife but yes, I am in pain. In my heart."

"You can certainly say it in front of your wife. If you cannot share it with her, who can you share it with?" Theodore shared all his feelings with Adelia. He was sure she did the same with him.

"You don't understand," Lord Mondial said.

"So explain it to me. Tell me, Mondial, were you and that girl carrying on in some way together?"

98

Mondial knocked back his brandy and stamped over to the decanters to pour himself a double, awkwardly juggling the stopper and the glass. "Hell, no. Absolutely not. Yet that is exactly what everyone else will think. The fact that you voiced it just now – does that not prove I *must* go on with the party? I could not bear for scandal to attach to me or, more importantly, to my wife. She is your daughter, Calaway. You know that I only act in *her* best interests. Oh, if people thought I had a mistress – Miss Lamb or whoever – that is one thing. I can weather that storm. It would be normal. But the taint attaches itself to Dido and not me, and that I *will not have*. Do you see? She is blameless and must remain so."

"Everyone understands you are an upright, honourable man," Theodore reassured him.

"A man of my word. A man who sticks to plans. The party will happen. It …" Mondial's voice broke and that shocked Theodore. Mondial threw back a third double brandy and sank into his chair at the head of the table. "I need to have something to focus upon. I need people around me. I cannot … I cannot bear how she looks at me, Calaway. I mean Dido. She looks at me as if I've let her down and the more that I give her, the more that I do for her, the more disappointed she looks. What else must I do, as a husband, to win her love?"

"You have already won her love! I am sure that she adores you. You have two fine sons. She speaks of you only in the highest terms."

But Mondial shook his head. "She speaks of the local butcher in the highest terms too. She is always just beyond my reach, as if she is the other side of a window. I can see her and

I can speak with her but her mind is a mystery to me. I am alone, Calaway. I am so utterly alone. I must fill the house with people. Sir Henry must stay. You must stay. In spite of your ... you know. Your opinions and how you pick at me. Yes, yes, I know why you do it. And bring your mother as soon as you can. Let her come; let them all come. Invite anyone you can think of. I need diversions, and what else can I do? Instead of company, what else is there; if I don't have company I shall turn to drink, or gambling ..."

"No. I would not suggest those things. Company and diversions, then, are better than drinking and gambling. Although don't those things go together? Do you not run the risk of falling into ... such ill-advised ways?" Theodore stared off into the middle distance. He didn't want to look at Mondial's face, reflecting the pain and loss that he himself had once experienced. Now he understood the depths of Mondial's confusion, and he understood the need to be focused on one thing. Before he had been rescued by Adelia, and after the death of his first wife, Theodore himself had faced a similar situation.

"I do not run any such risk," said Mondial. "I will be less inclined to excess with the right sort of people around me. And another thing. I spoke sharply to you earlier. I suggested that you leave. You must understand I will *not* be called out in front of my household."

"I do understand and I offer my heartfelt apologies. I overstepped the mark."

"You did. I was shocked and I am angry about it. Do not do it again. Yet this has been a difficult time for all of us. Nothing has prepared me for this. I would rather forget it all and move on."

"Quite so. We all would. However, there is someone out there who has committed the most dreadful of crimes. Mondial, I hate to suggest this, but it is entirely possible that Miss Lamb was not the target. Consider the possibility that *you* were the target. And consider, also, that they might return to finish the job."

Mondial inhaled deeply. "I maintain that it was a passing robber."

"Who fired two shots in quick succession?"

Mondial blinked. "He had two pistols."

"You saw them?"

"I did."

"But not his face? How close was he?"

"He was masked. He was close enough to speak to me and demand my pocket-watch. I fought back, naturally, and that is when the pistols discharged. I cannot tell you any more than that; it is a blur."

Theodore tried to imagine juggling two loaded pistols, fighting someone, and taking their watch. How many arms did the assailant have? "The police will want more information. You cannot prevent their involvement."

"The police can go hang. They are good for nothing and don't understand the ways of polite society. Let them go about their business of banging heads together in inns and chasing lost pigs, but I will not have them here. I am close with Judge Anderson and he is on his circuit here at the moment. He will take my side, I can assure you."

"And the detective from London? I know that you changed

your mind but you could still send for one."

"No. Listen, Calaway, if I did believe the attack was targeted, you may rest assured that I would call for a detective without hesitation. But I have had time to think over the past day or two and I do not believe it is worth incurring the expense or the hassle to call someone here who will poke into all our affairs and discover nothing. There will be nothing for the detective to discover; the robber is long gone."

"Yet if you are the target, he will not be gone."

"I do not think I could have been the target."

"Robbers don't attack in private grounds like this."

"Robbers are not known for their intelligence!" Mondial was growing increasingly agitated again. He had had a severe shock. Theodore prided himself on his own logic but he knew that not everyone was as blessed as he was with a cool rational approach to things.

So in the end, he replied, mildly, "I support your decision to continue with the party. I can understand your reasons now, difficult though they are. And my mother will be delighted to arrive as soon as we can send word to her. Let us fill this house, Mondial; I will assist you in whatever you need. However, I am concerned for your safety. Let me conduct a few discreet investigations around the place, on your behalf."

"No. It is not necessary."

Theodore tapped the ash from the end of his cigar. It was almost gone. It had been a good one. They lapsed into a silence that Theodore was not sure how to break.

Then Mondial spoke as he got to his feet. "Let us join the women. And Calaway? These investigations? I get the feeling that you shall not let up, whether I give you my permission to investigate or not. Your wife is likewise a woman of penetrating gaze. I expect you will discover nothing but if you want to speak to my staff or the people on the estate, you can go ahead and do so. I suspect it will amuse you and you are otherwise quite bored. So follow your whim. I ask only one thing of you."

Theodore thought that it would be a demand to keep any enquiry into Mondial's personal relationships off limits. But he was surprised when Mondial said, "I ask only that you allow me to be at your side throughout the investigation."

"But…"

"This is my house and I was one of the victims, intentionally or not."

Theodore could not argue with that. "Very well. As you wish."

Adelia was furious when Theodore told her what had transpired between himself and Lord Mondial, and she knew that he couldn't understand why, not at first. She could see it in his face. Theodore stood in front of her late that night, while she sat on her bed and brushed out her own hair. Smith had been sent to bed an hour before. Adelia didn't mind attending to her own toilet. She quite liked the intimate evenings when it was just her and her husband, talking about the events of the day.

Except for times like now, when he was telling her of his idiotic agreement to allow Mondial to accompany him in his investigations.

"But this is what you wanted," Theodore protested in confusion. "You wanted to look into the murder!"

"I did. But can't you see that Lord Mondial himself is not above suspicion?"

"He was injured." Theodore tapped his upper arm and mimed holding a pistol. "He is a victim. He was shot in his own right arm. He is right-handed. He is quite handy with his left hand but did not do this to himself, Adelia. It is impossible. I did think of that, you know," he added in a voice that was almost petulant.

"The man is brimming with secrets. There is much that he has not told us, Theodore. So much of this attack does not make sense and you have said it yourself. He only wants to be at your side so that you do not uncover what he wants to remain hidden."

"And that is his right. This is his house. Would you allow him to poke freely into every part of your house and life?"

"I would not; but…" Adelia trailed off.

"My love, come here." Theodore sat down alongside her and she put down her brush and let him pull her into his embrace. "We have gained a huge concession. We are not being asked to leave. I am allowed to make enquiries. Perhaps it will come to nothing but, like you, I am suspicious. I still have my doubts about Taylor the valet and, I must confess, Sir Henry too. And yes, Mondial is not all that he seems. I want to find out the truth because if … if there is something very amiss here, we need to know. For Dido's sake. Do you see? And if the only way I can do that is by conceding to Mondial's demands, then I shall do that."

"Of course," she said. "And thank you for all that you do for our family."

"My family." He kissed the top of her head. "Our family. Us. We are a unit that shall never be divided and if I discover that Mondial has hurt our daughter in any way, then I will not need a pistol to wreak my revenge."

She quivered, just a little, and it wasn't in fear or anger.

A note was delivered to Adelia the next morning at breakfast. The hot weather had finally broken, and rain was sheeting down, just as Sir Henry had predicted. Replies were still coming back to Dido accepting the invitations to the forthcoming garden party. Adelia had caught her daughter as they had entered the breakfast room, and drew her off to one side in the corridor.

"I am quite well, mama," Dido had insisted. "Perhaps it is for the best that I stay busy with all the things that I must now arrange." She had pulled away and gone into the room, leaving Adelia feeling annoyed, though she directed her anger more towards Lord Mondial. Theodore had seemed to be more sympathetic to the Marquis now, as if they had some common ground between them, but Adelia wasn't so happy to ignore things. Dido was struggling with something in her private life and Adelia longed for her daughter to open up to her.

Adelia resolved to bide her time. She adjusted her face into a bland attitude of indifference and entered the room for breakfast.

The note came to her as she was finishing her second cup

of coffee.

She could not help a small squeal of delight. Theodore raised one eyebrow and Dido frowned at her mother. Adelia adopted a more mature air once more, but she had to work at repressing her smile. "Harriet is in town!" she declared.

Theodore's face remained set. She had expected that look of bland indifference. He did not get on with Adelia's best friend. Harriet Hobson was the wife of a bumbling bishop. When she entered a room, it was as if the sun was breaking through clouds. She had been at Adelia's side through thick and thin. Of everyone in the world, Harriet knew her best. In some ways, she knew more about Adelia than Theodore did.

Adelia felt bad about that.

But she was sure that Theodore did not suspect it.

He simply didn't like Harriet and that was that.

She folded the note away and escaped to her rooms as quickly as she could so that she could send a reply by the earliest opportunity.

10

Even outside of London, there were plenty of postal deliveries each day and by making use of those and with the ease of sending a boy with a note between the castle and the town, a meeting was soon arranged between Harriet and Adelia. Rather than subject her friend to Theodore's almost inevitable disdain by receiving her at the castle, Adelia arranged to meet her in a cosy private room upstairs in the coaching inn where Harriet was staying.

Furthermore, it was nice to be away from Mondial Castle for a while. The town was only a few miles away and the roads were well-maintained. Unfortunately, Adelia didn't find herself quite as free of the castle as she had hoped. It sat on a hill and seemed to loom over the town even from its distant perch. Adelia turned her head away and closed her eyes while she rode in the enclosed carriage until she was in the market square and ready to alight.

Harriet was waiting for her on the steps of the pleasant and respectable inn. She enfolded Adelia in a firm hug as soon as they met, even while they were still standing on the public steps.

"Mrs Hobson!" Adelia protested, muffled against her friend's hair. But she didn't fight back. It was so reassuring to be with her old friend once more.

Harriet dragged her up the stairs and into the room she'd booked which overlooked the street. She had already had a table of finger-food ordered, and a selection of things suitable for ladies to drink was laid out on a clean red and white cloth: various summery fruit cordials, lemonade and barley water plus the welcome sight of a warm teapot. It was very much like an early afternoon tea. Adelia stripped off her outerwear. The rain had eased to a light drizzle and she was keen to get out of her hooded walking cloak. She even took her gloves off, as they were in private, and spread them on the windowsill to dry while Harriet played mum and poured the tea from the fine china pot.

"Murder!" squealed Harriet without any preamble. "I've seen the newspapers. That poor girl! My husband has prayed for her *ceaselessly*."

"How good of him. Do thank him."

"Oh, no, I shan't, it's positively tiresome. Because I knew Miss Lamb, through you, he has decided that I am utterly devastated, and of course I simply *am* but not, you know, so incapacitated that I must spend all my hours on my knees in the chapel, which he does, and seems to think that I want to do so too."

"It is his job to be on his knees in the chapel, surely."

"I thought I was marrying a bishop for the social life," Harriet sniffed. "The wife of a bishop gets invited to all the best parties. That's what I was led to believe."

"He wasn't a bishop when you married him."

108

"Maybe not but I knew he would rise because he was so very good at being good, even then."

Adelia rolled her eyes at her friend's constant revising of her own history. "A good man isn't going to become a socialite the minute he pulls on a mitre. Maybe he simply becomes an even better man."

"Well, it was unexpected, that's all I'm saying."

"That he continues to be who he always was?"

"Oh, stop it, you are trying to confuse me with your ... your logic and good sense! You are as bad as my Ophelia."

"And how is your darling daughter?"

"As judgmental as always. At least my dear husband has a generous Christian spirit. Ophelia is becoming more rigid by the day. I quite expect her to go over to the Calvinists and there where shall we be?"

"You shall be having very interesting conversations at the dinner table. Christmas will be fun."

"Oh, she will probably be on bread and water by then. Already she is teetotal and lectured me for fully an hour as I worked my way through an entire bottle of red wine to take the edge off her words."

"Harriet!"

"Well, what is one to do when one's own offspring take such a dreary approach to life? Philippa Lamb, though, she was a girl who could mingle at a soiree. She was always so much fun to talk to. Oh, I wish we had more than tea and lemon-water here. Perhaps I should ring for a bottle."

"Not at one in the afternoon, you won't. There is ginger-ale. Try that if you want a bit of a fizz."

"Oh, Adelia. But poor Philippa Lamb!" Harriet put down her tea-cup and looked dejected. Her eyes were swimming with genuine tears. "Tell me everything that has happened and if I interrupt, you may hurl something at my head."

"I will, don't worry. Here's the tale so far…"

Harriet was good and managed to contain her stream of comments until the end of Adelia's recount. They then discussed the matter from all angles – "Look to that Marquis, for he is a dodgy character!" was Harriet's opinion. "I bet he could have shot himself in the arm, whatever your Theodore says." She took up a thin pocketbook and tried to hold it like a pistol, pressing it to her upper arm. "See. I could shoot myself quite easily."

"Luckily, the book is not loaded. And yes, while Lord Mondial *could* have done it, the question must arise – *why* would he do it?"

"Love. Money. Spite. Jealousy. The usual things."

"And you'd know all about these things?"

Harriet wiggled in her chair. "Adelia. Adelia! The sanctity of the church is paramount of course, but my good husband does discuss matters in a very abstract way with me, and I know more of the seedy side of the world than you might imagine."

"Yes, from a distance, in the same way as someone might learn from penny dreadfuls or magazines."

"Not so. I accompany him to the darkest places in town. I am a woman of the world and it's a world you can barely imagine. Anyway, all knowledge is useful, whether from books or from life. Which brings me to another matter. I am not here to see you for fun."

"Are you not? I could be offended."

"Oh, but you won't be. No, I mean, I am here to bring you some knowledge, useful knowledge. Well, it's more like a warning. Perhaps? No, not quite a warning…"

"Harriet! I do not like cucumber sandwiches and I am quite prepared to sacrifice this one." Adelia held it aloft as if she were about to fling it into her friend's face.

"Yes, yes, fine. It is a serious matter so put the food down. It is about your brother."

"Alfred?"

"Yes. He is looking for you."

"I think that he has found me already."

"What?"

Adelia had to sit on her hands to stop herself fiddling with the flabby cucumber sandwich. She said, reluctantly, "The servants were talking about some man they saw hiding in the gardens."

"Before the murder?"

"Yes. He was asking to speak to me but refused to come to the house, which is how I know it must have been him. They said he spoke like a refined man of quality but dressed as if he'd been sleeping in a ditch, which is likely, knowing Alfred."

Harriet leaned forward, serious at last. "Adelia, this is important. Are you absolutely sure that the man in the gardens was Alfred? Did you see him?"

"I am relatively sure. But no, I haven't spoken to him yet. What do you know of it? Why do you know he's here?"

"He came to our house. Obviously we have an open door policy as the Bishop won't turn anyone away."

Adelia smiled to herself. Harriet never referred to her

husband by his name. He had always been a title to her, even in private. It was common enough for wives to call their husbands by their formal designation in public but Harriet kept just a little distance from him at all times. They utterly doted on one another; Adelia wasn't fooled by Harriet's uncharacteristic reserve. It was almost as if Harriet couldn't quite admit the depths of her feelings for him to anyone, even herself. Adelia was not sure why, though she had her suspicions. Like Adelia, Harriet had past pains of her own. One learned to protect one's heart.

"Was he looking for me?" Adelia asked.

"Of course he was. He has not suddenly had a religious epiphany. He had been to your own house and found you gone, so he came to me, as the next likely place. I had your letters and knew you were here but I didn't tell him. He went off, but later I found the doors downstairs – you know, at the back, that lead from the patio to the garden room – they were open and my writing desk, which I'd put in there to make the most of the summer light, was open too. He had read the letters and knew where you were."

"So he is a trespasser on top of everything else."

"He is not malicious. He took nothing, though there were items of value that he could have lifted. I offered him refreshments while he was with me and he refused them all, out of pride, though I am sure he was hungry."

"Oh, the poor, stupid man. His latest venture must have failed, then. Did he tell you why he wanted to see me this time?"

"I suspect it was the usual story," Harriet said. "He didn't mention any business dealings but he looked shabby and tired. He did say that his son has just turned thirteen and he was hoping

112

that he could be sent away to school."

"Alfred has very little to do with young Wilson."

"Apparently he's a bright lad and Alfred has just decided to take an interest."

"I am surprised Jane has let Alfred anywhere near her or their son. I thought that Alfred didn't even know where she had gone."

Harriet shrugged. "He didn't tell me anything personal."

"He wouldn't. Pride and dignity sustain him, at least outwardly. So he is circling here, waiting for a chance to come and speak to me and ask for money. He won't spend it on Wilson even if I give him some."

"I don't know. His plea seemed genuine," Harriet said. "I don't pay heed to my Bible half as much as the Bishop would like me to, but even I can argue the case for forgiveness. He is your brother and he is asking on behalf of your nephew."

Adelia gave her a rueful smile. Under her frivolity and chatter, Harriet was as good and upright a person as anyone could wish for. "His intentions might be to spend it on his son, yes," she agreed. "It is just that things happen between his intentions and his actions. His own nature intervenes in the very worst of ways. I suppose that I ought to go and seek him out and speak to him before he is caught on the grounds and makes a scene. Or, worse …"

"Worse, he is arrested on suspicion of murder!" Harriet said, her eyes now wide with horror. "Oh, whatever else he is, your brother cannot be a murderer. Can he?"

"I cannot see it. I will not see it. He is many, many things but he has never once caused anyone physical harm and he never would. I wonder if he has lodgings here? He cannot actually be sleeping in a ditch."

"I have not seen him in this inn but there are cheaper places where one can rent a bed or a share of one, in a room of others," Harriet said. "Even this town has flophouses and the like."

"I will have to make enquiries."

"I will, too."

"Thank you. Do not put yourself at risk in lowly places, though. If you do find him, will you send word immediately and engineer a meeting between us if you can? I will give him whatever he wants on the understanding that he goes away immediately. I cannot have him here, at risk of being arrested." Or at the risk of him bringing shame on my good name and upsetting the rest of my family, she thought.

"I promise." Harriet patted Adelia's hand. "Are we definitely agreed that he cannot possibly be the murderer? Not even accidentally? I am so sorry to have to ask," she added hastily. "It's only that I'd hate to be misled by my own desire to see the best in him, and end up as an accessory after the fact."

Adelia winced. "Me too, Harriet. Me too. I must go."

"It was lovely to see you again."

"I shall get you onto the list for this garden party."

"Oh, please do! And send my love to your husband."

"I won't."

Harriet laughed throatily and they embraced once more before Adelia swung her still-damp cloak around her shoulders, tied and pinned on her hat, gingerly squeezed her hands into her gloves, and headed out into the town.

11

Adelia took care to proceed slowly through the entrance hall back at Mondial Castle, greeting each servant that she recognised by name, and asking about their welfare. Clearly, such solicitations were familiar to them from her daughter's own household management, and they responded warmly to Adelia. She noticed, however, they always spoke to her with a certain alertness about their manner, keeping an eye out for the sudden appearance of Lord Mondial. She suspected that he was more old-fashioned in his approach to staff, insisting that they kept a distance.

On her way, she gathered up a handful of letters that had come for Dido and assumed they were mostly replies to the invitations or expressions of condolence for the loss of her friend. She carried them upstairs, telling the maid that tried to follow her that she was perfectly capable of taking the letters to her daughter, but that she would be grateful for a certain amount of attention to be paid to her walking gear. She left her cloak in the care of the maid, and her kidskin gloves she passed to her own woman, Smith, who was as trustworthy as anyone and had a fine eye for needlework and skilful repairs. Adelia did not like to be purchasing new gloves every time rain stained the previous pair, and preferred to have them properly cleaned even if it meant unstitching them to some extent.

She used to do it herself until Smith had found out, chided her, and wrestled them from her mistress's grasp. The pride of a good servant was a funny thing, but a useful one.

Adelia paused when she reached the landing. It was mid-afternoon now. She was not entirely sure where she'd find Dido. Although it was officially her day to be at-home to receive visitors, no one who knew what had happened here would have dared to request admittance so soon after the death of Miss Lamb. A garden party half a month later was cutting etiquette very finely; a social call a mere two days later was inexcusable.

All the people in the local area who were 'someone' would be frantically visiting one another to exchange increasingly scurrilous gossip and speculation, anyway. And Adelia thought about Lord Mondial's fears, and knew that he had a point. There was nothing else to talk about except the murder. Rumours would grow if given half a chance.

Adelia sighed. There was a very fine line between the useful sharing of information, which had paid dividends for her match-making exploits, and the spreading of gossip and rumour. She didn't feel as if she was always on the right side of that line. Gloomily, she carried on along the corridor, heading towards the sitting room. She stopped outside and remembered that the last time she'd been in there, she had been with Dido and Philippa Lamb.

It had been the last time she'd seen Philippa alive.

A lump came into her throat. She was no stranger to death; who was? Disease or calamity could strike anyone at any time. She was the only one in all her round of friends and acquaintances who had not lost a child but she had certainly lost other close family members. One couldn't walk down the street, it felt, without facing horrors everywhere one looked. Yet this death felt personal and she balled up her grief into an anger at the perpetrator. Part of her didn't want the murderer to have been a passing footpad, for in that case, they would have long since left the area. She wanted them to be found, and brought to justice. She wanted to look them in the eye.

She wanted to spit and shout and stamp her feet.

She heard a noise from within the room and remembered her task. She had the letters in her hand. She tapped once, lightly, and went straight in, not expecting to see anyone but Dido within.

There was one person in the room and it was not Dido. Sir Henry jumped up from the desk by the window, half hidden by a potted plant, with a look of horrified surprise on his face. "Lady Calaway! A thousand apologies."

"No, the fault is mine. I knocked but did not wait for an answer. I was looking for Lady Mondial. Have you seen her? This is her room," she added meaningfully.

He seemed flushed and his ears were very red. She moved so that she could see the table and his hands moved, closing a writing case hurriedly, and now Adelia was interested. That was not his writing case. It was Dido's.

"I am so sorry. No, I haven't seen her today." He began to inch to the side of the table. Adelia put herself squarely in front of him, and rested her hands on her hips like a market trader selling oranges.

"That is my daughter's writing case."

"I – er – is it?"

Such obvious lying could not be ignored. Adelia said, "You know that it is hers. Who else's could it be? What are you looking for, Sir Henry?"

The baronet darted his eyes this way and that. He didn't dare push past her, and she knew it. She used her untouchable femininity and his honour to her advantage, and advanced upon him. He backed away and found himself trapped by the table on one side and the aspidistra on the other.

"I have nothing to apologise for!" he blurted out.

"I am sure that you do not," she replied mildly. "I am not asking for an apology. Merely an explanation."

"I have mislaid an … item … and wished to find it."

"How might you have mislaid something in someone else's correspondence? Tell me what it is, and I will help you to look for it," she said. She spoke sweetly and innocently.

He was not fooled. He knew that he looked guilty and that she suspected him of something, hence his defensive reaction. He made it a hundred times worse by saying, "No, no, I cannot trouble you. It is a private matter between … my lady and myself."

"Then ask her."

"I – cannot, in the current circumstances."

"What is the relationship between you and my daughter?"

"Nothing! Nothing at all!" he stammered out desperately. "No shame attaches to her – to anyone – nothing! I must go. Please, *please* excuse me."

He looked so distressed that she feared to press him any

further in case she drove him to tears, a situation which most men would not forgive. So she stepped aside and let him flee from the room.

Still carrying the letters, she left the room a few moments later, and finally found her daughter in her private day room alongside her own bedroom.

Dido looked a little better than she had done previously. She seemed resigned to Lord Mondial's insistence that everything now return to normal. "In truth," she confessed to her mother, who had parked herself on a comfortable couch, "Perhaps John is right to press on with the party. There is so much to do and though I resent it, and want only to lie on my bed and weep, that won't solve a thing, will it? I am a woman of the British Empire and the British elite; we won't get anywhere if we succumb to the vapours every five minutes."

"There is a world of difference between succumbing to the vapours and allowing oneself to mourn the loss of a dear friend."

Dido nodded. "That is true. Though we had not been as close as we might have been lately, Philippa and I. I think since the birth of the boys, the second one particularly, it is as if my social circle has changed. I don't mean that in a bad way. Indeed, John thinks it ought to have not changed at all. He doesn't see why I have to – why I want to be so involved in the children's lives. But you were involved in ours, weren't you?"

"Of course I was. But remember, I was not raised in a castle like this. I was born to work, however genteel that work might have been. Listen to your husband as much as you can, because you need him to guide you in how to move with his sort of people. Had it not been for your father helping me navigate this sort of world, I should have got myself into far more scrapes than I did. John knows how to behave in this circle of people."

"I do listen to him. He does help me though he grows impatient with me from time to time. I try not to disappoint him but sometimes … oh mama, I love him, I do, but what if he does not love me?"

"He does!" Adelia moved to one side and let Dido sink down alongside her. Adelia held onto her daughter's hand and rubbed her thumb rhythmically over her skin. "He adores you but it is in his own way, according to how he has been taught to show love, that's all. He would do anything to protect you." She remembered what Theodore had told her about Lord Mondial's insistence that he was acting only to prevent gossip and shame attaching to his wife. "He loves you, I promise it."

"I hope so."

"Dido, I have been meaning to ask you. On the day of the terrible events, your husband came to the room and asked you to walk with him in the garden. What did he want to speak to you about?"

"Some matter to do with a tutor for the boys, he told me later."

"Was that all? Why was he so insistent?"

"That's his way. You know him. He is like that about everything. Everything has to happen immediately, for him."

"Hmm."

Dido hung her head.

There was something else. Adelia wasn't sure what maternal intuition really was, but she could tell that something was wrong. She spoke to Dido as if she were a foolish young girl again, saying firmly, "And another thing. What is happening between you and Sir Henry? Out with it."

"Nothing." The change in conversation shocked Dido upright again. "How can you ask such a thing? He was to be wed to Philippa!"

"I have just discovered Sir Henry in your own room on the other side of the castle, where you have left your writing case. He was looking through it and claimed to be hunting for something that he had mislaid, although he would not tell me what that was. And when I asked him about you, Dido, he went very red and panicked. There is something happening between you. I wish to know what that *something* is."

"Oh, mama! There is nothing between us. I can promise you that. I will swear on a Bible if I must."

"No, do not take such things lightly."

"I do not. You know I wouldn't joke about that sort of thing. I am trying to impress on you how serious I am. There is nothing untoward between us, not a thing."

"Nothing untoward, maybe. I only ask what *is* there between you both, untoward or not?"

"He is a friend to me."

"I know you are acquainted but has this friendship deepened?"

"Yes, mama, it has, but in a totally respectable way, I promise you. He is so easy to talk to and he has been an ear to my woes. He is dependable and solid and I trust him utterly."

"Have you met with him in private?"

"Mama! Do you think I learned nothing at your knee? Of course not. Our intimate conversations have *always* been in public places, surrounded by other people. At dances and the like, it is possible to talk with another person in utmost secrecy while being visible the whole time, such is the din. You know that. But we have never been alone. No shame and no scandal can possibly ever attach to either of us."

"Then what was he looking for? Have you given him some token? Or – this is more likely, and much worse – has he given *you* anything? Even the smallest gift, if done secretly, can carry far more meaning than it ought to."

"No, no, nothing at all."

Adelia squeezed Dido's hand.

She wanted to believe her daughter, she really did.

But Adelia had been young herself, once.

And she remembered how easy it was to slip into an indiscretion.

And how hard it was to dig oneself out again.

12

Mondial dogged Theodore like a pampered pug would follow its owner. Every time that Theodore stepped out of his own rooms at the castle, Mondial would be there, lurking casually – "Oh, I was just rearranging my fossil collection," he'd say, standing in an unconvincing manner next to a display case. Or "Oh, how marvellous to see you. I was also about to go for a walk in the grounds. I will accompany you."

Then Mondial would relentlessly ask Theodore questions about what he was calling "the unfortunate situation that happened outside" as if he was determined, at every opportunity, to divorce himself from any link with the murder.

"I should like to talk with your valet, Taylor, again," Theodore told him as they perambulated around the orangery late that afternoon.

"Why? He was in my room all day – until he heard the shots, of course."

"So he says, but there is no alibi to confirm that."

"Where else would he have been? Skulking around the ornamental ponds? He is an indoor man in all respects."

"He was seen coming from the stables a little while after

the shots were fired."

"Who said such a preposterous thing?" Mondial thundered. He stopped and faced Theodore head-on. "Who? I shall have them sacked and horse-whipped for slander. Or whipped first, and then sacked. I think that's the legal order of things."

"I cannot reveal my sources."

"You bloody well can. This is my house, damn it. Your sources are my damned servants. Let me tell you that whoever has suggested such a thing is either deeply mistaken, or is a trouble-maker of the highest order."

"Yet surely you must see that an alibi for Taylor would be incredibly useful?"

"Absolutely ridiculous, Calaway. Twaddle. Total nonsense. He is my valet and he was in my room. My word, Calaway, is my bond. And my word should be enough for you!"

"It is, it is. I believe you. It is only a matter of following the protocols in an investigation."

"What protocols? You don't know what you're doing, do you, man? You've read a few issues of the *Illustrated Police News* and now you're a detective. Protocols! What rot." Mondial snorted angrily and stamped off across the orangery.

But when the Marquis got to the door which was open to the outside in spite of the late summer drizzle to allow air circulate around the tropical trees, he stopped and turned around again.

"Very well," he said to Theodore. "Let us continue on your charade. The servants *will* vouch for Taylor, every last one of them."

Theodore found himself in an uncomfortable situation as

124

he was forced to stand next to Mondial while various members of staff were paraded in front of them and interrogated. They all kept their eyes on the floor and answered in short, clear sentences. Theodore tried to interrupt but Mondial overruled him. "I'll ask my own staff the questions," he said, and proceeded to ask the most leading questions possible.

"How many times did you see Taylor in my rooms on the day of the unfortunate event that occurred outside a few days ago?" the Marquis said.

"Er – a few times, sir?"

"Good. Dismissed. Next! At what time did *you* see Taylor in or near my rooms that day?"

"Er – in the morning, sir?"

"And later? You saw him in the afternoon, didn't you?"

"Sir?"

"Good. You did. Dismissed."

It was an utter shambles and Theodore could hardly wait for it to be over.

He escaped from the room before Mondial could button-hole him about the supposed witnesses, and loped up the stairs to seek sanctuary in his own rooms. He was pleased to find Adelia was there, relaxing before she had to begin dressing for dinner later than evening.

And he was even more pleased, although with a little trepidation, when she informed him that his own dear mother had sent word that she would be arriving the following morning.

125

There were yet ten days before the garden party. Almost everyone who had been invited had accepted, and every day, Lord Mondial recollected someone else that he felt he ought to invite. He was happy to have the Dowager Countess arrive early, and when he discovered that Adelia's own best friend was staying in town, he insisted that Harriet be accommodated in the castle too. "She is the wife of a Bishop," he had said. "She cannot *possibly* stay in a common coaching inn."

Lord Mondial had never met Harriet, so Adelia could forgive him his lack of insight. Harriet Hobson could have made herself comfortable in a Salvation Army dosshouse with half a bottle of gin and some cheap oysters bought on the street as long as she had people to talk with.

Nevertheless, Harriet gladly accepted the invitation to the castle and she arrived in the morning just before Theodore was leaving to meet his mother. He greeted Harriet stiffly and fled from the rooms, as Adelia expected that he would. Adelia only had time to introduce her friend to Dido briefly. Then Adelia was called away to pay the proper attentions to Grace, Lady Calaway. It could often be somewhat awkward when two titled ladies sharing the same designation were inhabiting the same space. Other women, less refined than the Dowager Countess, could use it to make their daughter-in-law feel unsettled or uncertain. But Grace, the Countess of Calaway, was happy to be as informal or formal as the situation demanded and did not take offence at any stumbling over mix-ups of address. In private she delighted in being called merely Grace and if she liked someone, she was positively offended if they insisted on the full formality of her rank.

126

"I'm just a silly widow, easily overlooked and forgettable," she'd say coquettishly, and the less confident would freeze in terror, because she was an ancient woman of an ancient family and someone less like a silly widow was hard to find. Once met, she was never forgotten. And you overlooked her at your peril.

Dido took Harriet up to her designated room, just a small single room quite close to Adelia and Theodore's suite, while Adelia bounced down the stairs to greet Grace who was currently embracing and scolding her son at the same time. When the older lady spotted Adelia approaching, she let go of her son and roughly shoved him to one side.

"Adelia, my most dear woman! Come here! You look younger every time I see you. What is your secret?"

"I merely follow your lead, my lady. You look fresh and lovely. The journey must have been pleasant?"

Grace took both of Adelia's hands and held them, shaking them a little and caressing the backs. "You are a flatterer and I love you for it. Now, you must tell me of every little thing that has been occurring here, for I have had it piecemeal and hardly know what to believe. But before all of that, food and drink. I have been travelling since seven o'clock this morning and I am too old for these roads. The journey was, in fact, a trial from start to finish. Ah! Here is the man of the house! Lord Mondial, look at you, quite the wounded hero. And where is your good lady wife? I saw her bound away. Now, here she comes! Yes, this is a true vision of pure angelic maternal duty. What a goddess she is! Hera, by all accounts. Come here, dear granddaughter! The sight of you brings light to my otherwise dull and grey life."

Dido came down the stairs as fast as her own personal sense

of decorum would allow her to. Lord Mondial was happy to accompany them all to the smaller of the many dining rooms that seemed to litter the castle and they all partook of a meal which might have been a late breakfast or an early lunch, but no one really minded. The conversation could not turn to the murder, that was to say, Lord Mondial's "unfortunate situation outside", but afterwards, Dido took Grace to her luxurious suite where her two maids had already prepared everything for their mistress. Grace freshened up and in spite of her age, just one hour later requested Adelia and Dido's company on a stroll around the gardens. The rain had cleared and the air was particularly fresh and pleasant.

"Tell me everything, and spare no detail," Grace demanded. They progressed slowly along the gravel paths, stopping from time to time to admire the roses that grew in such profusion. "You must be utterly devastated, my poor dear child."

Dido adored her grandmother as much as Adelia adored her as a mother-in-law. She took Grace's arm and said, "I was and I am." Adelia dropped back a little to let Dido unburden herself. The young dark head bent to the older one with its neat cream velvet hat, and Adelia felt that strange warm smugness one got when regarding people whom one truly loved.

Then she counselled herself to be wary of such pride. Had not Philippa Lamb's death shown her the folly of taking happiness for granted? She paused by a neatly-clipped box tree – one of those that Theodore had been so taken with when they had arrived – and spent a moment in silent prayer. She was not a regular church-goer but that didn't mean she didn't feel the presence of something much greater than herself. Harriet, who had to attend church more times in a week than Theodore did in a year, claimed to have actual conversations with God. Adelia certainly couldn't claim that kind of closeness with the divine, but she was more comfortable believing than not believing. And most of the people around her, in spite of their various states of secularism and fashionable declarations of atheism, cleaved still to the Church of England's annual traditions. Every week the papers printed diatribes from learned clergy bemoaning the death of God and falling church attendances, and every day people still crossed themselves and swore on the Bible and prayed in their hour of need, regardless.

Adelia was brought out of her reverie by a cry from Grace. She opened her eyes and leaped forward in alarm, her heart hammering with a suddenness that scared her. Murderers, she thought, robbers and pistols!

But Grace was not being held at gunpoint. To Adelia's utter relief, the older lady was poking into a pile of raked leaves with her stick. Dido was tutting in disapproval. "The gardeners are usually better than this," she said.

"We are off the main path and are they not busy enough at this time of year?" Grace said. "Still, I wonder why they are burning clothing out here like this."

"Clothing?"

"Yes, look here. And it is strange that the leaves have been piled on top *after* the fire that has burned the clothes." Grace stirred the leaves ferociously and a dark piece of fabric snagged itself around the end of her stick. She pulled it out and they saw that it was the remnants of a jacket. "Wool hardly burns," she said. "It must have taken some time to even get this far with it.

How silly."

Adelia came up alongside Grace and Dido. "This is a clue," she said firmly.

"Do you think it is linked to the murder? Oh! How delicious," Grace said. "I mean, justice for Philippa is everyone's priority, of course." She did not even manage to modulate her tone to one of serious sympathy.

"Of course," said Adelia as Dido sniffed discreetly. "And yes, I do believe it might be linked. It seems rather odd, don't you think? I suggest we leave everything exactly as it is for the moment."

"Has Mondial really refused to have the police involved?" Grace asked.

"He has. But Theodore is looking into things instead."

"Theo? My Theo?" Grace cackled. "Well. Well, well, well."

"Don't you think it is a good idea? He has powerful skills of observation and logic."

"A good idea? Well. It is an idea, certainly. No one can say if it is a good one unless he is successful. Ha! You had best fetch this gentleman-detective son of mine, and let us see what conclusions he can draw from *this*."

"I shall. Will you both wait here and prevent anyone from disturbing it?"

"Certainly."

Adelia could barely contain her excitement as she rushed over the lawns and into the castle to find Theodore.

A clue! She was sure it was a clue!

13

Theodore had managed to evade Mondial at last. When Adelia went out with his mother and granddaughter, making a perfect picture of familial harmony, Theodore slipped the other way and made it look as if he were heading back up to his suite of rooms. Mondial noticed but was too engaged at that moment speaking a final few words to Dido as the trio left.

Once up the stairs, Theodore went briskly along the landing and through a subtle, small door, placed behind the angle of a long-case clock and startled a few servants who were lingering on the narrow stone stairs beyond. He nodded as if he were behaving perfectly normally and they managed to politely turn their heads away as if he'd encountered them on the main stairs.

He thought, I am in their domain so roles are here reversed – perhaps I should stand to attention and face the wall, and let them waft past me on their essential business, whatever it is that they do. The idea amused him and he made a mental note to share it with Adelia. It would undoubtedly make her smile.

He was profoundly grateful, all over again, that his mother and his wife were close friends. Popular comedy would suggest that this was not usually the case. He had certain reservations, however, about the arrival of that Harriet Hobson. She was a woman that he suspected of … well, he was never entirely sure of what he was suspecting her, but he suspected her nonetheless. She was, in general, a bad influence. But he could not express that thought aloud. A bishop's wife, a bad influence? The suggestion was preposterous. She was a regular church-goer, a patron of umpteen charities, a visible beacon of hope to all the community. Everyone praised her. Yet he could not shake the nagging feeling that she was close to his wife in a way that excluded him. He knew, rationally, that was what female friendship was. He had no need to be jealous. It was a petty and unworthy emotion that had no place in his logical life.

Yet here it was.

He pressed his lips together and frowned to himself as he managed to find his way through some twisting corridors on the ground floor at the back of the house. He burst out into the gentle summery air, and breathed deeply, his frown clearing. He had to trust to his wife and his mother to resist Mrs Hobson's vagaries.

Yet when all three women got together and alcohol was opened, he was forever being put in mind of Macbeth's three witches, and that was an unworthy thought.

He glanced up at the tall walls of the castle, Macbeth still on his mind. Mondial Castle wasn't one of those romantic crenelated structures that dotted the Scottish highlands. It was a blocky and plain sort of place, which actually harked back to the Norman Conquest in some parts, with tiny arrow-slit windows and sloping thick walls. But the bulk of the building was comparatively modern and had been built in the eighteenth century when the Haveringham family who held the Mondial titles and lands grew tired of large draughty halls and dark rooms. Since then, Mondial Castle had been continually improved with each new invention that came along. The kitchens were said to be a marvel of cooking technology and certainly Mondial had no problem in retaining staff – usually. Theodore recollected that the maid he had encountered in the breakfast room had said that "Maud has run off". He wondered if she had come back.

He kept out of sight of the windows and headed into the cover of a shrubbery where he found a gardener at work trimming the edges of a neat square of hidden lawn. The man straightened up and regarded Theodore with a direct gaze. He was very old, and clearly had little time for forelock-tugging.

"You're doing a fine job, man," Theodore said. He appreciated a nice straight lawn.

"Thank you, my lord."

"I want to ask you what you might have seen on the day of the attack."

The gardener shook his head. "Nothing, my lord. I was on the front driveway, attending to the bedding plants around the fountain. Jem was with me, raking the gravel. He'll vouch for me, if you like."

"Oh, I am not accusing you of anything. I am simply trying to piece together everyone's movements. Did you see Tobias Taylor, the valet, at all that day?"

The gardener narrowed his eyes. "It would be a rare thing to see him out here at all. The sunlight never touches that man's skin."

"So if he were out and about, then he would have been noticed and remarked upon," Theodore mused, mostly to himself. He thanked the man vaguely and began to walk around the shrubbery towards the biggest rose garden, aiming to follow the route that Sir Henry had described to him. He needed to start at the patio where Sir Henry said he had left the castle. He glanced back and saw that the gardener had picked up his long-handled tool and was following at a respectful distance. Then the gardener stopped and squinted.

"Someone's hurrying up to the house," he said.

Theodore recognised his wife at once and he stepped out to intercept her. When she saw him she changed tack and rushed back across the lawn. She was almost out of breath as she said, "I was coming for you! Hurry, this way. We were walking in the gardens and we've found a clue!"

"A clue! You wonderful woman. Show me. You, there, will you come with us?"

The gardener nodded and Adelia said, "Yes, please come, Brody. You will be useful."

"Brody?"

Theodore realised his wife was smiling at the gardener who was more than happy to follow them. How did she know everyone's name? Women's brains were smaller than men's yet she seemed to hold so much more in hers. He couldn't even say that his medical training meant there was less space in his head for domestic issues because some women were even training as doctors now, and were apparently doing rather well. It was a mystery, for sure.

His musings were put aside as they reached the out-of-the-way spot where Dido and his mother were waiting for them. His mother was looking smugly pleased with herself and she pointed her stick into a pile of leaves. Theodore spotted the partly-burned clothing immediately, and threw up his arm to prevent the gardener from blundering right into the pile and ruining all his evidence.

"Stay back, everyone! I want to look at every inch of this scene in careful detail!"

Everyone took three or four paces backwards and fell into utter silence.

This was it, Theodore told himself. Here was his first piece of potential physical evidence. He circled the pile of leaves. He spiralled in closer and closer, fixing each stage in his memory. Eventually he found himself on his knees, finally allowing himself to touch and move the leaves and the clothing. He sat back on his haunches and nodded to himself.

"Well?" his mother demanded, breaking the respectful silence with no regard to his concentration. "So who's the murderer?"

"Mother, please! The investigation is in its very early stages. I will need to examine this clothing much more closely." He gathered up the ragged thick fabric which seemed to have been a jacket, and the thinner scraps of pale linen which he guessed was a shirt. As he got to his feet, he noticed the crowd had grown a little larger. Standing next to Brody, the gardener, was a neat young woman in a black and white maid's outfit, and she was standing close enough to Brody to suggest some association. Yes, Theodore thought; the nose is the same. She is his daughter or perhaps his niece.

Brody saw they were under scrutiny and he nudged the girl. "Go on, tell him. He's not like the other one so don't be scared."

She shuffled forward and said, "Sir, if it please my lord, sir, I wish to confess to telling an untruth and please don't have me dismissed, sir, but I was following orders and it is hard to know which way is right!"

"I cannot and would not have you dismissed," he reassured her. "It's not my place. Only Mondial can do that."

"And my lord certainly won't tell your master," Adelia said smoothly. Theodore thought that had been obvious but the girl looked relieved at his wife's words anyway.

"My lord, when my master called us in to speak in front of you earlier, I am afraid we were not all as clear as we ought to have been, but it was hard to speak out."

"Yes," Theodore said. "His questions were, regrettably, all wrong. He's a good chap, my son-in-law, but has no idea about people."

Adelia stifled a cough. It probably meant something but he ignored her. He went on, saying, "So why don't you tell me now, in total confidence, what you could not tell me before?"

"Taylor, the valet, he wasn't in my lord's rooms all day, sir, even though that's where he says he was. He was running up the back stairs from the kitchens when I was going down with the sheets, and he ran past me. Then when I got to the laundry room, I was putting the sheets into bundles to be collected and the laundry woman who comes for them was just coming in saying she'd seen folks running and shouting. And so we both went outside and someone said there'd been shooting and there was an injury and I thought it was to do with hunting, but it wasn't."

136

Theodore tried to get the timeline straight in his head. He said, "Did you hear any shots?"

"No, my lord, but I was inside at the back at the castle down the back stairs and you can't hear a thing through those old walls."

"Have you any idea how long had passed between the shots and when you saw Taylor?"

"No, sir. But the laundry woman said she heard nothing, neither, and it had taken her five minutes to come up the driveway in the cart and she had a boy driving it and he had heard nothing neither."

"Oh, this is excellent. The shots must have been fired *at least* five minutes before Taylor was then seen running up the back stairs back to Mondial's rooms. Do you know if anyone saw him outside?"

"I don't, sir, but I'll ask around if I can. Except I must be careful, sir, because some of the other servants will tell my lord everything and it's not always easy to know who to trust."

He heard his mother tut at that statement. "That is no way to run a household."

"Grandmamma, I do my best!" Dido protested. "I had no idea that …"

The poor maid went white. She had not seen her mistress standing in the background just behind the older Lady Calaway and she looked as if she wanted to crumple to the ground. "My lady, my lady, I should never have said a thing…"

"No, you have been right to speak up and you are very brave," Dido said.

Still the girl quivered. Brody put his arm around her. "You'll be all right. My lady will see to it."

"I will," Dido said fiercely. "Please let it be known that I am *always* available if there are any problems and …" She tailed off.

Grace stepped in smoothly. "Just remember that the lord of the house doesn't know half of what goes on and what it's like to actually work the way that you do, so if you have a choice, my girl, you choose my lady here. She is my granddaughter and she will see you put right."

The girl nodded. Brody began to turn her around, and they froze.

One more person was heading their way, and he had a look of frustration on his face as if he had been searching for them for some time.

Lord Mondial was on his way across the lawn.

"So this is where all my guests are hiding!" Mondial announced as he reached them. He smiled but Theodore wasn't sure that it quite looked genuine. There was something about his eyes, he thought. Something missing.

"What's that you've got there, Calaway?" Mondial said.

Theodore could not hide the clothing in his arms. "Someone's been burning something," he said. "I don't know if it was missed on the first search of the grounds, or whether it's been done since then." His money was on the latter.

"Good heavens. Brody? What's the meaning of this?"

The gardener shook his head. "I cannot say, my lord."

138

"I found it," Theodore's mother said, jabbing randomly with her stick. "No one knew it was here until *I* spotted it."

"Someone did," Mondial replied. "Whoever put it there knew it was there. Whose clothing is it?"

"I don't know, but I am going to find out," Theodore told him. "They have tried to burn it but being made of wool and linen, it hasn't flared up and been destroyed as they might have wished. Leaves have been piled on which have burned out before the fabric could get going, and so I believe in the end, the perpetrator has simply piled more leaves on top and left it, hoping that it would stay hidden. Perhaps they intended to return and burn it again but the recent rains have prevented any of that."

"We could hide in the bushes and apprehend them when they come back!" his mother said.

"I rather fear it is too late for such subterfuge," he replied. "But there remains enough of the garments for me to perhaps discover who owned them."

"But why?" Mondial said. "Do you honestly think that the attacker stripped himself of his clothes before fleeing? Is that what you are hoping? We should have surely heard reports of a man … in that state … running away from here." He couldn't say *naked* but Theodore heard his mother titter inappropriately anyway.

And Theodore thought no, they didn't run away in the nude, but they might have got changed in the stables and run back into the house to pretend they had been in your rooms all along. But he kept his supposition to himself, at least for the moment. It wasn't that he suspected Mondial in particular, he told himself, but he knew that the relationship between a man and his valet

139

was a two-way movement of trust and loyalty. Mondial might be protecting Taylor for all sorts of reasons, although if he really thought his own valet had tried to kill him, surely he would act? But Mondial would not believe such an accusation unless Theodore could provide irrefutable evidence. Nor would Mondial's friend the judge. Theodore had to have undisputable proof.

Perhaps now, with the clothing, that would be possible.

He had to make his case before Taylor tried again. Before he was successful in the act of murder.

"I am not sure what happened here," he told Mondial, "but it is strange and I want to get to the bottom of it."

Mondial painted on a false, tight-lipped smile. "Brody, and you, girl; get back to work. My dear ladies, will you step inside? Or can I escort you on your walk if you wish to continue? It is a delightful day."

"One moment, if you will so indulge us," Theodore said, and he cast a glance towards his wife. He hoped she would lend her powers of persuasion to the request he was about to make. "I am curious as to how the *unfortunate situation* played out here, and I wonder if you might aid my imagination by stepping through the actual events. We have enough people here to make a little play out of it."

Mondial's eyes widened in shock. "You cannot think I would be comfortable in going over those terrible things!"

"Indeed, I expect it to be a dreadfully uncomfortable experience but I hope to appeal to your strong-mindedness and sense of justice."

It was a clumsy attempt at flattery and he noticed that Adelia

140

winced. She said, "It might even do you some good to replay it. Sometimes we can find peace by facing what is difficult."

"It would be unseemly. There are ladies present."

Theodore's mother weighed in. "I don't know about that, but I do think it's a jolly good idea. I am dreadfully interested in all of this. Dido, dear, you might want to turn away. Perhaps the girl will take you back to the house. But yes, you, John, and Theodore, let's have you run through your paces. John, where were you standing?"

"Over there by the fishpond."

"Come along!" Theodore's mother ordered, turning and stamping off across the lawn with her stick jabbing holes in the grass. "Everyone come along with me. What japes! Let's be Shakespeare!"

14

Adelia found herself pressed into service with the role of poor Philippa Lamb, which made her profoundly uncomfortable. She was glad that Dido had been led away to the house. Theodore did not notice why it might have bothered her, and she was keen to help him in his investigations, so she did not speak up. She girded her loins, metaphorically, and let herself be positioned by a yew tree. And this was an ideal opportunity, she realised, to finally ask Lord Mondial why Philippa had been there with him in the first place. At any other time, such a query would have sounded as if it were insinuating something. Here, it was natural, if she could phrase it correctly. And it was easier now his wife had left.

"Was Miss Lamb standing still or did she come walking up to you?" Adelia asked.

"What was –" her husband started to ask, but he was immediately jabbed by his mother, who understood just as clearly as Adelia that he had to be quiet and not influence things.

Lord Mondial rubbed his thumb along his jawline. He looked as if he were recollecting the events of the day, although as Adelia also held him in some suspicion, he could just as easily have taken the time to make up some lie. Still, he sounded convincing as he said, "I was walking along this path, heading for the ponds. There's been some nasty blue algae in them so I decided, as I was out and about, to check on whether the gardeners had got on top of the problem yet. Killed a spaniel, you know, a few weeks ago. Dreadful stuff. As I came along here, I saw Miss Lamb come around the corner from the far end of the yew tree walk, and I hailed her. She came up to me around here, and I invited her to walk with me to the ponds and then back up to the house. I am always happy for my guests to walk in the grounds but when a young lady is alone, one worries."

That was all fair enough, Adelia thought. He carried on, now asking Adelia to walk alongside him in her role as Philippa. "So Miss Lamb and I continued along this branch of the path and suddenly a man came out from behind that tree there."

Theodore scurried into position. "This one?"

The Dowager Countess mewed in disappointment. "Oh, that's not fair. I wanted to be the murderer."

"Mother, please," Theodore muttered in disapproval. Sometimes Adelia thought that the older Lady Calaway deliberately challenged convention, safe in the knowledge that no one was ever going to dare censure her. Lady Calaway laughed and let them continue with the reconstruction.

The scenario ploughed on exactly as Lord Mondial had described previously. Theodore, pretending to be a rather stiff and formal assailant, leaped out from behind the broad-trunked yew tree and pointed his hand at Lord Mondial, who said, "No, he waved it towards the young lady first." Adelia wiggled her eyebrows at her husband but he ignored her and remained serious.

"From this distance?"

"Exactly so. He shot at her, and she fell and I caught her. I was shouting but also trying to help her and I cannot recollect exactly how it next played out except that there was another shot and the most curious pain, almost delayed, in my upper arm. It is strange but it was as if my vision went to a very narrow point. My ears were thundering, like I was underwater. I tried to get a grip of myself. And I was aware that Miss Lamb was … I am sorry. I shall not continue with this in front of the ladies. All I can say is that I assisted her to no avail, and the attacker fled."

Theodore scratched at his chin like an uncouth field-hand. He seemed deep in thought and Adelia had to speak three times before his attention was roused.

"What? No," he said in answer to her question. "That will be all, at least for now. I must take these clothes and … examine them."

They began, by silent mutual assent, to walk back to the house. Adelia fell into step with the Dowager Countess while Lord Mondial attempted to engage Theodore in conversation. Theodore was oblivious to Lord Mondial's overtures and Adelia could hear the Marquis's annoyance growing in his voice. She decided not to catch up and interrupt them. It wasn't far to the castle. There, Theodore wandered off in a thoughtful daze, apparently heading upstairs to their suite. Adelia smiled in wan apology to Lord Mondial, smiled in genuine warmth to her mother-in-law, and followed her husband up.

Theodore was already sitting at the small table in the window, scribbling his ideas feverishly onto a fresh sheet of paper. The burned clothing sat in a heap on the floor at his feet. He didn't look up when he heard Adelia enter. She sat herself on a couch, and waited until he was ready to speak.

It didn't take long. He began to tap the pencil repetitively on the paper and muttered, "But why did Mondial not see the attacker? How masked can a man be, and still hit his target? Adelia, my love, in your long and varied life, have you ever been in such a situation of intense dread that you were unable to see?"

"Theodore, darling, don't suggest to a lady that her life has been *long*. It may be misconstrued. Likewise, *varied* can mean all manner of things. That aside, I am not sure." She cast her mind back but apart from the pain of childbirth, which had certainly done strange things to her perceptions at those moments, she could not recall anything. "No. I have never felt in fear of my life though. And yourself?"

"I thought that I had. I've – well, not quite duelled, but I told you about my youthful arguments. Mostly drunken, mostly forgettable. I thought back then that I was quite the daredevil but I suspect that we all did, and it was in truth nothing more than posturing. We were playing at dancing with death, that was all. This is something different. Yet it does not add up. Taylor is hiding something."

"The valet? He could have been possessed of a fit of madness. Does it not happen," Adelia suggested, "when someone can have an attack of unreality so convincing that they act quite out of character, but at all other times they seem perfectly normal? Perhaps Taylor has been at the mercy of such an episode, and due to his long service, Lord Mondial feels charitably towards him and is protecting him."

Theodore burst out laughing, which rather affronted Adelia. He said, "I can understand Mondial protecting Taylor for some reason. I have considered the same thing myself. But not on account of a fit of madness. If Taylor had been seized by insanity and – I don't know, ripped up half of Mondial's shirts in some fever – then perhaps. But he has *killed*. Killed a woman and injured his master. That is unforgiveable. Even your Mrs Hobson's good bishop husband would struggle to forgive so completely and not seek recompense."

Adelia nodded. "I agree. Yet he *is* protecting Taylor in some way, and for what purpose?"

"I don't know but I shall find out. Can you talk to Dido and get her to press the servants? They seem to know things and now we know that some can be trusted. Start with that girl…"

"Betty Brody?"

"Is that her name? Well, whatever. Yes, her." Theodore bent and stirred the clothing with his hand. "I will lay this out and perhaps we can see if we can find a matching pair of trousers. I will try to work out the size of man who wore it. Beyond that, I am not totally sure what they might tell us, but I must try."

"If there is anything to learn from it, then I have no doubt that you shall discover it," Adelia said. "You seem to be enjoying this investigative lark."

"Yes. It is a mental challenge but I should do much better if Mondial could leave me alone. It is not so much that he dogs me but his constant presence encroaches upon my ability to think."

"He is anxious to stop you from discovering what he does not wish you to know," Adelia told him.

Theodore looked surprised.

"For goodness' sake," she said. "Has that not occurred to you?"

"I confess this is all somewhat perplexing," Theodore said, looking like a small boy faced with algebra for the first time. "Because although we all have secrets, and Mondial no less than anyone else, I still strongly believe that he is a strictly honourable and upright man. He is married to our daughter and I do not regret that match. For all his faults, I cannot imagine that he would protect a murderer for whatever reason. And before you suggest it, yes, I have contemplated whether he is under some thrall of blackmail. A man's valet knows a *lot* about that man, and Taylor could have many sorts of incriminating information about Mondial. Yet ... what? What could that possibly be? No. The idea becomes too ridiculous the more that one examines it."

"But if all other ideas are cast away, then even the most ridiculous one must be the correct one. Perhaps you only resist the idea of Lord Mondial being involved because you feel he represents your class and if he could be involved in such a dreadful deed, so could anyone."

Theodore shook his head. "While I agree in principle, dear one, I don't think we've considered all the other available ideas yet. And he was utterly distraught when I encountered him. He was in tears, genuine distress, and that wasn't just the pain in his arm. We could still be looking at a passing robber, though I know I've discounted that idea many times. Or maybe ..."

She finished for him. She knew how his thoughts ran. "Or maybe it was Sir Henry after all."

"Exactly so."

He looked glum at the thought of discovering the bright young man was a murderer, and Adelia herself felt no better.

But there was one other person whose presence preyed upon her mind. Abruptly she stood up and went to the door, feeling agitated. There were a few hours before she had to dress for dinner but she didn't think she would have time to get into town and back. And anyway, what excuse could she come up with? She stopped.

She would go tomorrow. She would go at first light, and seek out her brother, and pay him whatever he needed to go away. And she would ask him about what he might have seen in the grounds of the estate. She couldn't bear to think of him as a potential murderer.

Perhaps, though, he was a witness.

She hoped that she was right. She knew, in a sick feeling in her stomach, that feeling such hope and longing suggested that there was also the possibility in her mind that she was wrong; that her brother had sunk to new depths, and would very soon be dragging them all down alongside him.

Adelia muttered something that Theodore didn't quite catch, and left the room. He assumed that she was off to see Harriet, Dido or perhaps his mother. He was glad of the freedom now to do something that would have certainly got him reprimanded if he had tried it in front of his wife. He spread out the dirty, charred clothing on the bed so that he could examine it all more closely. He did try not to get too much dust and dirt on the bedclothes but really, such housekeeping details didn't matter when it was all about the pursuit of justice.

He pushed the image of an angry Smith out of his mind and set to work.

The jacket had multiple scorched edges as if someone had tried to set it alight in various different places. Being tightly-woven woollen cloth had made it pretty resistant to the flames. One sleeve was burned up to the elbow but the other was mostly intact, though the stitching at the shoulder was loose and torn. The pockets of the jacket both inside and out were all empty. It was lined with rough cloth of a more open weave which had burned far better and was mostly gone. The colour was a muddy brown and there were no labels, notes or distinguishing features.

The shirt was in a worse state as it had burned a little more effectively but it, too, had resisted a total conflagration. The stitching was small and neat but there were a few patches that showed repair, albeit very skilfully done. So this shirt had belonged to a man who could not afford to simply buy new ones, but who did have a talented wife or daughters, or who could afford to pay a good seamstress.

To Theodore's mind, that ruled out a lowlier sort of servant but did not exclude Taylor. I must be careful, he reminded himself, to not become so set on the idea of the valet being a murderer that I overlook or ignore other important clues that might point in a different direction.

Yet the valet remained his prime suspect.

He held the jacket up. It was fitted for a tall, thin man.

150

One more clue that pointed to Taylor.

He pictured Sir Henry and thought that the man's youth and outdoor pursuits made him too wide for the jacket to fit him well.

Impulsively, he folded it up to hide the burned areas, and left the suite of rooms abruptly. He wanted to confront Taylor immediately with the evidence. Soon, he had no doubt, word would have spread among the servants about the discovery in the pile of leaves, and he didn't want Taylor to have any time to prepare his excuses. He knew his rash act of speaking to Taylor might annoy Adelia but he resolved that he would argue that she hadn't been around for him to consult, or he would have.

He was also aware that impulsive acts did not sit well with the idea of being a cool, calm, rational detective. But didn't Adelia always tell him to be less rigid? So off he went on his mission.

And he failed utterly.

He didn't fail in the way that he had expected.

He reached Mondial's rooms and asked a passing maid where he might find Taylor the valet. He was fully prepared to learn that Mondial cleaved to the very ancient style of household servants and have Taylor sleep on a truckle bed at his feet. In the event, that turned out to not be the case. Taylor had his own small room alongside his master's.

"But you'll not find him, my lord," the chambermaid said. She was middle-aged, yet fresh-faced, and one of the more confident ones. She'd likely been in service for twenty years or more. "He's been called away on urgent business."

Theodore stared at her in complete shock. He managed to blurt out, "What manner of business?"

"I don't know, my lord."

"Where?"

Again she shrugged. "No idea, my lord."

"What urgent business could a valet possibly have?"

"Sorry, my lord."

"Where is Lord Mondial?"

"I don't know."

Theodore gave up. She melted away and he stamped back to his rooms. Just when he wanted to speak to the damn man, the Marquis was now nowhere to be found.

15

Adelia was pleased to have plenty of company at the dinner table that night. Things were certainly livelier with her best friend and her mother-in-law present, and she was heartened to see a little colour back in her daughter Dido's cheeks, too. Dido was dressed in mourning colours even though Philippa had been only a friend; she argued that she felt like a sister to her, and that mourning was appropriate. Her dark, sombre dress had a high neckline and an air of chastity about it that was not usual for eveningwear.

The Dowager Countess had sniffed and said that she was not intending to dress in mourning as a visitor, and no one could argue with that. The expectation that one would make such ongoing displays of grief that affected everyone even remotely connected to the deceased were dying out these days anyway.

Unlike the Countess whose gloved fingers were absolutely stacked with rings, Adelia had made one concession to Dido's sensibilities in removing most of her more ostentatious jewellery, and wearing only one small dull grey brooch. Theodore had laughed at her when he noticed it as they sat at the table. "You hate that thing; why did you bring it?"

"Smith always packs a range of colours for me. She says 'you never know'. In this case, she was right."

"Smith is always right. If women like her were able to run the country, we'd have no more scandals or upsets. Britain would rule the world."

"We *do* rule the world," the Dowager said snippily, unashamedly listening.

Conversation at the table roamed widely over many topics but, noticeably, did not mention the "unfortunate situation that had happened outside" at all. Adelia kept her eye closely on her husband. He'd told her about the strange case of the missing valet, and she had agreed it sounded odd, but she had given him strict instructions to not raise the matter at dinner. She was pleased to see that he was doing his best to comply.

Due to the expanding company, the conversation after dinner continued to be rather sedate. Word had come back from Miss Lamb's household that someone would be arriving at some point during the following day to collect her companion but they would be grateful for a bed for the night, due to the distance travelled. Adelia felt sad for the old nurse. She had remained in her rooms ever since the murder, and had resisted all attempts from anyone to draw her out for a few hours. She spoke only to the housekeeper.

They all went to bed late but sober.

In spite of her scant few hours of sleep, Adelia rose early. She dressed well, and informed her husband that she was going into town to purchase some "necessities."

"Do you need some money?" he asked.

She did, but she was cautious about it. He had never overseen her purchases like many husbands did. Luckily here in this strange town she had none of her habitual lines of credit in Theodore's name, so she would have to pay cash and he would therefore not scrutinise the accounts of everything she was going to buy.

Or everything that she was going to pretend to buy.

The money was for her brother.

Theodore unrolled some London-issued bank notes but also gave her some coins which were more likely to be accepted by the more provincial shops in town. She pocketed the lot and hurried out before he could think to ask her what, exactly, she needed.

She felt as if she were lying to her husband by saying nothing, and she hated it.

Theodore didn't give Adelia's trip to town a second thought. He assumed that she was going with Harriet or perhaps his mother. It didn't matter. It was probably good for her to go off and indulge in some shopping for fripperies. He had more important things to do; there were his investigations to conduct, and he was determined to find out where Taylor had gone, and why. And did Mondial know about his valet, or was he a mere dupe of a cunning servant?

He left their suite of rooms and headed down to the breakfast room. Adelia had not even eaten before going to the stables where she had already apparently pre-arranged a man and a carriage to drive her into town. On the way to the meal, he fell into step with Sir Henry, who was going the same way. Sir Henry still looked pale and Theodore asked first after his health.

"Oh, I fear that I have discovered I am a weaker man than I once thought I was," Sir Henry said gloomily. "I am making plans to leave but…"

"Before the garden party?"

"That is the sticking point. Lady Mondial tells me she would be mortally offended if I were to go. Yet under the circumstances, how can I stay? The whole thing is a sham, sir, a sham. It should have been cancelled and I don't mind who hears me say it."

"It is certainly unusual but hardly completely unthinkable, at least by the standards of the ton." Theodore recollected his own misgivings and how his conversation with Mondial had changed his mind when he had discovered their common ground. He could not break the Marquis's confidence, of course.

"The standards of the ton? The demimonde, if you ask me. I wish that I had lived a hundred years ago when we had a stricter and fairer approach to what is considered appropriate behaviour in polite society," Sir Henry said in a stiff way.

Theodore laughed. He couldn't help himself. "What nonsense! You are a young man of – what, thirty? Now, look at me. I am ancient. Nearly twice your age. Let me tell you that things were never better in the past, not at all. It's a lie we tell children, though for what ends I do not know. We live now in an age of true enlightenment and I, for one, am grateful beyond measure for fast steam trains and telegraphs and coal-gas to light our rooms and heat our food. And if standards change and loosen, that is generally a good thing. It might feel as if the rug is rucking up under our feet and catching our step from time to time but one cannot stop progress."

Sir Henry stared at Theodore and he realised he had been ranting. He ground to a halt and harrumphed awkwardly. "Anyway," he finished, "That is my opinion. Tell me, what do you make of this urgent business that has apparently called Taylor the valet away?"

The turn in topic took Sir Henry by surprise. "Who – what now?"

"Mondial's valet has disappeared on supposed urgent business. Had you heard?"

Sir Henry continued to shake his head. "No. What Lord Mondial does with his staff is up to him."

Theodore was disappointed in the lack of information but he had other people to ask about it, so he put it aside. "You have a man with you?"

"Only Carter. I can't bear to be plagued by servants at every turn. Carter's only tolerated because he was my man when I was at sea, and he's seen the very worst of me. I could hardly let him go; he knows too much."

"I did not realise you were a naval man."

"Briefly. It did not suit me. Far too much of the up and down, and I missed green hills and trees. I am an outdoor man, as you know, but you can have too much of the – outdoors. So I am content to be a landowner now, and I am as hands-on as my tenants and bailiff will allow me to be, which is not so very much. Why are the workers of the land so resistant to new devices which can only benefit them? Sorry – forgive me. It is a pet topic of mine."

"No apology needed! I rambled on and now you should do the same. Please, tell me more. What is the latest in agricultural technology?" Theodore asked with genuine enthusiasm.

Sir Henry and Theodore went into the breakfast room together and bit by bit, Sir Henry warmed up and outlined his theories and hopes for the future. Theodore was genuinely enthralled. He even followed Sir Henry out again, once they had dined, still probing him about threshing machines.

Sir Henry stopped awkwardly at the foot of the stairs.

Theodore finally intuited that Sir Henry no longer wished to speak about farming machinery but he wanted to seize the chance now they had established a rapport. He couldn't wait to tell Adelia how well he had done in making Sir Henry feel at his ease. Now at last he could ask him about his business with Dido. Adelia had told him all about finding him going through their daughter's writing case, and he meant to get to the bottom of the situation.

"I say, have you spoken to Mondial about all these improvements? He's very interested in having all the modern conveniences," Theodore said.

"In passing, yes. He refers me to his estate manager mostly."

"Ah, he's not so hands-on as you, then? What about Lady Mondial?"

"What about her? What interest would she have in pumping and drainage, tilling and ploughing?"

"She is my daughter through and through. She is as interested as I am in such things, I am sure." Perhaps, he thought. It was a small lie. In fact it was his youngest daughter, Edith, who

158

had the most analytical mind he had ever encountered. She could glance at a steam engine, listen to its thumpings, and tell you exactly what was going wrong and how to fix it. "After all, I understand that you and Dido have grown close?"

Sir Henry's face went blank and rigid. "You understand no such thing, sir."

"Oh, I am not implying anything. But it is known that you and her…"

"Nothing is known! Good day, sir."

Theodore watched in amazement as Sir Henry took the stairs two at a time and disappeared around the bend on the landing.

Well, he thought. I suppose that's a success, of a sort. I have certainly touched a nerve.

But if Sir Henry has touched my daughter – my married daughter, my respectable daughter – I shall take a pistol to him and I shan't even bother to be masked. Let them hang me for it.

16

When Adelia climbed into the closed carriage that was awaiting her in the courtyard, she was surprised to find Harriet was already nestled in a plush hooded cloak in a corner. It was too thick for summer but at least would muffle the worst of the bumpy journey. Adelia was wearing a silk and cashmere cape over a respectable tailored jacket and matching skirt. Her puffed sleeves made wearing anything other than a cape very awkward.

"Good morning!" Harriet warbled. "Would you care for a mint?" She pulled out a twist of paper from her deep handbag and wafted the humbugs under Adelia's nose. "I am a terrible traveller."

"You are a terrible person and we are hardly travelling far. I am only going into town. It's barely a few miles and I should walk if it I were allowed."

The door was closed and she nodded through the window at the coachman who was happy to have a trip away for half a day. They rumbled off. She had to speak up over the noise of the wheels on the gravel and the squeaking of the springs. "Anyway, why are you here?"

"Lord Mondial invited me to stay."

"No, why are you here in this carriage, you harridan?"

"Oh, I heard in passing that you had asked for a ride into town and I thought you'd enjoy the company."

"Harriet…"

Harriet leaned forward although she didn't drop her voice. "I know why you're going and you'll need my help. Didn't you ask for it? I nearly invited Lady Calaway to come with us too."

"Oh goodness, I adore Grace with every inch of my being but no, I really don't want her to know about my particular private matter. It's a family thing. I regret even telling you."

"You cannot keep anything from me. I promised to help you and I haven't managed to do so yet. Anyway, you will be safer with me at your side. We shall have to go into all the lowest dives in town."

"You look positively excited at the prospect."

"I am a bishop's wife. I am used to accompanying my husband as he ministers to the very worst and poorest and lowest of London's streets. I find it invigorating and humbling, all at the same time. You, however, are going to be shocked and troubled."

"I doubt it. I was not born a lady."

Harriet looked disdainful. "You were not born poor, and that makes all the difference."

It was too early in the morning to bicker, even as friends. So Adelia nodded with mild restraint and let Harriet have the victory this time.

Soon they arrived in the town and she gave the coachman a coin or two to spend in the respectable inn where Harriet had first stayed. He took the horse around to the back of the inn and

162

rang the ostler's bell as he went. Adelia faced Harriet. "Well, then, oh fount of all knowledge both depraved and unseemly, where do we start?"

Harriet looked up and down the busy street, and pointed. "We go that way and start looking down the side alleys."

They set off, picking their way along the raised pavement. "Why did you choose to go this way?" Adelia asked. "There are no docks in this place, being so far from the sea. I know that shabbier places are near the docks in a city, but not here. We're going downhill. Is it perhaps to do with the wind? Are we near a tannery? Perhaps there is a clue in the width of the street…"

Harriet laughed. "I didn't want to walk in the shadows, that was all. This way is as good as that. There was no art to my choice. We will simply start to ask around. I'll go and talk to that market seller. He will know where the dosshouses are."

"The one with the pretty hat pins?"

"Oh, I hadn't noticed what he was selling," Harriet said with pure innocence in her voice.

Yet she still bought a new hatpin with a green emerald button. It was inevitably going to be made of paste but it looked well enough even in the light of day. And Harriet also got her information. It wasn't long before Harriet and Adelia had found a strong hint that Alfred Pegsworth – "such a nice gentleman, shame he's down on his luck" – would be in a public house at the back of a coffee warehouse on the road east out of town, surrounded by looming hills and rocks. They walked with small, careful steps through the muck. There were no pavements here and the road was busy with carts and barrows.

Adelia found that she was feeling a little uncomfortable. She must have walked too close to Harriet because she bumped her friend with her elbow. Harriet laughed and took her arm. "Steady now. Hold your nerve."

"I am perfectly fine."

Adelia was grateful that this time, Harriet didn't argue back. They came up to the rough wooden door of the public house. Adelia nearly missed it, but Harriet spotted the faded sign hanging from a chain and pole above the darkened window. It was impossible to see inside and the door was closed. They were going to have to enter. It didn't look like any inn that Adelia had ever been in.

"This is not the right thing to do," Adelia said, pulling her cape around her shoulders even more tightly and wishing she'd opted for a dark rough wool rather than russet-brown cashmere. "My reputation hangs on a thread at all times; you must know that."

"You are correct. But if anyone sees you here, and they are the sort of people to judge you for being here, then they ought to not be here themselves. You will both be trapped in a case of mutual silence and each will be unable to call the other out. It is an elegant solution to transgression."

"You speak as if you have had cause to rely upon such a solution before."

"Oh, these things do not trouble *me*. Being a clergyman's wife gives me a free entrance anywhere – visiting a hovel like this merely improves *my* status. The worse the public house, the greater my holiness, don't you see?"

"Well, in that case, you may enter first." Adelia nudged Harriet to the door. Harriet laughed and pulled it open without hesitation.

Conversation wavered and fell as the two women slipped in. They stepped directly into a low-ceilinged room thick with smoke both from pipes and also from the open fire. It was crowded with men dressed in shades of grey and brown. Through the strange quietness, Adelia thought she heard a baby cry out but she had no idea where it might have been. It might have been in a basket under a table.

There was a portly man in an apron who stood behind a high table at one end of the room, which she assumed served as the bar. He came forward with a look of concern on his face, and confusion as he tried to work out what manner of women they were.

Harriet had obviously encountered such uncertainty before. She said, boldly, "We are respectable women, sir, on a mission. We're looking for Alfred Pegsworth and if he is here, might we have a private room in which to talk?"

"He's in the back, but are you sure you want to be here and are you sure that you want to see *him*?"

He was then assured that they were sure, and that was backed up by a small coin. He took them to a room off to one side, separate from the main room by a thick curtain rather than a door, and asked to wait while Alfred Pegsworth was fetched.

Alfred arrived at the same time as the publican brought a small decanter of his "best" wine and some smeared glasses. He fussed around the table as if his diligence could conjure up doilies and crustless sandwiches, and no one could speak freely until he had gone. Adelia used the few moments to study her brother carefully.

He was forty-one, ten years younger than Adelia, but he looked unkempt and old. He had a beard and moustache which both needed trimming, and his hair was too long, touching his ears and grubby collar. His dark suit matched but it was shiny at the elbows and knees, and his waistcoat was missing a button. They were good quality clothes, made to last, which was one advantage at least. He smelled of carbolic acid. There were worse things to smell of.

Looking at him brought her back some painful memories of their father. And with that memory came blame, blame directed at her even though she had been innocent of any of the troubles that had befallen the family in times past.

Alfred, her brother, had been eleven when she had married Theodore. She was twenty-one then and Theodore was twenty-eight. She had risen from being a mere gallery owner's daughter to the wife of an Earl, and their father had lavished a huge dowry upon her. His business was doing well and they were a popular and rich family amongst the well-to-do trades of London.

So off she had gone to her new married life, leaving Alfred to learn the ropes at their father's side, and all should have been well. Yet within a year, their father had seen a few business ventures fail, a gallery expansion eat money and return no profits, a few major sales fall through, and their mother — always sickly and weak — had died in her sleep.

When Alfred had been fifteen, their father had killed himself.

The shame that had attached to the family after that event had been devastating. Even while people assured them of their sympathetic feelings in private, the public gossip was one of studied horror and judgmental sneering. Harriet had stuck to

Adelia's side throughout, ignoring even the worst of the comments that were cast their way. Her father's action, taken in the very depths of his despair, cast long shadows and most people did not care to ask *why* this had happened. They were content to gloat in their own apparent "strength".

While Adelia had had her friend, her husband and her first children to comfort her, plus her title and her status, the fifteen-year-old Alfred had not been so lucky. Now orphaned, he had been apprenticed to his uncle Oliver Pegsworth but he ran a tannery business which was not to Alfred's liking, even though he had been placed as a clerk in the offices rather than out in the leather workshops. The dreadful smell from the pits permeated everything. The tannery was on the edge of the worst slums of London as no one else would put up with the noxious fumes, and though it was a profitable and essential business, it was a horrible one dealing with animal carcases and the filth that was used in the tanning processes.

At twenty-two Alfred struck out on his own in the world but he found himself adrift, sustained only by a lingering feeling of resentment that he focused on his sister.

If such money had not been wasted on her dowry and wedding, he said, then his father's business could have weathered its storms. Mother would not have died and father would not have done – he would not have done the thing that he did.

And Alfred would have been Master Pegsworth for a little longer and not ended up merely known as "that Alf who smells of dog's mess."

"That Alf" then roamed London getting into jobs and out of them; and finally he got himself into a marriage that, though he was in many ways now out of it, still hauled him back to his responsibilities from time to time.

Such responsibilities as he was talking of now, here in this lowly public house.

He sipped at his wine, taking his time with it, and shot a dark look at Harriet before saying to Adelia, "Does she really need to be here?"

"Yes, she does. She has helped you in the past. Don't forget the time that she got you that position as a clerk to the bishop." Which he had left after only three months, she thought but did not say.

He knew what she wasn't saying. "It wasn't my thing. Too preachy."

"What is your thing?"

"It would have been printselling. Gallery owning. That sort of thing. You know, what I was born to."

"Oh, for goodness' sake." Adelia closed her eyes and asked for strength. She opened them and spoke as calmly as she could. "So, how is your good wife?"

"Jane is as Jane does."

It wasn't much of an answer but in truth, Adelia did not like Jane and she certainly didn't trust her. She was as much of a chancer as her brother was. She suspected both had lied to the other about their wealth before the wedding. It would have been an uncomfortable wedding night as the truth was revealed. Both had married the other on the promise of great riches: both had lied. It was an inauspicious start to married life and the outcome had been predictable.

"And how is your son, my dear nephew Oliver?" she

168

continued.

"Right, well, you see, it's about him that I need to speak to you."

Harriet nudged Adelia as if to say, "You see? I was right." Adelia nodded and said, "I understand you want him to go to school?"

Alfred shot another filthy look at Harriet. "She's been spilling my business, hasn't she? It's not done, you know, to be gossiped about. I might look like this now, but I was raised to conduct myself with certain standards. I don't like to be talked about. I still deserve respect, you know."

"You do. And she didn't spill your business. I just know that Oliver is thirteen now, so it's about the time you'd think of his future."

"Huh. Well. I want to send him to a good school. I want him to have a proper gentleman's education so that he can take up the lifestyle that ought to have been mine."

"I see."

"You can't argue with that, can you?"

"I cannot," she agreed. "But first, I'd like to ask you about when you were prowling around the grounds of Mondial Castle the other day."

"Me? I've never been there."

"Don't lie to me, Alfred."

He picked at a cold lump of wax that was welded to the table top. "Well, yes, I did come down to see if you were about but I resent that being called *prowling*. And I am not stupid. I know you're going to ask me about that murder that happened there, like I had anything to do with it. That's not nice, you know.

169

I'm hurt, I am, that you think so low of me."

She could have slapped the mulish resentment right out of him. She wanted to. But she restrained herself and said, stiffly, "Actually, I only wanted to ask if you had seen anything or anyone acting suspiciously."

"No. I didn't see a thing."

"Are you sure?"

"There you go again, acting like I'm no brighter than a house-brick. Just because I never had the advantages that you have had. Yet instead of feeling charitable towards me, you kick me while I'm down. It's only on account of my good Christian nature, all forgiving and forgetting, that I even come back to see you like this from time to time."

Adelia wanted to hit him and laugh at the same time. So, she was supposed to be grateful that he was here? "Well, if anything occurs to you, please send me a note."

"I could come to see you."

"At Mondial Castle? I fear it would be impossible at the moment. It is a house in mourning."

"That's not what they're saying around town."

Harriet leaned forward and poured him a little more wine out of the decanter. Black lumps swished at the bottom. "So, what are they saying around town?"

"That there's going to be a big party and lots of people are turning up soon."

"The party was arranged anyway, before it all happened." Adelia suddenly felt the need to defend Lord Mondial's decisions. "But Dido has lost a very dear friend. Yet you have not even asked after your own niece's health."

170

His face fell. "As to that, I am sorry," he said in a lower voice. "I am. And I feel for you all. Death is death, isn't that right?"

Adelia nodded, accepting his apology because she knew that he meant it. He saw that as a moment of weakness, and struck immediately. "Such tragic events make us treasure our young folk even more closely, isn't that so? As for my Oliver, he's such a bright young man. So much potential if only it could be unlocked in the right way. I know you do only want the best for *all* of your family and we only need a little boost, a little temporary easing of the passage of your nephew into a good school, not Eton, not Westminster, but a good one nevertheless, you know."

She knew that was why they were there and decided she wanted to get on with it. She pulled her handbag onto her lap and slipped a hand inside. "I am happy to help out with Oliver's education," she said. "But this must go towards a school for him, and not get diverted in any other direction."

He feigned utter astonishment at the mere suggestion.

"Furthermore, as I am away from home, I don't have access to very much money and therefore what I give you now is *all* that I can give you. You must leave this area and not return."

"I shall do my best."

"Listen, Alfred, it's for your own good. You were seen in the grounds before the murder. Don't you realise you're a potential suspect?"

"Only if someone names me, and the only people who could do that are you – and her," he spat out. "Would you do that? Would you throw your own brother to the wolves like that?"

It was tempting, she thought. But she kept her mouth closed

as she unfurled the banknotes. He protested at first, saying it was hard to get places to accept them. "Just take them to a bank and have them exchanged."

"I prefer coin."

"They are for school fees. It should not matter," she argued back, and she noticed that in spite of his words, he didn't hesitate in pocketing the notes immediately. She then laid out a few coins for him. "And these will tide you over to help you get home," she added.

"This won't get me far."

"It is all I have."

"You must have more back at the castle. I will come with you. I should like to meet your husband again. He was always so very kind to me."

"You must not. You would not dare."

"I am his brother-in-law. He said he would always have an open door for me."

Theodore did not know the depths to which Alfred had sunk. As far as Theodore was concerned, Alfred was still living with his wife Jane and was gainfully employed as a clerk in an office. Adelia had maintained that fiction for so long that she simply didn't know how to disabuse her husband now. In desperation, she grabbed the ugly grey brooch that was pinned at her collarbone, and threw it onto the table too. "There. Sell it or pawn it."

He picked it up. "Is this a grey diamond?"

She would not have been giving him anything quite so valuable, in spite of its ugliness. "No, it is a sapphire."

"Sapphire? This colour?"

"It is true. It has value."

He squinted at it as if he could tell, but he couldn't and she knew it. Yet she was not lying. "Take it to a few different valuers," she told him. "Not here. Go to London and go to the best advice. You will not be disappointed. And you can make use of the bank notes more easily if you go home, too."

Her words convinced him. He grabbed the decanter, poured out the rest of the wine including the sediment, and drank it down in one gulp. She felt her teeth itch at the thought of the lumps. She couldn't find anything else to say, and he was clearly done with conversation now that he had got what he wanted.

Without further ado, he left.

Harriet sat back. "Shall we order more wine?"

17

In the end, they held back on having any more wine. It had left a furry taste on Adelia's tongue and the whole meeting made her feel despondent. They trudged back to the coaching inn and refreshed their palates with a reasonable meal before clambering back into the carriage and returning to Mondial Castle.

"Who is the top suspect in this murder now?" Harriet asked as they rumbled back along the narrow roads. "I should have expected your clever husband to have solved it all by now." She was always nicer about Theodore than he was about Harriet.

"I am starting to think it was a passing robber as Lord Mondial claims," Adelia said. "I wish it weren't so, but here we are. Although Theodore is still convinced that Taylor the valet is involved and I can see why he thinks so, but I simply can't suggest a motive for the man. I am beginning to wish I had never told Theodore he ought to investigate. We are running in circles."

"What of the local police?"

"They are still keen to step in, according to Dido and some of the servants, but Lord Mondial won't have it. He sent the inspector away with some stiff words. Lord Mondial has friends in very high places. He is a friend in a high place himself. So the magistrates and county judges will bend to his demands. He drops the name of the circuit judge whenever the matter is raised. I have no doubt he also knows the police commissioner for this area and if Lord Mondial doesn't want police involvement, then there shall be none."

"Even with a death such as this?"

"People die every day in all manner of ways. Justice falls only to those who can pay for it, after all."

"That is sadly true," said Harriet. "We see it all the time in our line of work. The Bishop quite despairs at the unfairness of it all. What of that Sir Henry Locksley? He's a likeable man but he's far too upset and I can't understand why he's still here if he *is* that upset. He's awfully prey to his emotions, isn't he? Quite the wayward romantic sort."

"He is very mixed-up and confused and there is more to him than meets the eye."

"Oh? I bet he has a secret. I wager he's an *artist*. That would explain it, wouldn't it?"

Adelia wasn't sure she wanted to tell her friend everything. She didn't like the way it could reflect badly on her daughter. Yet by the time the carriage rolled back into the courtyard at the back of Mondial Castle, Harriet knew everything anyway; she just had that way of winkling someone's secrets out of them.

But she was never judgemental. Harriet reassured Adelia that she thought Dido was perfectly respectable and blameless and innocent of any clandestine affairs. Adelia believed it, but she needed to hear it from someone else, and was glad of Harriet's vehemence. They parted in the entrance hall of the castle. Harriet wanted to have a lie down for a few hours, and Adelia decided to get changed and go and see how her daughter was faring. She was only halfway across the hall when she was accosted by Theodore emerging from the library.

"And how was your visit to town?" He eyed her empty hands. "You have either bought things that are very small and hidden them in your bag, or they are very large and will be delivered by cart directly. Either way, it does not bode well for our finances." He smiled and held out his hand to take her bag as they proceeded upstairs together.

"I have bought nothing," she said. "I had hoped for some silk ribbons and other trinkets but the choice was sadly lacking."

"You said you needed necessities."

"Silk ribbons are a necessity, dear one."

He laughed. Once in their suite, Smith came forward to help her out of her cape and whisked it away immediately so that the dust and dirt of travel could be brushed from it. "You have lost your brooch," Theodore said, watching proceedings. "I could have sworn you wore it this morning."

"Oh. You are that attentive?"

"You know that I am. It is my trained medical eye. But how did it work lose? Was the clasp broken?" he said.

"You are taking this idea of being a detective far too much to heart. It could have come free at any point today. The roads are bumpy. I'll ask someone to check in the carriage."

Theodore smiled as if a cunning thought had occurred to him. "Oh, I can guess exactly what has happened to it."

She felt cold. Perhaps having a detective for a husband was a very bad idea. "Oh?" she asked as lightly as she could manage.

"You never did like it, did you?" He grinned in triumph. "No doubt you have 'accidentally' lost it and I am sure that all the searching in the world won't bring it to light again. Well, it is no matter. Listen, I too have news. I spoke earlier to Sir Henry."

Smith came back and took Adelia into an adjoining dressing room. Theodore conversed with her through the partly open door while she got changed, telling her of their ill-fated conversation. She sighed and rolled her eyes multiple times throughout his recount. She had *told* him not to talk to people! This was exactly the problem with his practice as a doctor, too. Too much blunt speaking. People simply couldn't cope with certain kinds of truth.

Still he made a good point about how he had obviously touched a nerve with Sir Henry. Once again, she felt she didn't quite know what was really going on.

She left Theodore sitting at the window, tapping his pencil to his teeth, and went out in search of her daughter.

This time she was going to get to the very bottom of things.

She found Dido in the garden room downstairs, standing up and looking out over the lawns. She was dressed in comfortable day wear and so was not at home to visitors. She had correspondence on a tray nearby, but she was obviously taking a break. She turned when she heard her mother approach, and gave her a big warm smile.

"I am pleased to see you looking brighter today," Adelia

said.

"I think that my husband was right all along. Having grandmamma here has made the whole place feel happier somehow. And Mrs Hobson is a delight. She is always amusing."

"I've just been into town with her," Adelia said.

"It is a pretty town."

"It is."

Adelia walked slowly around a tall orange tree that was outgrowing its terracotta pot. The large doors were thrown open making the room feel like it really was part of the garden. Butterflies flitted from bloom to bloom. She let the silence lengthen until Dido felt compelled to break it. "Mama, do you really think any of us are in danger from the attacker?"

"Perhaps. If it were not a passing robber who committed this crime then it was someone from within the house. Your father will find it all out, I am sure. He is looking very closely at someone now."

"Taylor, the valet?"

"No. Sir Henry Locksley, in fact."

"Mama!" Dido sat down with a thump on an ornate metalwork chair. "We have talked about Sir Henry. What could he have done that could possibly arouse anyone's suspicion?"

"The fact that he was in your room, going through your writing-case."

"But…"

"What was he looking for, Dido?"

"I cannot say."

"You can say. You must say. Someone's life may depend on it. Will you see an innocent man hanged?"

"It could not come to that!"

"Forgive my drama, but it could. So whatever you need to tell me, you must tell me now."

She bent her head. "He has written to me," she said in a whisper. "But I have not replied, of course."

"That will be it. Oh, so simple and yet so dangerous. He wanted to get the letter back. But why? What on earth did it say?" Adelia pulled up a nearby chair and sat close to her daughter so that they could converse in low tones. "I assume it is awfully incriminating."

"Oh, Mama, it was an ill-advised sort of letter and one that I suspect he regretted that he wrote as soon as it left his hands. He may have been drunk at the time. He declares his undying devotion to me. I know that he means only to be an absolute ally to me, a friend as close as a brother might be, but the way that he expressed himself was … unfortunate. He is not good with his choice of words. It is a letter that I blushed to read. So I hid it away. I should have destroyed it, of course."

"Why didn't you? Such a letter can only bring trouble, to you and to him."

"It felt disrespectful to burn it or tear it up because I know that his intentions were always, and will always be, strictly honourable."

"Ask your father if even the best of men have only ever honourable intentions," Adelia said darkly. "Even women. When we are facing the extremes, our emotions can take us to places we would never admit to."

"Mama! What do you mean?"

"Only that a man's intentions may be honourable most or

even all of the time, but sometimes his actions are in contrast to those intentions. And writing a letter of love – yes, that is what it sounds like to me – the act of writing such a letter opens the door to less honourable things. He has taken one step along a dangerous road. All other steps come more easily. In this way, an honourable man and woman may find themselves too far down a path of sin to turn around and escape. It happens by inches."

"No!"

"Yes," Adelia said firmly. She thought she might have been over-egging the pudding a little but her daughter's honour was the most important thing to her. If she was brought into disgrace even by words, not even by deeds, then Lord Mondial would have her cast out or committed to an asylum without a second glance. He was strict and upright and his own brand of honour would not allow for a moment of flexibility.

Not that she would express those fears to Dido.

"Where is the letter now?"

"In the hidden section below my wedding tiara in my locked jewellery case that lies in my own private safe in my room," Dido said in a rush.

"It must be destroyed and Sir Henry must be told that it is gone."

"But why?"

"While it exists, it brings danger to you and your whole family, and to Sir Henry. If you care for him at all, let it be destroyed utterly and let him know it. He will understand why. I suspect he is trying to get it for the exact same purpose. He can only be filled with regret at his actions."

Dido thought about it for a moment before acquiescing with a heavy sigh. "Very well," she said. "Let us see to it immediately."

18

Adelia acted as chaperone between Dido and Sir Henry as he was told of the letter and what they had done to it. She called him into the garden room after Dido had fetched the letter and burned it in front of her mother's eyes.

Sir Henry looked pale and nervous as he glanced between mother and daughter. Dido kept her head turned away and didn't speak, letting her mother take charge. Adelia assured him the matter was at a close now the letter had been destroyed and he escaped from the meeting as quickly as he could.

Dido went to speak to the housekeeper on everyday matters, seeking solace in the ordinary running of the household, and Adelia headed upstairs to find Theodore. He wasn't in their suite nor any of the public rooms, and eventually Lord Mondial, who was lounging in his study, indicated he had left him in the stables, "talking to the horses."

She went out and found him doing exactly that.

Theodore was leaning on the stable door of a loose box, peering into the gloom and apparently muttering a stream of nonsense. As she got closer, she saw the long thin head of a handsome bay mare. Theodore would blow gently at her nostrils and she would huff and blow back.

"Is this the only way you can get intelligent conversation?" she asked as she approached and he jumped.

"Ah! I was lost in my own thoughts there."

"Well, I have some news for you concerning Sir Henry. But first you must understand that no blame is to be attached to either Sir Henry or Dido."

The warning made his face cloud over. "This sounds serious."

"It is, but I believe that nothing reproachable has happened. And we have averted any possible rumour of impropriety."

"You need to start at the beginning." He glanced around. "Come, let us sit down and discuss this. Follow me. I find the hay barn to be both private and strangely comforting."

He led her into a vast lofty space that was piled high with straw bales on one side, rich and deep yellow in colour, and hay bales on the left, a lighter and thinner substance altogether. Both smelled wonderful. She had been raised in the heart of London and any hint of bucolic countryside filled her with romance. She almost giggled as she sat on a wide low straw bale and spread out her skirts, feeling like a milkmaid in a pastoral painting. The hay was scratchier than she had expected but she could ignore it for the sake of looking appealing.

Theodore did not sit down. He prowled around as she explained what had occurred between Sir Henry and Dido. He cursed the young man a few times but she managed to persuade him that Sir Henry was merely impulsive and reckless but not a lothario, and Dido was entirely innocent.

184

"Yet has he no care for our daughter's reputation?" he said angrily. "Sending letters of love to a married woman!"

"He does care for her reputation and for her, very much, and that is why he was looking for the letter. He explained that he wished only to get it back and destroy it himself to ensure it could never come to light and harm her. But he could not approach Dido and ask her because a private meeting would have been misconstrued and a public one would have been overheard. He also did not wish to cause her any embarrassment or distress by referring to the letter directly. He accepts it was a foolish thing to have done, and wants to never think of it again. And I believe him."

"Foolish? Criminally irresponsible. Did you read this letter yourself? I need to know what it said. I cannot now believe anything he might *claim* that it said. I need to see it for myself."

"I did read it. It was not a passionate declaration of love. It was an affectionate letter from one friend to another, that was all. He was offering his support. The unfortunate thing was the wording and the fact it comes from an unmarried man to whom she has no familial connection. He said that he *dedicated* himself to her, which could be misinterpreted by those of evil mind. And we know the world has enough of those."

"Fool. Was the man raised in a barn?" Theodore muttered, kicking at a bale.

She laughed at his joke but he didn't even realise he'd made one.

"Theodore, calm down," she said. "You are worked up far too much over this. I suspect it is not the letter that is truly bothering you."

"No," he grumbled. "It's this whole thing. I thought that I'd look at the evidence, speak to people – and you would speak to people – and that would be that. Things would add up and the killer would be found. It ought to have been easy and logical. I had not realised that people would lie. That they would lie *to me!* And, worse, that because people would be lying about unrelated things, it would become this tangled mess. And even worse than that: the tangled mess might reveal things that could have stayed hidden because they are nothing to do with the murder!"

"If it were straightforward to investigate a crime, everyone would do it. This is the test," she told him. "A true man can continue even when the darkness comes."

"You flatterer. But yes, I am determined to see this through, though if I press too hard, Mondial's patience will snap. I am having to be careful and … well. You know me." He dropped his voice. "Taylor is involved; he might be guilty. But Mondial's protecting him and I don't know what Mondial knows, and this makes it all so very difficult. I feel for Mondial, and his sorrow seemed genuine, but he is not all that he seems to be. Most of the staff are either loyal to him or terrified of him and the result is the same anyway. They won't talk. I've reached the limit of what I can find out from that girl Brody and I can't get any further."

"I'll see what I can do. But the main thing is that we are ruling out Sir Henry, aren't we?"

He grumbled again but said, "Yes. Very well. Though he needs to leave this place and never be seen near our daughter again."

186

"He is a good friend to her in spite of the error. And she needs friends."

"Why? She has a husband now."

Adelia bit her tongue. He would never understand. He was a self-contained sort of man who found all his emotional needs could be met in his wife.

Theodore continued on his perambulations, sinking back into thought. Adelia was finding the hay bale uncomfortable. Her layers of skirts prevented the stalks from irritating her except around her ankles, even though she was taking care to keep her feet clear of the hay. Her nose was tickling and her eyes beginning to itch. The countryside was much better being appreciated from a distance, she realised. She was about to complain when Theodore spun around on his heel at the far end of the barn and began to stride back to her.

He said, as he came, "We must speak to every member of staff again and you must work your magic with them. We must find where this Taylor has gone, find out his history, find out his secrets. Is he a gambler, a womaniser, a cheat, a fraud? Then we will have a motive! Yes." The energy that rippled through him as a result of making some clear plans led him to jump up onto a hay bale dramatically and Adelia tittered.

She was obliged to counsel caution in spite of the amusement of his sudden display of boyishness. "Theodore, remember your bad hip…"

"It's not a bad hip, it's the state of our mattresses…" he began to say as he jumped down. But he misjudged how far he had to go to clear the edge of the bale, tried to correct himself, and grabbed onto a nearby pile of bales that were stacked four high.

They fell.

He yelled and she screamed.

Bad hip or not, Theodore managed to twist away and the heavy bales fell to one side of him. Adelia was on her feet but frozen to the spot in case the falling bales sparked some kind of chain reaction.

They settled in a haphazard array on the floor and nothing else happened. She laughed in sudden relief.

But Theodore was not laughing. She thought he might have been injured or, worse, it had given him a shock to his heart. Then she realised he was not doubled over in pain but actually bending over one of the fallen bales and looking at something that lay on the floor beyond. She went over to his side and looked. A bundle of cloth had been dislodged. All manner of horrible things went through her head then and she didn't want him to reach over and unwrap whatever was being hidden. She straightened up and turned away while he stepped around the bale to examine the bundle more closely.

"Adelia," he said in a grunt. "We have found the murder weapons. This was no passing robber. I knew it all along! I knew it! Ha! Who would have hidden them here but Tobias Taylor?"

Her curiosity propelled her to look at what Theodore had found. Two short wooden pistols lay wrapped in brown sackcloth. Theodore picked one of them up and examined the butt of it.

"Brass," he said, a note of puzzlement coming into his voice.

"Is that unusual?"

188

"Generally, yes. These pistols were made for use at sea."

"But they work on land, too, don't they?"

He looked at her as if she'd said something ridiculous. "Of course. They work anywhere. They use brass to stop the salt corroding the metal, that's all. I doubt Tobias Taylor ever saw the sea. Oh, perhaps he is cleverer than we have given him credit for…"

"Taylor?"

"No, Sir Henry Locksley."

"What?"

"Yes. Sir Henry was a naval man, you know. And a clever one, too. What would a guilty man do to hide his guilt? Overlay the large secret with a small one, of course. When the detective discovers the smaller secret he is fooled into thinking he has discovered all that can be known about the man. We may be dupes, Adelia. Sir Henry is not out of suspicion yet."

"Surely…"

"No. Do not let your finer feelings cloud the ultimate aim of objective rationality." He bundled up the pistols and began to leave the barn.

She followed, feeling a dark sense of foreboding about the weapons in her husband's arms.

19

Theodore had to remind himself not to let the excitement that was bubbling through his veins influence him. It was all very well for him to reprimand Adelia, he thought, but he himself could easily fall victim himself to the allure of emotional responses. Sir Henry could yet be guilty. He had *shown* himself to be emotionally involved with Dido. What better motive, then, for him to shoot Mondial? Get the husband out of the way and swoop in to take the wife.

In fact, that was a far clearer motive than anything they had come up with for Tobias Taylor. Taylor looked suspicious because of his movements but there was no earthly reason for him to wound his master. Mondial was a strict man but he was not cruel and he was far better a master than many a titled man often was. A little bit of discipline, they said, was good for the staff anyway. They needed to know where the boundaries were. It gave them a sense of reassurance. Theodore often thought that Adelia's more hands-on approach of learning names and trying to be considerate to a servant's private life was ill-advised. Some of them scented weakness and would only take advantage of

Adelia's kindness.

Perhaps that was Taylor's story. Perhaps he had taken liberties, bit by bit, until he had grown arrogant in his place, and knew too much of Mondial's life, and blackmailed the Marquis. Mondial then would...

Here was the stumbling block. Mondial would have simply shot the man himself or taken him to the magistrates or any number of other things to be rid of the troublesome valet. Theodore could not imagine Mondial submitting to blackmail. Perhaps he didn't. Perhaps he refused Taylor. *Then* Taylor tried to shoot him.

And that was a second stumbling block. Mondial would have known that the assailant was Taylor. So why keep him on in his position as valet?

Aha! Theodore picked up his pace and took the stairs at an unseemly speed, leaving Adelia far behind. He vaguely heard her greet someone. *Maybe* Taylor was not "away on urgent business" at all. Had Mondial taken matters into his own hands at last? Had he killed the valet and had the body disposed of? It would tie it all up very neatly.

And there Lord Mondial was as if Theodore had conjured him up by merely thinking about the man.

He was standing at the top of the stairs alongside Theodore's mother. She greeted him cheerfully but Mondial's face was dark. Theodore found that he was a little out of breath as he reached the top and his mother tutted at his lack of physical condition before bidding them both farewell and moving off along the landing. Adelia had disappeared. Theodore was left alone with the Marquis, and the man was not happy.

"What's that you've got there?" Mondial demanded as soon as the ancient lady was well out of earshot.

Theodore did not have time to come up with any kind of excuse or subterfuge and anyway, he thought that such tactics would only go wrong in the long run. There were too many lies floating around in this household. So he pulled back the cloth to reveal the pistols and while he did so, he kept his attention firmly on Mondial's reaction.

Mondial did not react. And that, thought Theodore, was a reaction in itself. In fact Mondial went stiff and silent and still.

"I found these in the hay barn," Theodore offered, still watching Mondial. "They had been hidden."

"What on earth were you doing in the barn?" Mondial spat out.

More interesting still, thought Theodore. *That* is his first question? "I was talking with my wife."

"In the barn?"

"In the barn. I enjoy the company of horses."

Everyone knew that and Mondial could not argue further. So he reached out with his uninjured arm to the pistols and said, "I shall dispose of these. One cannot have weapons lying about the place, especially with the garden party fast approaching."

"Do you recognise them?"

Mondial exploded in anger. "Do I recognise them? No! Do I hell! Why would I recognise them? I am not in the habit of keeping such things scattered about. You've seen my gun room. You know it's locked and secure. Who'd keep things like this in a barn? No. These were dropped there by the robber as he fled. This, Calaway, merely corroborates the very strong suggestion

193

that the attacker was a passing highwayman or footpad. It is more evidence which simply supports the theory. Are you not yet convinced? I dine tonight in town with Judge Anderson and I shall be sure to inform him of this development. And I have absolutely no doubt that he will agree with me."

The implication was that Theodore was now on his own with his ideas and without the backing of the local judiciary, he was bound to get no further in his amateur investigation. They both knew that.

Theodore had no choice but to hand the pistols over. He meekly apologised for any offence he might have caused in his eagerness to find someone to blame for Miss Lamb's death.

He walked sullenly on to his suite.

Mondial was a difficult, stubborn, pig-headed man, convinced of his own rightness and secure in his own authority.

Theodore was starting to doubt everything. The idea of giving up was galling to him, but he had to consider his own reputation and his family's good name. If he pushed things too far – especially against the local great and good – he was going to see himself side-lined from society. As to that, he didn't care too much.

But it would also ostracise Adelia from polite company and she wouldn't bear that. Nor would he. Adelia's wellbeing was even more important to him than his own.

To Theodore's frustration, he was unable to find Adelia.

He found their suite empty and remembered he had heard her speak to someone when they had entered the castle after leaving the barn. He explored all the public rooms and knocked on the door of Dido's usual day room but found everywhere, including the parlour and drawing room, to be empty. His mother was sitting in a patch of sunlight on the patio, just outside the open doors of the garden room, with solicitous servants hovering in the background. Everyone adored Lady Calaway, even the staff. She treated everyone generously if somewhat peremptorily. It was generally understood that her bark was far worse than her bite.

So she was being waited on with careful attention and Theodore took the chance to speak to a few of the servants who lingered around. None of them, he found, were willing to tell him anything about Mondial or Tobias Taylor.

He flopped down into a chair alongside his mother, who sipped at a cool mint drink. She dismissed all the remaining servants with a wave of her hand.

"I was listening, of course," she told him. "Just now as you spoke to the staff."

"I expect that you were."

"Your bedside manner has not improved."

"I wasn't using my bedside manner."

"That's probably for the best. Everyone seems to die once they've listened to you minister your medicine to them."

"Mother! That is harsh. They do not. My medical knowledge is unparalleled."

"Yes and much of it ought to be kept to yourself. You might well have a thoroughly enviable understanding of the intimate

195

workings of a person's internal organs, but much like those internal organs, no one wants to see them laid out in front of them on the dining table."

"I believe that honesty is important and, in fact, the more that a person knows about their own health and body, the more they can take control and ensure that they remain healthy. You should read what Doctor Beddoes says about the matter."

She shook her head and laughed at him. "No. A person who is ill wants to be told that they are going to get better."

"I would hate a physician to lie to me."

"But I would hate to hear the truth so you had better not come anywhere near me with your black bag of needles and potions. Now, on to this Tobias Taylor, a man of whom you have singularly failed to learn a single useful thing – am I right?"

Mulishly he had to agree.

"He is a good-looking man, don't you think?"

"I have absolutely no opinion on the matter. I actually thought that he looked like a heron."

That observation made his mother laugh. "He has a look in his eyes that makes a woman feel quite girlish. There is a dark smouldering. A hint of danger. A suggestion he might sweep one off one's feet. One can overlook his knobbly shoulders if one feels smouldered at."

"Mother, must you be so … earthy? I don't know how to listen to you saying such things."

"I thought you prized honesty? Anyway. Let me tell you that the female staff in this household, when they are young and new, fall easily prey to this man. This has made him arrogant and over-confident."

"Ah, I see. And his status gives him the pick of them. But how does this help us? Unless – no, surely not! Are you suggesting that he made advances to Miss Lamb? Surely he would not shoot so high above his station. A parlour-maid is one thing, though it risks dismissal for them both, but Miss Lamb is quite another. That is utterly unthinkable and the penalties would be far higher."

"You are right," his mother agreed. "It is unthinkable and I do not suggest that it happened. He would have been a fool to try and I doubt that he did. However, have you not also noticed that the man is less intelligent than a potted plant?"

"I admit he is not blessed…"

"Not blessed? He has been completely cursed with the intellectual abilities of a politician but without any insight into his condition."

"Your brother is a politician. Uncle Charles would be mortified to hear you say such a thing."

"Charles is fully aware of the shortcomings that prevented him from entering the church or taking up a profession such as the law. Parliament is his last refuge from the real world. As for this Taylor chap, consider that Mondial Castle is *his* refuge."

"From?"

"From earning his living in the real world. Here, he is a king. He would do anything to remain here, I would wager."

Theodore sighed. "This is all very well, but does any of it connect him to the murder and the wounding of his master?"

"Well, that's for you to find out, isn't it?"

"Has there been any hint that he has taken things too far with the female staff?"

"As far as I understand it, they have mostly fought back and the housekeeper is something of a Valkyrie in that regard. She watches over her charges and she knows of his menaces. Taylor may try his hand – but Taylor generally won't succeed."

"That is of some comfort. Does Mondial know of his valet's indulgences?"

"I am sure he is fully aware of everything that happens in this house." Lady Calaway glanced around. "It would not surprise me to now see him rise from the middle of that aspidistra and declare he has heard everything we have said."

Theodore could not stop himself. He took his leave from his mother and on his way back into the house, he examined the potted plant very closely. Just in case.

"It's a bit off of Lord Mondial to leave us all without a host tonight," Adelia remarked to Theodore as they headed down the main stairs. "Not really done, you know."

"I rather think he has business with the magistrate or judge or someone of that ilk," Theodore told her. "May I say how stunning you look tonight?"

"Hush! You may not. Our daughter is in mourning even if the house is not."

He smiled at her. "Diamonds and pearls look better on you than any grey sapphire."

She winced as he spoke and he wondered if he had said the wrong thing. But she didn't reprimand him so it couldn't have been anything important. He offered her his arm and she took it willingly. She glanced down at his feet as they descended.

"Did you hurt yourself when you fell off the bale of hay?"

"No. Only my pride has been wounded."

"Oh look – there is Lord Mondial now."

They were halfway down the stairs, going slowly on account of Adelia's dresses. Her train was fashionably long and the front of her dress snug and narrow. Mondial was in full evening wear and they saw him crossing the hallway. His injured arm was no longer in a sling but Theodore knew it would be tightly bound and Mondial was keeping it relatively still while the muscles healed. The Marquis glanced up and paused when he saw them.

"I am so sorry to be leaving you in this manner but I have no doubt that my dear wife will preside over a small and intimate meal with utmost aplomb," he said. "If she can tear herself out of the nursery, that is."

Theodore wondered if the children were ill again. He was aware that Mondial's statement made Adelia hiss under her breath but he wasn't sure if it was because Mondial was going to be absent this evening, or for some other reason to do with the children. Theodore said, "I am sure we will have a very pleasant time and I wish the same for you."

"I hear the judge's cook is an absolute miracle worker with a syllabub," Adelia said, astonishing Theodore all over again. From where would his wife hear such things? He shook his head in wonder and pride.

"I am looking forward to it. And now if I could possibly beg your forgiveness, I must hurry…" Mondial gave a short bow to Adelia and nodded to Theodore. He pulled out his pocket watch and glanced at it pointedly before he turned to go. Theodore resumed his descent of the stairs.

Adelia nudged him.

The housekeeper and butler were both busy with preparations for the dinner so the main doors were swung open by a footman in livery for Mondial to pass through. It was not yet dark outside. Adelia and Theodore reached the ground floor and were able, therefore, to hear Mondial shout out in surprise. Theodore let go of Adelia's arm and hurried forward to see what the matter was.

"Taylor!" Mondial was saying in fury. "What in blazes are you doing, man?"

Theodore reached the front steps. Tobias Taylor was crossing the wide lawn and coming from the direction of the main gravel driveway. He appeared to be heading to the side of the house, not the front steps, which made sense. The servants wouldn't ever enter by the main doors.

"My lord!" Taylor said, stopping in surprise and looking up. "I had understood you were to dine out tonight…"

"I am on my way, but that's no business of yours. You were supposed to be – away."

That was a curious phrase. Mondial suddenly seemed to realise that Theodore was at his side. He said to Theodore, through tight lips, "Do excuse me as I attend to this *private* matter. I beg you, go back inside." He strode down the steps and headed for Taylor, clearly intending to prevent him getting any closer. Theodore remained where he was and strained his ears.

Mondial had his back to Theodore. But that meant Taylor was facing the house and his words carried on the breeze. "It didn't last like I thought it would. I'm sorry. I knew I shouldn't have come back but I was going to stay downstairs though."

Mondial said something and Taylor was shaking his head, his hands upraised in denial. "No, sir, not gambling *as such* but I wasn't as lucky as I usually am."

Mondial grabbed Taylor's upper arm and steered him off around the house. Their remaining conversation was lost to Theodore.

Adelia joined Theodore. His head was spinning with what he thought he'd seen and what it might mean. The footman was hovering close by, waiting to close the door, so Theodore drew back inside and took Adelia with him to a small anteroom where guests usually divested their outerwear and umbrellas. He stood close to her, unwilling to be overheard.

She was smiling. "You've discovered things, haven't you? You've made connections."

"I believe that I have." He couldn't contain his confusion and upset. She caught the tone in his voice and her smile faded.

"What's wrong?"

"I don't know what to make of it. Of any of it. Mondial said he was robbed, didn't he?"

"Yes. They took his – oh, yes!"

"They took his antique heirloom pocket watch. It was a large thing, unmistakable. Exactly like…"

"Exactly like the one we've just seen. I thought so. That's why I nudged you."

He nodded and chewed on his lip reflexively. And then there was the matter of the return of Taylor, Mondial's reaction to it, and Taylor's words.

They had to go in to dinner and Theodore was aware that his silence throughout the whole meal caused sideways looks and comments but he made no excuse or apology for it.

He was feeling as if he had been duped – and not by Tobias Taylor.

20

Adelia found that no amount of pointed comments, angry looks or even subtle kicks to the ankle could draw Theodore out of his unsocial mood during dinner. She was glad, therefore, that no other guests of note had arrived yet. At least his mother and his daughter were aware of Theodore's habits and would not judge him too harshly. Quite what Sir Henry made of it, though, was another matter.

She had spent much of the afternoon with Dido, helping her with the mountain of work that was piling up now that the garden party was less than one week away. The guest list was checked and double-checked. Replies were ticked off and filed. The accommodation plan had been worked and reworked, with everyone housed according to their status. The housekeeper had engaged extra help from the town so that the rooms could be properly and promptly serviced.

In truth, it was misleading to call it a garden party as if it were a mere few hours of drinks and chat in a vicar's village garden. Many people would arrive the day before, which was just a few days' time, so there was a large dinner to plan for that night.

Then there was the catering for the breakfast and luncheon, which would lead into the garden party proper. Entertainment had to be laid on. Music, dancing, and the right sort of cultured people were needed to lead the pleasurable activities. The ballroom was to be decorated. The party would last into the evening. More food had to be planned.

Then there were the drinks to organise; champagne had to flow as if it were endless, and there would be a wide choice of alcohol cups of summer fruits and liqueurs. Lord Mondial was insisting on plenty of "Judy" which was something of an acquired taste but reckoned to be very sophisticated, being a mix of champagne, lemons, sugar, green tea, brandy, rum and mint. There were sherry cobblers and mint juleps for the less adventurous plus all the very best that his wine and beer cellars could offer.

Also needing overseeing was the planning of the evening entertainment; cards, dancing, more music. It would last late into the night and there was an obligation to serve a special hot meal called the grand ball supper for the dancers between one and three in the morning, with crystallised fruits and the messy, complex business of spun sugar to decorate everything.

Many people were only attending for the afternoon festivities but those who were invited to stay for longer were the very best of the best. Even at a party, one had a hierarchy and there had been complex decisions to make about who earned a place in a bedroom and at the dinner table, and who was expected to leave before the exclusive late night celebrations.

Dido had drawn the line at fireworks.

"Utterly uncouth, totally unnecessary; unthinkable, given

the circumstances," she had said flatly.

But even without fireworks, there was endless work to do. Dido was holding up well under the pressure and her staff were very capable, which made all the difference. The household was used to holding extravagant events and this one had been planned, in one form or another, for some time. The devil, as usual, was in the details and it was to those details that Dido paid the greatest attention.

Adelia had simmered with rage when Lord Mondial had alluded to Dido apparently "wasting time in the nursery" during their conversation earlier. On top of her extraordinary household management skills, Adelia considered Dido to be a devoted mother and not a second of her time with her boys was any kind of a waste. If Lord Mondial ever lowered himself to step into the nursery, he'd know that. Unfortunately he seemed to be waiting until the boys were old enough to go hunting and to clubs with him. By then, Adelia thought, it would be too late to start a relationship with them.

More fool him; it would be his loss and regret and neither Adelia nor Dido could do anything about it.

Without the presence of Lord Mondial at dinner that night, conversation between everyone except Theodore flowed more freely than it had done for some time, although it was noticeable that no one mentioned the recent events or the absence of the Marquis. They dined at a smaller table than usual and Dido sat alongside her grandmother, Lady Calaway, who delighted in presiding over proceedings. Miss Lamb's chaperone had gone now, slipping away at first light with the man from Miss Lamb's grandfather's house. The house did not seem to notice she had left at all.

For a brief moment, Adelia let her imagination explore the possibility that the chaperone was an over-looked suspect and had been faking her infirmities all along. It didn't work out. She could barely lift a spoon to her mouth if it were overfilled with soup. Handling a pair of pistols would have been impossible for the old lady.

Sir Henry had stayed and Adelia kept in mind what Theodore had said about his naval career, and about the effect of having layers of secrets. She watched how he behaved very closely but he was utterly blameless in all things, as he always was – at least in company.

She did noticed that he avoided making eye contact with her, however. But she put that down to embarrassment.

With Harriet making up the sixth person at the table, bringing her wit to play alongside the older Lady Calaway's, it was a lively but intimate evening and one that went on for a little too long.

Both Adelia and Theodore rose very late the next day. Adelia's head was sore and she could tell from the strained look around Theodore's eyes that he, too, was suffering although he tried to deny it. He disappeared and returned about twenty minutes later with a tonic he had prepared in the kitchens, much to the disgust of the cook and her staff who felt her realm to have been invaded. He also brought up some lightly buttered toast. Smith followed, carrying a tray of coffee things and some fresh fruit. Theodore made her take the fruit away again as being too cold and sharp for a delicate stomach.

"Dido is already up and about," Theodore told Adelia as

they lounged around their suite, picking at the toast.

"She is young. We were like that, once."

"I wonder what it is about the body that makes it more in need of rest as it ages?" Theodore mused.

"If you must speculate, do so in silence, I beg you," Adelia said. She knew she could not bear to hear medical terms about body parts while she was in her weakened state.

He muttered to himself and poured more coffee. Adelia followed Smith to get dressed in the adjoining room and when she returned a quarter of an hour later, she found Theodore slumped in a wide armchair which he had dragged across the floor so that he could look out of the window. Smith tutted and began to straighten out the rug again, but he dismissed her with a grunt. She was used to him, and took the dirty tray and crockery away with a quick nod to Adelia.

"My love, perhaps you should return to bed for an hour or two," Adelia said gently. He was almost grey in the face and his eyes were fixed on the horizon. "I fear you are pushing yourself too hard. Late nights and all this brain-work cannot be doing you any good."

"It is the fact that the brain-work is going nowhere which is the problem," he said. "No, sit with me. Listen. Let me lay it out to you because I am sure, now, that I am missing something very obvious."

She settled herself carefully on the couch. He kept his head turned away from her and she let him speak slowly, feeling his way through his thoughts.

"Tobias Taylor is guilty of involvement in some way in this crime," he said. "I had my suspicions revived about Sir Henry when I found the pistols but that went nowhere. Taylor was seen by more than one person, Sir Henry included, outside the house at the time of the attack and he has lied about his whereabouts. The jacket that my mother found would fit the man exactly and he habitually wears such colours. I don't think it would fit Sir Henry, who is too broad. Taylor evokes my suspicion greatly. Yet it is the man's nature that I do not understand; what possible motive does he have, and why would Mondial cover it all up?"

He fell into silence. She let him muse for a long time. Eventually she said, "So Lord Mondial is involved in the matter too, isn't he?"

"I suppose that he must be," Theodore said awkwardly. "Yet why? And how?"

"Is it important that we know why? If you have proof, surely you can take that proof to the authorities and it is down to them to discover the reasons as to why."

"Without a motive, all the proof is worthless; it's evidence that is needed, evidence which may or may not point to guilt. A clever man could explain it all away without hard evidence. And without such absolute proof, I cannot go up against Mondial. He would simply destroy me and what, then, of our daughter, left here in this place? And our grandchildren? It would open up such a rift in the family that I am beginning to think this is all better left alone. Don't you? Would you risk Dido's relationship, health and happiness?"

"I would not."

Theodore groaned and put his head in his hands. "There is one good thing that has emerged from all of this tragedy. No, two. Firstly, the knowledge that the man who gave so much to me, though he might not know it, still lives. I must visit him, the old Doctor Hardy. It doesn't matter if he doesn't remember me. And secondly, the distance I have had from home has allowed me to see that perhaps ... perhaps you are right. Medical practice is not for me. Those complaints, those libellous cartoons, those threats of legal action. There is perhaps something in it. Logic dictates that I must contemplate, most seriously, the fact that I am a terrible doctor."

"No, Theodore, you are not terrible but..."

"Enough. You do not need to mollify me. Throw no sops to my ego, if you please. I have been in denial for a long time and merely the knowledge that I have lied to myself is a difficult realisation to come to. I am ashamed of it."

She felt her heart breaking for him. Yes, he had finally come to the knowledge that she had hoped he would – but it was still terrible to watch as his lifelong dreams crumbled around him.

He needed new dreams.

Before she could say so, he went on. "I am ashamed that I deluded myself and I am ashamed of my poor medical skills. And now it seems that I am as bad an investigator as I am a doctor."

That stung. It felt as if it were an accusation against her – after all, she had encouraged him to play the part of detective. She tried to keep the annoyance out of her voice as she said, "You cannot think that you are a bad investigator. You have been thwarted by circumstance, that is all, and I am sure that when police detectives are at work they do not succeed in solving every crime that comes their way. And anyway, think of all the things that you have discovered! You have been listing them to me just now."

209

But Theodore was sunk too far into a morose self-pitying mood. He muttered, "Me? I could not have done any of this without your input."

She hated the way he would let his misery beat him down. She hated the way it suggested weakness, weakness in the man she believed to be the most strong in the world – well, in her world. She wanted to know that she could rely on him at all times. She *needed* to know it. This indulgent questioning and crisis of confidence unsettled her and she felt it turn to anger within her. She knew she wasn't being rational but she could no longer hold her tongue.

She said, "So, my input somehow tarnishes your own achievements, does it? The fact that you could not have done it without me makes you feel less of a man? Makes you feel like you have failed as an investigator? Is that it?"

"No, Adelia, of course I didn't mean that," he said, his own anger rising.

She stood up. She was glad that he was angry. His anger was a positive force and far better than his misery. "Well, you will be glad to know I shall give you no more of my worthless input," she snapped at him, hating herself for saying it and somehow unable to stop herself. She could perhaps blame her hangover.

In spite of her queasy stomach and spinning head she stormed out of the room.

21

Adelia walked off her fury in the gardens. It didn't take long for her to calm down. Her angry words were born out of many emotions all jumbled up, but her love for her husband stayed true underneath it all and the argument would not linger between them. Their disagreements never did last and anyway she knew she had been somewhat irrational in her accusations.

The air outside was once again stifling and hot, and it reminded her too much of the day of the murder. She could not help scanning the bushes and shrubberies. Would she see Tobias Taylor, intent on some secret business with an innocent maid? Would she see Lord Mondial, hiding his part in events or perhaps hiding some other nefarious secret? Would she see her own brother, still skulking around, waiting for a chance to grab her and demand more money? She hoped that he had taken the grey sapphire to London, not just because he'd get a better price there, but because she really did not ever want to see him again.

A few fat spots of rain fell and she had to hurry back inside. She was met by Smith who always seemed to know what she needed before Adelia herself had realised it. They walked almost side by side back upstairs. Distant voices could be heard down the winding corridors of the castle. A young boy laughed. The boys had been kept out of her way, mostly, due to the events of the past week, and she regretted that. It was probably Lord Mondial's old-fashioned orders to keep the children hidden except on Sundays when they might be permitted to attend church, and the sporadically attended morning prayers. Everyone was supposed to be there for a short while before breakfast but Lord Mondial himself rarely put in an appearance.

A door thumped somewhere far upstairs. A servant appeared at an entrance, saw Adelia, and melted out of sight until she had passed. Everything had the air of a usual day with a normal busy-ness and in spite of the lack of children playing, it was nice to feel the place lived-in and alive. Dido had brought that to Mondial Castle, Adelia thought with pride.

"Smith," she said in a low voice as they ascended the stairs. "What do you make of Tobias Taylor? Please speak plainly."

"As you wish, my lady. He is an idiot, my lady. A pretty idiot."

Adelia had to stop and press her hand to her mouth, stifling her laugh. "Oh goodness."

"Really he is, my lady. He is a charmer and an innocent girl might have her head turned at first but ten minutes into conversation with the man should disabuse anyone of his character and abilities. In that, he has no character and little ability. I suppose the wrong sort of girl doesn't care about conversation." She sniffed with disdain. "He has enough fun, I imagine, to suit him, but that will be in the town and not here in the castle."

"You have spotted what I suspected. Why does Lord Mondial employ such a man? You'd think he would want his valet to be clever."

"He is clever enough merely to do what he is told," Smith said. "One does not want a servant who is clever enough to go beyond orders; it is dangerous to have one that is clever enough to question things and think for themselves."

Adelia shot Smith a sidelong glance.

Smith smiled slightly and they carried on up the stairs.

Adelia found it hard to imagine that such a man could have made a dupe of Lord Mondial.

At the top of the stairs, Adelia said, "Oh, I believe that Lady Mondial has invited one of her sisters to the garden party. The Parker-Greys will be in attendance, I hope." She had hoped for more of them to come but everyone was otherwise engaged.

"God willing Lady Mary's health permits," Smith said warmly. Everyone adored Mary, who was Adelia and Theodore's eldest daughter. She had married a wealthy and educated commoner of very high standing and respect, Mr Cecil Parker-Grey, and had carried a courtesy title with her into the marriage though of course he had remained a mere "Mr". Mary had seemed as if she were about to expire from the moment she had been born and had consequently spent her life treated as if she were made of the finest glass. Even her husband, who was considerably older than her, would have carried her on his shoulders if he thought he would be allowed to. In spite of the extreme care and attention she'd been lavished with, all her life, Mary was a humble and self-effacing girl. If she were described to someone like that, as a sweet and charming woman of little ego, there was a tendency to assume she was cloying and unlikeable. Nothing was further from the truth.

Everyone really did love her when they met her.

Someone like Mary would be exactly the right sort of company for Lord Mondial, Adelia thought with growing pleasure. She was married and therefore quite safe to converse with the Marquis. She was pure and lovely and also his sister-in-law. She would be like a calming oil poured over the troubled waters of the household.

I should have invited her as soon as the murder happened, thought Adelia.

Smith moved off and Adelia turned without looking where she was going.

"Watch your step!" crackled an older woman's voice.

Adelia nearly bumped right against the Dowager Countess, but that was only because Grace had deliberately put herself directly in Adelia's path. "Oh, my word, do forgive me, my lady!"

"It's Grace when we're in the parlour and my lady when you attempt to run me down on the stairs like a runaway carriage," Grace laughed. "You were so lost in thought I feared you would not hear me. Come along, my dear. I cannot stand here on my frail old feet and talk like I'm a woman at market. Let us sit down like civilised people and you can tell me everything."

"Oh, there is nothing more to tell…"

Grace glared at her and Adelia was beaten instantly. "Very well. The rooms along here are generally full of light at this time of day. Shall we?"

Grace was already ahead of her and flinging open doors as

214

if she owned the castle, hunting for a room with comfortable chairs and a reasonable view. "This is a little showy," she said, swooping into a long room full of dark oil portraits and over-stuffed red velvet armchairs, "but it will do."

Adelia prowled to the windows while Grace settled herself in a chair and sniffed at the needlework on the cushions. "I hear Lady Montsalle is to arrive tomorrow," she said. "That woman takes any excuse to be here."

"Yes, she was here before. She has a house locally."

"She has a house thirty miles away. That's as local as France, quite frankly. One wonders about that woman, one really does."

"Does one?" Adelia turned to face Grace. "I mean, I have not wondered. She doesn't like me so we don't often converse."

Grace pursed her lips and said, "Well, *I* wonder. But others will be arriving tomorrow too, and so perhaps I will wonder about other things. Such as – of course – what is on your mind? Come and sit down. I cannot have you hovering like a buzzard, not at my time of life. It makes me think things about mortality. Now, speak: I want to know everything about the case."

"I don't think there is a case anymore."

"Has my foolish son given up?" Grace thudded her cane on the carpet. "I can't put him over my knee and thrash him but I can possibly order a footman to do it."

"Please don't." Adelia sat down, smiling at the image, and told her mother-in-law absolutely everything. The feeling of closeness that she enjoyed with Grace was always underwritten, just slightly, by a sadness that she had not enjoyed this same closeness with her own mother, who had been so distant and rigid. She even told her about the little tiff with Theodore, because she knew that Grace would understand.

And she did. "Oh, you were rather restrained, my dear," Grace said with a laugh. "I should have thrown something at his head. There's nothing like a good temper tantrum from time to time."

"I have never had one."

"You are altogether too correct."

"I have to be. I am not of your class; I am scrutinised at every turn."

"Oh, the world is changing," Grace said airily. For all their closeness, this was one thing that the older lady simply couldn't fathom. "Just be who you are; a dear, good woman. No one who is of real quality could mind that. I don't."

Was there a veiled insult under that? Grace was smiling. Probably not. Adelia sank into deep thought, going over everything to do with the murder. If only she could believe it was the work of a passing highwayman.

After a few moments of contemplation, she said, "I still wonder if Lord Mondial is protecting his valet in some way."

Grace snickered and said drily, "You have met the Marquis, haven't you? You must have worked him out by now. If he is involved, he won't be anyone's dupe. He's no performing monkey. He'll be the ringmaster himself."

There was a rushing sound, like waves breaking on a shore, in Adelia's head. Her palms were clammy. "He … he set it all up himself?"

Grace shrugged slightly, as much as her tight clothing would allow such a movement. "I am not suggesting that he did. But *if* he is involved – as you suspect he might be – then he will be at the very heart of the matter. Lord Mondial will never be on the periphery of anything."

Adelia stood up quickly. She paced to the windows and when she turned around, the Dowager Countess had left. She must have slipped out silently to leave Adelia to think.

And think she did.

We have been hunting for Tobias Taylor's motive, she thought, and coming up short. He does not have a *hidden* motive. He has *no* motive.

But what of John Haveringham, the Marquis of Mondial? What of his motive? He could not shoot himself – but he could arrange a shooting.

Why was Philippa the target, though?

And then Adelia smacked her forehead and gasped as her blood ran cold. Lord Mondial didn't intend to be out in the gardens with Philippa Lamb.

He was supposed to be there with *Dido*.

Adelia wanted to be sick. She gathered all her wits and she ran to find her husband.

22

Adelia rushed back into their suite. She didn't bother with an apology to Theodore about her earlier behaviour. It was hardly the most important thing at the moment. She sat on the bed, stood up, sat at the window, stood up, paced around, sat down, stood up again and all the while she blurted out what she had put together.

Theodore remained seated throughout and listened intently, also willing to put the matter of the small argument to one side for the moment. He bid her explain her reasoning to him three times. Each time she did so, she slowed down a little and together they pieced together a possible chain of events. He pulled out the drawings that they had made right at the start, and followed the paths of the principle acts as they talked it over.

"Taylor the valet," Theodore mused, tapping his pencil repetitively on the table as he went over the possible events. "He is asked to attack … our daughter." He coughed and cleared his throat. "Mondial arranges to walk with her in the gardens, here. But she is called back to the house. Miss Lamb is already down there. Is that a co-incidence? We may never know."

"I believe Lord Mondial was lusting after her," Adelia said, no longer willing to see anything good in the Marquis. "And she knew of his unseemly attentions and she wanted to avoid him."

"Well, they met anyway and probably accidentally, and Taylor did not know it was the wrong woman. He fired as arranged and fled from the scene. He changed his clothes and hid the pistols and came back into the house. Later he burned the clothes, but unsuccessfully. And then Mondial tried to send him away. But he came back. I gather that he ran out of money. Is he a gambler, do we know?"

"I don't know but I can find out," she said.

"It's not the most important thing. From his words, I suspect that he is – he said he was not as lucky as he usually is. So, this is all plausible," Theodore said, now pressing so hard with the pencil that the lead point snapped. "But is it true?"

"I do not want to believe so. Yet it fits as no other explanation did."

"Explanations are one thing – a clever man can explain the moon is made of cheese and we can believe it if the lie is good enough. What don't lie are facts."

"Which you have unearthed," Adelia said. "The clothing, the pistols, the movements of Taylor. There are witnesses, too. Sir Henry Locksley, for example."

"Motive," Theodore spat out suddenly, and his face was twisted with anguish. "Miss Lamb or our Dido – why would either woman be a target?"

Adelia was still pacing around. She got to the window and looked out across the lawns. It was a bright day but the grass was untouched. No one played on the perfect lawn. No children

220

hunted for beetles in the flower borders. The castle was filling up with guests all carefully chosen to be the best of the best, the elite of British society. There were barely a dozen marquises in all of England and Lord Mondial liked you to know it.

"Do you think he is truly a devoted husband?" Adelia said. She was talking to herself as much as she was addressing Theodore. "I'm not talking about love. He doesn't need to love her."

"He should!" Theodore said.

"You old romantic. You know that's not how it works. We were happy to have him as the husband for our daughter because he was rich and his reputation was spotless. And she was happy to have him as she found him kind and attentive. He's also good-looking and they shared the same aims." Adelia stopped.

"What? I agree with all of that."

"No. Their aims. I think they have always had different dreams and different ideas of what this marriage was supposed to be!" Adelia said in a rising panic. "I can see it now – I think."

"It was a mutually beneficial transaction between them, if you wish me to be logical," Theodore said. "But I do believe he loves her, and she loves him. That is a great bonus."

"They might have done so, once. I need to confirm my thoughts with Dido herself, but she will never confess this to me directly." She turned and smoothed down her clothing. "I'm going to speak to your mother again first."

"Wait. Wait one moment – tell me honestly, my dear heart, do you believe, really believe, that Mondial could have engineered some harm to befall our daughter, for whatever reason?"

"Yes. I am sorry to say that I do but I need to find more

221

proof."

He was on his feet by then. "I don't need proof anymore. I believe in your intelligence and if you say this to be true, then I shall call the cad out and be done with it."

"No! You must have patience. Remember that you are the rational one, my love. Do not be swayed by my feminine excesses. Bide your time. You told me about the importance of evidence; now take your own advice. Please." Adelia was afraid that one more push would have sent Theodore striding down the corridors, threatening a duel with the Marquis.

"What proof can you possibly get into the inner workings of a man's dark heart?" Theodore demanded.

Adelia could not resist a grim smile. "You would be amazed what a woman can do."

She found the Dowager Countess deep in conversation with a gaggle of recent arrivals, all ladies, gathered in the garden room. Dido was there too, playing the part of graceful hostess with calm magnanimity as if nothing had been happening in her life but an endless whirl of tea parties and fancy cakes. Adelia greeted everyone with the due respect they were owed, which took far too long, but she kept making meaningful eye contact with the Countess until the older lady sighed and declared she needed to stretch her legs.

"Otherwise," she told everyone, "I shall simply set like stone in one position and have to be carried from chair to bed and back again for the rest of my days. My dear daughter-in-law, would you do me the honour of accompanying me on a turn around the garden? No, no, dear Dido, you stay with your guests. Don't allow a doddery old fool like me to ruin your day."

As soon as they were out of earshot and progressing down a neat pathway, Grace said, "Well, I must say, no one has mentioned the murder yet but they're all simply dying to. My money is on Lady Montsalle to be the first to open her mouth. She is utterly crass."

"If you hear any gossip or rumour, however idle or spurious, will you come directly to me?" Adelia begged. "We believe we might be close to a breakthrough but…"

"Of course. What is the nature of this breakthrough?"

Adelia hesitated. "You bid me look more closely into the nature of Lord Mondial," she said at last. "I am fearful that his relationship with Dido might not be …"

They walked on in silence. Adelia struggled with finding the right words to express herself. She could barely frame her fear that Lord Mondial might be plotting his own wife's death and anyway, really, why would he? Except that…

Grace put voice to those fears. She said, "Dido is the most dear, sweet thing but she's not at all what he was expecting in a wife, is she?"

"What do you think he was expecting?"

Grace snorted. "What do all men of his class expect? A pretty woman who will stay looking as if she is twenty-one her entire life. A witty woman who will sparkle, night after night, at soirees and dinner parties and social engagements, without tiring or flagging or growing bored. A woman that others envy. A woman that others lust after. A woman that everyone admires, everyone looks at, everyone wants to be seen with. Her glamour and beauty and skills as a hostess reflect all the more on him and his status. He wants a bride, a perpetual bride. He did not expect her to become a good, sensible, mature wife and mother."

"You have expressed well what I have been struggling to come to terms with," Adelia said as a profound sadness washed over her. "I am not sure if he has been unfaithful but I suspect that he wants to and little would stop him once he found a willing partner."

"Miss Lamb?"

"She was decidedly unwilling. She was packing to leave at one point and now I suspect he had made advances to her which she repelled."

"And so he arranged for her murder?" Even Grace sounded shocked at that idea.

"No, worse. He arranged for ... oh, this is beyond horrible. When the attack took place, he was supposed to be walking in the garden with Dido!"

Grace did not speak for a long minute. They stopped walking and stood side by side, staring across the lawns at the rolling hills and carefully planted copses of trees that dotted the idyllic landscape. High hills rose up behind, making the perfect backdrop. "There are other ways to be rid of a wife," she said at last.

"Yes. The asylum is the most common choice for a man of means."

"Yet I feel certain that he loves her, or at least holds her in high regard," Grace said. Then she gave a bitter laugh. "Do you

224

know, I rather fancy that's why he would rather have seen his wife dead than committed. In death her reputation is spotless and unsullied and no blame can attach to the husband. A mad wife, though, is a source of pity and shame and public speculation. Oh, my poor dear Adelia – my poor dear Dido. If this is true, it is a tangled mess. Do you think she knows how he thinks or feels?"

"No," said Adelia. "I doubt she even suspects the specifics but she must have some idea of her husband's mental state in general. I cannot ask her. I am her mother and she will never tell me everything, especially if she thinks it will upset me. But you…"

"Consider it done. I shall go and speak to her this instant." Grace offered her arm to Adelia and they walked back up to the gathering together. The patio doors were open and the conversation spilled out onto the upper lawns and terraces. There was light laughter and gentle teasing. No one was saying anything of importance. And Adelia had to fight the urge to run through the garden room, picking up cups of tea and hurling them against the walls, kicking over the tables and shouting – "Shut up! All of you, all of you, can't you see you're all fake?"

Of course she was as fake, outwardly and in public, as anyone else. She plastered on a smile and entered the throng, and wondered how many other people there harboured secret desires deep in their hearts to kick over a table or two.

Grace went off to speak to her granddaughter Dido, and

225

Adelia found that now she herself was the object of meaningful eye contact. Harriet Hobson was on the edge of the growing crowd and wiggling her eyebrows frantically. They slipped away before anyone else could waylay either of them.

"Tell me some good news," Adelia said. "For I am going to burst with worry."

"I am so glad that I can! I've been sleuthing for you and you can thank me in many ways, but let them be alcohol-based ways. Your darling brother has left this area and is bound for London."

"Oh, thank goodness!"

"And are we absolutely sure that he's nothing to do with the murder? I should hate to have aided a murderer to escape, thrilling though that sounds as an abstraction."

"Absolutely. He's an annoying distraction, nothing more."

"He's a distraction that keeps turning up. He will try to bleed you dry for as long as he knows you have money. You can't hide it from your husband for ever, you know."

"I rather think that I can. I'm going to try. Surely when Wilson's old enough to earn his own living, Alfred will have no more excuses to come and beg for money."

"You don't believe that. I don't," said Harriet. "He'll dog you till you die unless you wash your hands of him completely."

"And that I cannot do. You know that and you can hardly be encouraging me to be so unchristian, surely?"

"Oh no, of course not. I mean me, in your position, I'd be an absolute saint, of course. But we're different people and I make concessions to people like you."

"Harriet!" Adelia gasped, not sure if she was even joking.

226

Her friend burst out laughing. "Why are you so serious? You wouldn't usually take that sort of thing to heart." Then her face fell. "Forgive me. The matter of the murder is still a heavy burden on you. Tell me everything."

"There is much to tell and it's not good."

"I am here for you. Go on."

Adelia spilled out her heart once more, and wondered at what point would a worry shared become a worry halved because so far, she wasn't feeling any better at all.

23

Once Adelia had left their rooms after unveiling her suspicions and speculations, Theodore had remained in silence and solitude for a few hours. He poked his head out of the room from time to time, aware of increasing numbers of people arriving for the garden party. It was happening the very next day. Once again he felt a surge of anger as he thought about Mondial's pressing need to have everything carry on as normal.

Nothing here was normal!

He had no desire to join the growing crowds of people milling about the castle. He was aware that another of his daughters, the sweet Mary, was hoping to arrive and he had left instructions that he was to be informed the minute she crossed the threshold. However, the nature of her delicate constitution made last-minute changes to her plans often unavoidable and so far he had received no word.

So there was little reason to join the others yet. He was also afraid that if he encountered Mondial, he would speak his mind and show his cards too soon. But Adelia had been wise to counsel caution. His best chance for justice and to ensure the safety of his daughter lay in using his intellect to gather compelling evidence to lay before the Judge.

But he could not contain himself all day. By late afternoon, he was almost exhausted from simmering away in private. Eventually he ventured out and rather than descend to the lower floor and its public rooms, he went upstairs in search of familiar comfort.

He found himself, by accident or by unconscious design, on the upper floor in a far wing of the castle. Who lives in a castle these days, he thought to himself as he went along the bare corridors. Even all the modern improvements in the world can't make a chilly passageway like this into an inviting space. Yet this area was not unlived-in. In fact he could hear high voices up ahead, asking impatient questions, and then he recognised the answering speech of his own daughter, Dido. He hurried to the room and peeked through the half-open door.

He was looking into a schoolroom, although the boys were not engaged in any educational activity. No one seemed to notice him as he peered in. Dido was sitting on the edge of a plain wooden chair, leaning forward. She had a book in her lap but she wasn't looking at it. Instead, she was gazing at a spot on the floorboards, apparently lost in thought, mechanically answering the boys if they blurted out a random question. The two boys were romping around with wooden swords in their hands. Both were dressed as sailors.

Theodore coughed and everyone stopped. The boys came to attention in a reflex action until they saw who it was, and then they dropped their swords to come thundering towards him in a great rush. Dido called out to stop them but they paid her no heed. He dropped to his knees and opened his arms to them.

"Grandfather! Do you want to play pirates with us?"

"Of course he doesn't," Dido snapped. He was concerned when she raised her head and he saw her face. She looked tired and pale. It didn't take a doctor to see that she had been crying.

He said to the boys, "I should love to play at pirates with you. Why, in my youth, I was a veritable scourge on the high seas!"

Their mouths dropped open in a most pleasing display of astonishment which was utterly punctured by Dido saying, "No, he was not and I don't think it's a very agreeable thing to be playing, anyway. Run along to your room and find your nurse. It is surely nearly time for your supper."

He wanted to let them stay. He winked at them both as they reluctantly left, trying to hint that he had really been a pirate, no matter what their mother said.

He said, "They didn't need to go so quickly. I've missed them. I thought we'd see them around a lot more."

Dido shook her head. "Oh, you know how it is. We're so busy here that it's better for them to be out of the way. My John prefers to take the more established approach to child-rearing."

"Out of sight, out of mind?"

"He's very traditional. You'd see them if you came to church or morning prayers."

"You know how I struggle with all that."

"Well, I find it to be of great comfort."

"And it seems that you are in need of comfort at the moment," he said. He perched himself somewhat uncomfortably on the edge of a sloping desk.

"Yes. I know why John wanted all these people here but part of me simply wants to run away and … and mourn poor Philippa, quietly and in my own way."

"That's a very understandable sentiment."

Dido looked sideways at her father. "Is everything all right?" she asked.

"Yes. No. I mean, well, that's why I'm here. To ask you that question, you see?"

She merely blinked at him. He knew it was unusual for him to speak to her like this and he felt very uncomfortable. But then he reminded himself of his purpose.

"Dido, my dear, if your husband does anything to cause you a moment of unease, I need you to know that I shall always believe you and take your side, no matter what the world might say."

"What is the world saying?" she asked in horror.

"Nothing. I only mean, if they … I mean, if you … if *he* …"

He stumbled to a halt as she bent her head. He hoped that he had not made her cry. He wasn't sure what he ought to do or say if he had.

She said, "Grandmamma came to speak to me a little while ago. That's why I'm up here. I just needed some peace. She was asking me about John, too." She suddenly looked up at her father. "He has never been unfaithful to me. And I don't believe that he ever would be. But I know that I'm not enough for him and I've tried to be but I can't. My boys are my life; it's like a physical pain when I'm not with them and he can't understand that. No one does!"

He thought very deeply before he answered. What would Adelia say, he wondered. With great care, he said, "When I hear the pain in your voice, it is like a knife in my own heart. When I imagine harm coming to a single hair of your head, I am ready to take up arms on your behalf. No, these are not fashionable things to say. No, you will not hear them expressed in sophisticated drawing rooms. But it is what I feel and I know I am not alone. You are not alone. In truth, Dido, I think it is Mondial who is the abnormal one. I have been present in the moments of grief afflicting rich and poor, old and young, as a doctor; all people feel as you do. The difference is only that you are brave enough to say it."

She cried like her heart was breaking and he had to wipe away a secret tear of his own before she saw it. "Father," she whispered at last, "I think he wishes to be rid of me. I have failed as a wife!"

He grabbed her and held her as if he was a mother with a new-born. She leaned into him as he stroked her shoulder. He had exhausted all his calm and soothing phrases.

Now all he wanted to do was to rain vengeance down on Lord Mondial's head.

Theodore did not believe that his daughter was in any danger while the house was full of people, and he also did not think that Mondial would attempt a similar attack so soon after the first. That Mondial wanted to replace Dido with a more "suitable", fresher, younger wife was now clear to Theodore, but he also would not risk underestimating Mondial's intelligence. The Marquis was unlikely to act rashly now that he was under scrutiny. He'd lay low for some time. No wonder he was so insistent the attack had been the work of a passing robber! No wonder he had not wanted an investigation! And when he had realised that to leave it uninvestigated was more suspicious than not, of course he'd allow Theodore to do it – an untested, untried, unprofessional man of advancing years, close enough that Mondial could watch his every move. His every failure.

It all made a perfect sense.

Theodore assured Dido of her safety and that he would "make everything all right" although he could see that she doubted him. He refused to tell her what he truly suspected had happened though he wondered if she herself already knew. He walked with her to her rooms where her closest maid took her from his hands. He then found himself standing in the corridor, feeling a little lost.

It was nearly time to dress for dinner. It would be a large and formal affair with so many guests. There would be card games and drinking late into the night. Anyone with any sense had spent the afternoon resting. With a sigh, for he was absolutely not in the mood for socialising, he headed for his own suite of rooms to get changed.

On the way, he bumped into Sir Henry Locksley. Theodore stopped and stared so intently at him, taking his time in working out what to say, that Sir Henry grew uncomfortable. "I say, Calaway, are you feeling all right?"

"No. Something's rotten in this house. Do you know what

it is?"

"Er, is that a rhetorical question? Only I was awfully bad at that sort of thing at school. Riddles and so on. More of an outdoor man, you know —"

"Yes, yes. So you've mentioned. No. I do not waste time with meaningless questions. Do you know what's wrong in this household?"

"It's your daughter's household. I am sure that she manages everything exceedingly well."

"Mealy-mouthed answer, man. Have the guts to speak the truth to me."

"I fear causing offence. I am already so close to being thrown out…"

"What?"

"Sir, forgive me. I must go!" And with that, Sir Henry fled.

Sir Henry's refusal to speak, on top of the stress that Theodore was feeling about his daughter's situation, made him irritable and quite unable to face Mondial himself with any degree of civility. The Marquis appeared at the far end of the corridor and rather than continue on his way, he stopped and waited for Theodore to catch up. Theodore increased his pace, therefore, in an attempt to look as if he were in a hurry.

Mondial smiled politely. Now that Theodore was brimming with suspicions, he wanted to punch that smile clean off the other man's face. Mondial opened his mouth to speak and Theodore simply couldn't gather his wits fast enough. Unable to trust himself to be calm and decent, instead he simply pushed right past his host in total silence and stamped off on this way.

Mondial gasped.

Theodore didn't even turn around. And he cursed himself as he went. His irrational snub of Mondial would surely now have suggested to the Marquis that Theodore suspected him.

If Theodore really was close to the truth, then perhaps this would force Mondial's hand.

Perhaps Mondial would react.

Theodore was angry with himself in case he had now precipitated an over-reaction – but a part of him was icily determined to face whatever happened next. Perhaps bringing things to a head as soon as possible was the very best way forward. Force a reaction now – before the clever Marquis had time to conjure up yet another plot.

For he would have certainly learned from his past mistakes, and Theodore didn't think his daughter would be so lucky as to escape a catastrophe for a second time.

24

Adelia was dressing for dinner when word came that her eldest daughter Mary had arrived with her husband Cecil Parker-Grey. Adelia could barely contain her delight and even Theodore, who had been consumed by an introspective grumpiness, finally raised a smile. Smith made the finishing touches to her hair, fixing a pin of glittering jewels into place. As soon as she could free herself from her servant's clutches, she hurried through the upstairs corridors to the rooms that had been assigned to Mary and Cecil. Theodore was at her side.

Mary was in a complete flap. She was in a sideroom, attended to by her constant companion, lady's maid and nurse all wrapped up in one capable package, the indomitable figure of Sophia Cobbett. Cecil, who was considerably older than his wife, was already dressed for dinner and rose from his armchair to greet his parents-in-law with warmth. Adelia could not see Mary but they conversed through the door while Cobbett performed the same duties for the daughter that Smith had been doing for the mother a few moments earlier.

"Do tell Cecil he's the most monstrous worry-wort and I

shouldn't have missed this party for the world!" Mary warbled through the door.

Cecil shrugged. Theodore leaned in and whispered, "Is she unwell?"

Cecil shook his head but shot a glance towards the door, and Mary called out, "I know you're whispering about me because it's all gone quiet!"

When she finally emerged, Adelia was relieved to see that Mary looked relatively healthy. She was not too pale and there was a decent amount of flesh on her bones. Adelia wanted to embrace Mary but they were both too finely dressed and anyway, they were very nearly late for dinner.

"How is Dido?" Mary asked with concern as they made their way downstairs. Other guests were appearing from doors and corridors and the castle was alive with bustle.

"She is well – though we ought not to speak of the more eventful things that have been happening, at least, not tonight," Adelia said. They had just reached the top of the main staircase when she spotted the very object of their conversation further along the corridor. "But there she is now!"

Mary squealed, "Dido!" and rushed along the passage, breaking free of her husband's arms. Dido turned and her face broke into a wide smile as soon as she saw her sister. She was just opening a door that led to another staircase, and the two boys were at the top.

"Mary! You made it. I am so pleased. I was just about to say goodnight to the boys."

"Oh, may I come with you?"

Adelia felt Theodore lightly touch her hand and she glanced

towards him. She knew what he was thinking. Mary had not had children and was unlikely to do so but she adored them with her whole heart. Mary was just about to follow Dido up the smaller set of stairs when Lord Mondial appeared alongside Adelia and Theodore. He barked out, rather crossly, "My lady, our guests are waiting." He put out his arm and clearly expected Dido to rush to his side.

Mary turned and said, "Oh, my dear Lord Mondial! How lovely to see you! We shall be down directly – do indulge a doting aunt such as myself."

Any other man would have crumbled at the sight of her innocent face clouded by a pile of blonde hair. But Lord Mondial had his duties as a host and they came far above mere family matters. "With my deepest apologies, there is time for that later. My lady!" he said again, sternly. And this time, Dido did rush to his side, leaving a flurry of apologies in her wake, and the door was closed on her children. Dido and her husband descended the stairs. After a moment, they were followed by Adelia and Theodore. Mary and Cecil brought up the rear and were soon absorbed into the throng of other guests.

The loud, busy dinner party which took place that evening turned out to be a blessing in disguise. Intimate conversation was utterly impossible and everyone took care to be on their best behaviour, even Lady Montsalle. After all, the company of the Marquis was highly sought-after and no one wanted to anger him by referring to the "unfortunate incident that happened outside", at least, not too early in proceedings. In fact it almost became a competition in who could show the very highest breeding and good taste as they all tried to outdo one another in their politeness and restraint. Wine and brandy didn't exactly flow, though there was plenty of the very highest quality on offer. Mary added a high point of light, Adelia thought, though she knew she was biased. But she couldn't help the special place in her heart for Mary as her firstborn and as the one who had spent her childhood continually teetering on the edge of death.

Theodore stayed silent but it didn't matter too much as there were so many others present to pick up the conversation. He remained with the men after the ladies withdrew and then they all joined together once more, but after the barest minimum of time to be polite, he begged everyone's indulgence for an "old man" – to some hoots of laughter – and retired to bed. Mary and Cecil left, with Cecil fussing around his wife as usual. Dido remained up, staying until the last of the guests wished to go to bed, though they were looking to their hostess to give them a cue.

Adelia accompanied Theodore, glad of the excuse to flee the gathering.

She looked at him anxiously but could see that he was in no mood for speaking. What was there left to say, anyway? And Adelia herself was disinclined to chatter. They withdrew to bed in silence.

Theodore rose earlier than most of the rest of the household and guests the next day. He already felt exhausted by the social whirl and the real party had not yet begun. He felt the urge to get out and clear his head. Mondial had offered Theodore the use of a splendid hunter for the duration of his visit. So far Theodore had been content merely to admire the muscular, prancing stallion, recognising that Mondial had chosen this particular horse to demonstrate what fine animals he had in his stables. It was not the most suitable mount for a desk-bound bookish man past his prime, like Theodore.

But it was exactly the right sort of horse for a man fizzing with frustration and foul temper.

A perky stable-boy jumped briskly to the task of tacking the hunter up and offered to warm him up with some gentle walking but Theodore was itching to get away. He just wanted to be on his own and have some space to think. Properly on his own, not surrounded by servants lingering in corners. So he ordered the boy to lead the horse to a mounting block and swung himself up into the saddle. He adjusted the stirrups, ignored the early protests of his inner thighs and took up the reins, urging the horse out of the courtyard and along the gravel drive. He needed to leave Mondial Castle behind, just for a while.

He started out sensibly and sedately, just a walk that kept bursting into bouts of trotting. But the horse was lively and wanted to test out this new rider it found upon its back and soon Theodore found that he was barely clinging on, fighting to keep the horse down to a rocking canter. He was dragged down lanes and bridleways that were totally unfamiliar to him and he had to trust to the animal that it knew where they were going. It left no space in Theodore's head for anything else. He used every ounce of his concentration to stay on the horse but he was fairly sure it was the stallion who was calling the shots.

It was over an hour later when he finally managed to persuade the stallion to bring him home. Even after such a long time out, the horse trotted into the yard with a high and prancing step, tossing its head in satisfaction. Both Theodore and the horse were soaked in sweat, not helped by the oppressive atmosphere. The sky was leaden grey with low clouds, an inauspicious start to the day of the garden party.

The stable-boy rushed out to take the reins when he heard them enter, and this let Theodore slither to the ground. He managed to keep upright and dignified until he was out of sight around a corner. Usually Theodore would have taken care of the horse himself, rubbing him down and sorting out the tack although he generally stopped short of cleaning the saddle and bridle himself. This time, however, he was content to leave it to the servants. He just needed to lean against a wall and wait for his legs to stop wobbling.

He guessed that he would have missed breakfast by now so once he was able to walk again, he entered the house by the main doors but went along the ground floor towards the kitchens. A maid waylaid him before he could encroach upon their domain too far, and told him she'd be happy to bring him a selection of breakfast foods into a smaller dining room or his own suite. He refused and requested only bread and ham to be handed over where he stood, as he knew they were all busy with the preparations for that day's party.

"Oh don't worry, my lord. We're used to this sort of thing," she said. She smiled prettily and was just dropping a curtsey when her face froze and she whirled off to the kitchens, saying in a stiffer voice, "I'll see to it directly, my lord."

Tobias Taylor approached from behind Theodore.

Something snapped in Theodore. He couldn't explain it. It wasn't just the knowledge of the part Taylor had played in recent events, but it was also the reaction of the maid when she saw the valet. It told Theodore so much. Before he could muster his rational sense, he had grabbed Taylor by the lapels of his liveried jacket and slammed him against the wall.

"I say!" Taylor gasped out as Theodore laid his forearm along his throat and pressed down hard. The valet was a little taller than Theodore but the older man had weight, experience and righteous fury on his side. All of this temporarily overrode the trembling in his exhausted muscles.

"You!" Theodore snarled. "What did you do? I know you did something – you had some part in the murder – that poor girl! I ask you again, what did you do?"

Taylor couldn't answer. He was choking and going red. In exasperation – partly at himself, as it seemed he couldn't even get intimidation right – Theodore let go and Taylor sprang away, clutching at his bruised neck.

"My lord shall hear of this!"

Theodore wanted to say, "Good, and tell him I'll do the same to him, too!" But sense finally prevailed. He could not risk being ejected from the house at this late stage and already he was suffused with regret. He managed to make a stiff apology, saying, "I am so very sorry. That was inexcusable. I have no defence except that I have been so very overwrought lately. Please, I most humbly beg your forgiveness."

Taylor stared at him like he didn't believe a word of it, and Theodore didn't blame him because he certainly didn't mean it. The valet strode away and the maid, who must have been hiding and listening, popped up with his makeshift breakfast.

She had filled a basket of goodies for him. "Oh, do please take it and enjoy it, my lord." She looked as if she wanted to say something else but she restrained herself, held in a small smile, and tripped away.

He took the food up to the suite and prepared to face the day.

Today was the day he'd bring Lord Mondial to justice.

25

Adelia looked strained, Theodore thought. She was looking around the room and then out at the garden, all the while tapping her fingers against her dress.

"You mustn't worry," he told her as they lingered in their suite during the dead hours before the garden party was to begin. "I promise you that I shall bring them all to justice."

She turned from the window and blinked at him in surprise and confusion. "It's not that. Well, that is part of it all, of course. But I thought that Mary looked well until I looked more closely and realised she was wearing an inordinate amount of powder and rouge, though carefully applied to make herself look as if she were perfectly healthy. And I was thinking about Lord Mondial and our Dido. And I was thinking about this afternoon's party and whether everything is ready and where the band is going to be and if Lady Montsalle will keep her opinions to herself. And also, I am sure that it's going to rain. Don't you think?"

"We could do with the atmosphere to break and freshen things up."

"Perhaps, but it needs to wait until tomorrow. Did you think that Mary looked ill?"

"No, I thought she looked very well."

Adelia made a non-committal noise and continued to stare out of the window. Someone tapped at the door and Theodore called out for them to enter. Smith poked her head inside.

"No, thank you; we're all ready," Adelia said over her shoulder.

"Begging your pardon, my lady; but there's a gentleman downstairs who's asking to see my lord." Smith handed over a card.

Theodore glanced at the name and felt a strange dropping sensation in the pit of his stomach. Suddenly he was a small boy again, nervous and unsure of the world.

"What is it?" Adelia asked.

"I must go down. It's – he has come at last. I mean – it's Doctor Hardy."

He barely heard his wife's reply. His vision had narrowed to a point. He followed Smith down the stairs and he was glad of her confident step because he wasn't sure, in his suddenly overwrought state, that he could have found his own way down. She steered him through the bustling great hall and into a side room set out for receiving any last-minute arrivals.

And there he was.

He was old, so much older than even Theodore had imagined he might be. He was sitting in a straight-backed chair with his hands on his cane and a solemn-faced male attendant stood behind his shoulder, glaring at Theodore in case he offered any threat to his master. Theodore said, "Sir! Doctor Hardy! Please don't get up..." and then he felt foolish for the old man

246

was making no move to do so anyway.

Doctor Hardy smiled broadly and his face instantly became the one that had etched itself into Theodore's memory since his childhood.

He was gazing upon the face of his hero once more.

"My lord," the doctor said, his smile fading. "We meet at last under the most terrible of circumstances. You were there at my dear Philippa's passing…"

Theodore went to the doctor's side. He wanted to pour out his heart to the old man, tell him of his own struggles to become a doctor, tell him of the influence that he had had on Theodore's whole life.

But Adelia seemed to be with him, in his head, and she was saying – very firmly – *no. This is not about you. He is here for his granddaughter and don't you dare divert him.*

Theodore realised that his soul's unburdening could and would have to wait. He said, "Yes, sir, I was there…"

"Tell me everything."

"Are you sure?"

"I am old and ill and not long for this world. My heart weakens with each passing day. Let me go to my grave with nothing but truth."

Theodore nodded. "Very well." And, still kneeling on the floor as if his own aging knees were not complaining, he told Doctor Hardy everything, including his investigations, his suspicions, and his plans for justice. He summed it up as succinctly as he could, not wishing to tax the old man.

His legs had almost seized up. As he got to the end of his recount, Doctor Hardy sunk into silence as he took it all in, and

Theodore got awkwardly to his feet. The attendant had to put out his hand to steady Theodore and he nodded with gratitude. He stretched and said, "Sir, do you stay here tonight?"

"Oh, goodness me, no, I understand there is to be something of a party tonight and I have not been invited. Nor do I wish for an invitation. I have engaged a room in the local town and tomorrow I will return home. I wished only to see the place where she … and speak to you, and thank you for your solicitations. You took such care of her while I was away during her youth and I never did make the time to thank you in person. It is a dreadful business, dreadful, but we do what we can and the rest is in the Lord's hands."

"Sir, might I accompany you to your lodgings?" Theodore asked as the attendant helped Doctor Hardy to his feet. He felt a dragging reluctance to let the man go. There was still so much that Theodore wanted to tell him; it burned a hole in him, this flame which had been fanned up again from a smoulder of many long years.

"Of course, that would be –"

But Doctor Hardy did not finish his sentence. The door burst open and Smith was there, but this time her usually placid and benign face was stretched, and her skin was pale.

"My lord – come at once. It is Mary!"

Theodore ran to the door and stopped and turned to face Doctor Hardy.

The old man rested on his cane, his attendant holding his master's elbow.

"My daughter," said Theodore. "But…"

"Go to her," Doctor Hardy said. "You know what's

important; you should have learned that by now. Show me that you have."

Theodore gulped, nodded, and raced off after Smith once more.

Adelia was already there, of course. She looked up as Theodore entered the room. Cecil was hovering alongside the couch where Mary was lying, her skin clammy and her lips blue. She said, "Oh, I am gathering quite the audience!" in a voice that was faint and slow, punctuated by too many breaths.

"You have overtaxed your heart," Theodore said at once.

"Well, all of you crowding in won't help," she managed to reply with archness even in her weakened state. "I only need to rest; you know nothing else will do."

Cecil nodded. "She had fainted but she is much revived now. I am sorry to have alarmed you all. As she says, all she needs now is a little rest."

Theodore took her pulse. It was slow and weak, but it was regular. Adelia twisted her fingers together and he knew she was remembering all the illnesses and attacks that Mary had suffered throughout her whole life.

"This has happened before, of course," Theodore said. "And you have never died before so I doubt you will this time."

Mary started to laugh, and after a pause, so did Adelia.

Adelia said, "I have never been so happy to hear your blunt bedside manner before."

"You see?" he replied, almost crossly. "The patient always deserves the truth."

He still had hold of Mary's hand. She squeezed it. "Go and enjoy the party – is it not about to start?" He glanced at Adelia, who nodded.

Cecil said, "I shall stay with her and we shall be most content."

"Call me at any sign, however small, of a change."

Cecil assured Theodore that he would. Adelia left, saying there was something important to do involving artichokes, and Theodore followed.

When he got back to the receiving room downstairs, it was empty.

26

And then more disaster struck.

It was now two in the afternoon and all the guests had arrived. Theodore hadn't seen Adelia since leaving Mary's rooms, either. She was busy with helping Dido attend to the last-minute preparations for the event. However efficient and experienced the household staff were, there were still always a slew of late disasters to deal with.

People began to mill around the gardens, admiring the roses, gathering in the large marquee to listen to a string quartet, and already the champagne was flowing.

And by half past two, torrential rain had forced everyone out of the garden and into the great hall as even the marquee could not cope in the heavy downpour.

The guests wandered around in confused chaos but the staff, who had prepared for all eventualities, calmly worked like a well-trained army to bring the food and drink inside. Musicians dashed past trying to hold their precious instruments under their clothes, preferring to risk indecency than allow the wood to get wet. Theodore stayed out of the way as his offers of help had been refused. He caught snatches of conversation as the throng ebbed and flowed around him.

"…dress was quite transparent in the rain, most shocking! Did you see her?"

"…thought that he looked rather ill, if I'm honest; Geneva cannot have suited him at all…"

"…into Mondial's wine cellar, wouldn't you?"

And then came the snippets of gossip about the more serious matter.

"Yes, the pair of them, both shot at close range, but just what were they doing together in the garden, that's what enquiring minds want to know."

"Surely you're not suggesting…?

"Of course not! He is always above reproach. That girl, however, well, she should have been married a long time ago. Don't you find it strange that she was still unwed?"

Theodore bristled at the insinuations being thrown at the memory of poor Philippa Lamb. But of course no such scandal would attach to Lord Mondial. It was easier to slander a woman, and one who could no longer defend herself was even easier.

It was time for him to act. He scanned the room, aware that he was rudely ignoring the overtures towards initiating a conversation that other people were making towards him. After a brief hunt through the open reception rooms of the main part of the castle, he finally spotted Judge Anderson standing by a window, alongside another man. Both were looking out at the rain. This room was a small and unremarkable receiving room, generally unused in day to day life. There was a smell in the air of dust and wet wool. A few other people were gathered in small knots around the room, including a pair of ladies who had taken over a long couch by a screen and whose heads were bent together in deep conversation. There were three sets of double doors opening into the room and all were flung open to allow the free movement of the guests.

Theodore had been introduced to the judge on a few previous occasions and they knew one another well enough to nod if they passed in the corridors of a club. Theodore wasn't sure enough of the man's character, however, to be able to guess how he was going to predict when he was rudely interrupted. And how close were Mondial and the judge, exactly? If Mondial were to be believed, they were in one another's pockets.

But it was not wise to trust to what Mondial claimed was the truth.

Theodore realised that he was stalling by sinking into reflection. He shook himself and surged towards the pair before he could convince himself not to.

Judge Anderson turned and greeted him with a brief smile. He was not, generally, a jovial character. He was tall and broad, as well built as a village blacksmith, and though he was older than Theodore he looked as capable as a man of twenty. He would not have let a headstrong stallion pick his own route for a ride, Theodore thought. And that gave him hope that the judge was unlikely to be unduly influenced by Mondial, whatever the Marquis might believe.

The other man was introduced as a local landowner, someone of the minor gentry. He seemed perfectly respectable and soon melted away when he realised that Theodore needed to speak to the judge.

"Sir," said Theodore urgently. "I shall not prevaricate or beat about the bush. I need to outline a most serious crime which has occurred here. I am going to make some shocking allegations and I beg your indulgence for just ten minutes. Please will you listen?"

Judge Anderson's deep black brows drew down in a frown, making him look even more like a pugilist about to enter the ring. "Is this to do with the attack that occurred in these grounds?"

"It is, sir. I have a great deal of actual evidence, not just eyewitness accounts and speculation, to demonstrate beyond reasonable doubt that the murder was planned from within this very house – although the intended victim was never Miss Lamb."

Judge Anderson did not comment or make any other facial expression except displeasure. Theodore could not read what that expression might have meant. So he ploughed on with his recount, regardless.

"Sir, is the county commissioner of the police here this afternoon? I intend to lay it all out before you both and my information must then be acted upon immediately."

"As to any action, that will be for us to decide. But yes, Sir Michael Tennyson is here. Are you absolutely convinced we must listen to this now? You are welcome to call upon me in my lodgings at any convenient date as I would rather attend to professional matters in a professional space; I am here to enjoy myself."

That was untrue, Theodore thought. Everyone knew that professional matters, business deals and important political information was dealt with at social occasions just like this one. So he said, "I could come tomorrow. But I should prefer to strike this very instant, as this may be our best chance of apprehending the guilty party or parties and to that particular end, it is helpful that Sir Michael is here. If he might be summoned?"

Within five minutes, all three men were at the window watching the rain sheet down against the glass. Sir Michael was a grey and pale sort of man, with a receding head of thin white hair and drooping jowls. He looked unimpressed to have to listen to Theodore, but he was also polite and mindful of Theodore's status. Sir Michael had been raised to the knighthood only recently, and was pleasantly deferential.

Theodore decided to start with the most shocking part of the whole affair, to get their attention fixed upon him.

"Lord Mondial arranged for his valet, Tobias Taylor, to shoot his wife and for himself to be injured, making it look like a chance robbery."

Judge Anderson blurted out a laugh that he changed instantly to a cough, and Sir Michael merely twitched his cheeks.

Theodore had not expected mirth as a possible reaction but he ploughed on. "Tobias Taylor was seen coming from the stable area after the incident by a respectable man and various servants, but he lied about that and claimed to have been inside the whole time. Clothes that fit the man exactly were found burned in the gardens."

"He sounds like a potential suspect on that bare information, yes, but how do you account for Lord Mondial's alleged involvement?" Judge Anderson asked. "Not to mention that it was not his wife who was shot."

"Yes, how dare you!" came the thundering and unexpected cry of Mondial himself. He burst into the room and now everyone was looking their way. He must have been in the adjoining room and had heard everything. Theodore felt this was to his own advantage. Surely he would not be able to lie in front of the judge and the county commissioner of police?

Theodore pointed at Mondial and held his nerve. "Your wife is the very best of women – I know this for she is, of course, my own daughter – but she disappoints you, does she not? She is, in your erroneous opinion, too concerned with your children and no longer young enough, pretty enough or social enough to deserve a place on your arm."

Many of the women listening to this speech gasped and nudged one another. Someone nodded.

Theodore went on. "But in your strange and twisted logic, you knew you could not bring shame to her or to your own reputation by taking a mistress, nor could you cast her aside into an asylum which many a husband in your position has done before you."

There were murmurings of agreement and a few names were whispered among the listeners. Everyone knew of at least one troublesome woman who had suffered the fate of receiving a diagnosis of "madness" or "hysteria" and been sent away "for her own good", leaving the husband free to do as he pleased.

"Only one course of action seemed to lie open to you. You decided that you had to have her shot, indeed killed, and then you could elevate her memory, seem to be an object of pity, and have your pick of women to serve as the next Marquess of Mondial Castle. In fact you had already chosen Miss Lamb though she rejected you, did she not?"

"Are you suggesting that I had Miss Lamb shot for some

imagined refusal?"

"No. Even you would not sink so low. She was not your target; your wife was." Theodore tried to keep the impatience out of his voice. Had he not already said as much? "I am suggesting, however, that your plan misfired when you put it into practice. You told Taylor to find you and your wife in the gardens that afternoon, to shoot her, and to injure yourself. You came to the room where my own wife was seated with yours, and insisted that she accompany you into the garden. Little did she know she was walking into a trap!"

"But she did not come," Mondial spat out.

"She did not. She returned to the house to see to the children and instead you encountered Miss Lamb, quite by accident. Before you could do anything, Taylor had kept to his part of the plan and shot you both – her fatally and you only lightly. No wonder you were distraught. Your distress at Miss Lamb's death was genuine and your remorse at that moment was great."

"This is utterly preposterous."

"You refused police involvement, instead agreeing to allow an untried man – myself – to look into the crime, insisting on staying close to me in case I discovered anything."

"If I had been guilty, why would I have allowed you to investigate at all?"

"Because you thought me a fool, incapable of revealing the truth."

"You are a fool and there is not a scrap of truth in it! Except – perhaps…"

The room fell silent. Everyone seemed to be holding their

257

breath.

Mondial had been backed into a corner. But he had one way out and he took it. "Bring Tobias Taylor here immediately!" he yelled.

Theodore was expecting Mondial to interrogate Taylor and use him to prove his innocence. Everyone was now trying to press their way into the reception room. He caught sight of Adelia and he was heartened to see his mother alongside her. He also saw Dido, and wished that he had not. The truth was going to destroy her and he longed to spare her. But it was not possible.

Taylor walked into the room wearing his finest official livery and came to a halt before Theodore and the judge. He smiled ever so slightly in a smug way and Theodore began to say, "We cannot trust a word this man says."

He was cut off by Mondial. "Indeed, we cannot!"

That took the wind out of Theodore's sails and he closed his mouth.

Mondial took a moment to let the shocked murmurs die down before continuing. As he spoke, every word made Taylor's jaw drop a fraction further open. "This man has been my trusted valet for ten years, maybe more. In that time he has lied, cheated, stolen and gambled. He has tried my patience in every sense. I have, of course, done my Christian duty by not only forgiving him his transgressions each time, but I have sought at every opportunity to encourage him to reform. He is a dissolute womanizer – ask any female member of the household staff. He recently fled this place taking money he had stolen from my own rooms. I, fool that I am, covered for him once again by saying that I had sent him away on business but certain people were astute enough to not be fooled by that. Yes, I lied, but only to give my valet yet another chance. He returned as soon as he had gambled it all away."

Theodore was shaking his head but every sentence was entirely plausible.

Mondial barely paused for breath. "But these allegations are the final straw. Do I believe that my own valet could have committed such a monstrous act? I do not *want* to believe it. I am, perhaps, too inclined to see the best in people. I am notoriously kind-hearted. You, Calaway, for example, though you are spouting forth some of the most vile accusations about me and my wife, yet I do not rise to your provocation. I am mindful of the recent stresses that you have been under. You speak out of concern and care for your daughter and surely the potential lawsuits which currently plague you must be affecting your mind; and this causes me to be more generous in my opinion of you."

Theodore wanted to smack those weasel words right out of Mondial's mouth. How dare he allude to the lawsuits! He began to speak but someone was at his side, jabbing a sharp elbow into him. It was his mother, the Dowager Countess.

Mondial smiled slightly. He knew that he was winning with the force of public opinion easily on his side. He said, "And of course I recognise that I owe you a particular debt of gratitude in bringing this vile miscreant to justice and for that I thank you."

He nodded at Taylor, who began to yell.

In between foul language and words that made the ladies pale and the gentleman urge restraint, Taylor shouted, "You liar! You lying...! It was you, it was all you..."

Mondial waved his right arm vaguely towards Theodore. "Are you saying I shot myself? Calaway here will certainly vouch for the injuries that I sustained. He did a fine job in patching me up, in fact."

Once again, Mondial looked like a magnanimous and forgiving sort of man while Theodore simply felt foolish. He tried to argue his point, saying, "You must have known it was Taylor all along. You simply could not have failed to miss your own valet standing so close in front of you!"

"He was at such a great distance, and I was injured and of course tending to the poor *dead* girl in my very arms..."

Ripples of sympathy rose for the heroic figure of Mondial. Theodore clenched his fists and tried again. "He was close enough to take your watch!"

Mondial dipped his hand into his pocket. "He took no such thing."

"But ..."

"You were almost as overwrought in the terrible situation as I was. It is natural you might misremember things."

While Mondial and Theodore had been sparring, Taylor was obviously taking the chance to work his way towards the nearest doors. A woman screamed, and suddenly all was pandemonium as the valet sprang free of the crowd and sprinted off through the rooms. A man cried, "The hunt is up!" and it triggered a great and unseemly pursuit of the errant valet though many of them skidded to a halt at the front door and looked out dolefully at the rain.

Theodore remained where he was.

He felt utterly beaten.

27

Adelia was one of the crowd who had run after Taylor through the great hall, though quite what she hoped to achieve with such unwomanly behaviour didn't even cross her mind. She stopped with most of the others at the main doors as a handful of men bravely dashed out into the pouring rain. She wondered how strong and fit Taylor was. He lived his life behind closed doors and some of the pursuing men were able sportsmen.

She turned and went instead in search of Dido, her heart breaking for the terrible situation her daughter now found herself in. She would be the object of so much speculation and gossip. But they'd known that it would happen when they made their accusations to the judge; and it was better than leaving her at the hands of a man who wanted to kill her.

Except that the planned exposure of Lord Mondial had not worked and it now appeared he was going to get away with everything by simply throwing his valet to the wolves and washing his hands of the whole affair.

Adelia loved Theodore deeply but she couldn't feeling just a tinge of frustration that he had not been as clever in expressing himself as Lord Mondial had been. He hadn't quite managed to put his case forward convincingly. She wished she could have spoken out on his behalf but that would have undermined his position and anyway, who would have listened to her when there was Lady Montsalle around to remind everyone of Adelia's background? But then, Theodore had so much occupying his mind at the moment – Mary's sudden illness didn't help matters.

Various people reached out to her as she passed and she ignored them all, even Lady Montsalle who was not used to being snubbed. She just caught the woman's loud tut before she spotted her daughter being led towards the stairs by the reliable Dowager Countess and the indomitable Harriet Hobson. Adelia skipped forwards to catch them up but as she reached them, a hubbub at the doors behind her made her stop and turn around.

Sir Henry Locksley, with his hair plastered to his face, breathing heavily, was dragging the screaming, kicking Taylor into the hall. She only caught the briefest glimpse of him before they were swallowed from view by a surge of people around them.

It was a job for the men now. The judge and the county commissioner of police would do what they needed to do. She hoped Theodore was going to be all right but at this moment, her place was at her daughter's side and she went on up the stairs to find her.

Dido was not gripped by paroxysms of grief. She was not wailing or crying. At first, Adelia assumed that her daughter must

264

have received a massive dose of laudanum but it would not have worked so quickly.

No. The truth was that Dido was showing her mettle and strength in the face of adversity. Adelia looked upon her straight-backed daughter with pride.

"You are so like your father!" she burst out as she closed the door of the private upstairs day room behind her. "Life may offer you blows and you may be knocked down but you will survive – no, indeed, you will rise!"

Dido didn't smile but she met her mother's eyes. "I try to take after you, dear mama. Can't you see that? Oh, what a dreadful mess we are in. But there is one glimmer of happiness in all of this; Mary's woman, Cobbett, has just sent word that Mary has eaten a light meal and is reading, just like her old self once more. As to everything else, however ..." She dropped her gaze and sighed.

Harriet positioned herself by the door that Adelia had just entered through as if she were on guard and ready to repel all intruders. Adelia went directly to Dido's side and sat down. The Dowager Countess had taken the most comfortable armchair which was in the bay window, not that there was any kind of view of the grounds to be had through the sheeting rain that clouded the glass.

There was just the barest hint of a wobble in Dido's voice as she asked, "So, what happens now?"

"I don't know," Adelia said. "But I am sure your father will sort everything out."

Grace snorted from her perch in the window. "As my son, I love him dearly. As a man – well, like the rest of them, he's going to need some help. Off you go, Adelia dear, and play your part as a dutiful wife. He might be the brains of the affair when it comes to science but he's not as rational as he likes to believe and it takes us womenfolk to help them navigate through the seas of emotions. He's in a storm now; go and pilot him out."

Perhaps it was the slowly-flooding garden that gave rise to Grace's sudden passion for nautical references. Adelia looked to Dido.

"My dear child, this is not my house and I don't want to overstep my mark…"

"Why not? Try it; it's fun, I find," said Grace.

Adelia ignored her, which was as overstepping as she felt she could get with the Dowager. "Dido, what do you wish me to do about the guests?"

"I don't know. Whatever you deem to be the best. I support any decisions you make. Do apologise to everyone on my behalf."

"Do not," put in Grace. "This is your house and you owe no apologies to a single soul."

Adelia wasn't comfortable with it but she had a duty to perform. She could see that Dido was in safe hands and in no immediate danger of throwing herself from the highest battlements of the castle in grief and shame. So Adelia took a deep breath and sailed out of the room, going back downstairs to take charge of the party that had been left in such disarray.

There was no sign of Judge Anderson, the chief of police,

Lord Mondial, Tobias Taylor, her husband or Sir Henry. It was immensely frustrating to Adelia to find herself sidelined from the investigation after having had such a role at the heart of the case. All the garden party guests were milling around in groups, gossiping and nudging one another when they saw Adelia. She went straight to the housekeeper and the butler who were, against all the odds, managing to keep their staff in order. This meant the guests were replete with all the food and drink that they expected to have. Without that, there were sure to have been mutterings and mutinies.

Adelia made some snap decisions. "The supper will go ahead as usual. Feed the military band in the servants' hall and give them some beer as they expect but ask them to leave; do not let them become too drunk to go. Retain only the string quartet who must play calm and gentle music this evening. It is to be a dignified and restrained affair with no dancing. Let it be known that we expect early hours to be kept by those staying overnight. Anyone with good breeding will understand why this is to be the case." She was speaking to the senior servants but loudly enough for anyone close by to hear. She knew her words would spread. No one would want to be painted as the disrespectful one. The servants nodded and agreed and set off on their tasks.

Thank goodness it was such a well-ordered and experienced household, Adelia thought once again. Honestly, Lord Mondial doesn't realise half of the efforts his wife goes to on his behalf. He thinks a wife is merely an ornament to boost one's status in society. But woe betide the man whose wife is nothing more than a sparkling object! She remembered one old Duke, twice

267

widowed, who had taken a fresh young thing while he was almost in his dotage. In three years flat he had ended up penniless and ruined and no one could say that she had done so deliberately or with malice; she was simply hopeless at everything except spending money and throwing parties.

Now it was Adelia's own turn to be capable and in control. She plastered on a polite smile and entered the fray, answering questions, greeting people, dealing with problems to do with the food or accommodation or where one might powder one's nose or make a hasty repair to a dress or sit for a moment in peace or a thousand and one other things. She had the very best of light food sent up to Mary and Cecil and received word back that they wer perfectly content. She kept one eye out for the reappearance of her husband.

But none of the men returned until supper was over.

Theodore came in, looking ready for a drink or three, as the conversation fell silent.

Taylor was not with them.

And nor was Lord Mondial.

Adelia herself was longing for nothing more than a bottle of wine to herself, a deep bath and a sleep that would last about twenty hours. By the time she was able to retire, it was nearly midnight. She had food sent up to Dido and Harriet in their room. Cecil also came down and joined in, saying that Mary had been well enough to sit with Dido and Harriet.

Grace came down to supper and hissed at anyone cross enough to mention either the murder or the public allegations and revelations from earlier in the evening. Adelia was grateful for her support. Her feet ached, her head thumped, and she was utterly exhausted with the worry and the management of things; and with the pressure of having to appear serene and calm, as if nothing bothered her at all.

She bid the last of the guests a goodnight. As the late night dancing had been cancelled, there was no need for a grand ball supper to take place after midnight, and by one in the morning, she was at last able to retire. When she slid into their suite, she found Theodore standing by the window, the curtains open, clutching a very large tumbler of spirits. His jacket was cast untidily on the back of a chair and his cummerbund was in disarray. He stared out into the night. He heard her come into the room but he didn't turn to face her. He just started speaking. Smith came out of her side room to assist Adelia with her hair but she was dismissed as soon as Adelia was at a point with her toilette that she could cope with the ties and buttons on her own.

Theodore was telling her about what had happened and he was not pleased at all.

"Mondial's fled," he said. "Gone. Disappeared. We were all focused on Taylor and Sir Henry Locksley, and when I looked around, the dashed cad had made a run for it. I said to Anderson, surely this above all else simply confirms the man's guilt?"

"I agree. I assume that men were sent out to fetch Lord Mondial back?"

"That's the thing!" Theodore said explosively. "Anderson simply replied that we have nothing to stick to him. All the evidence points nicely to the valet."

"Does the judge not believe that Lord Mondial was involved at all?"

"He does! I am riled beyond all measure, Adelia. Anderson as good as told me that he thinks Mondial is guilty. He even said to me that 'knowing the truth and applying justice can be two different things'. Can you believe that?"

"I can. Men of Mondial's class are often beyond justice."

"That is utterly reprehensible. Indefensible. Unspeakable. I am ashamed of my fellows."

"That's awfully noble of you, dear, but this is the reality. And try to see it this way: the man that pulled the trigger and killed Philippa Lamb has been caught and he will feel the full force of the law upon him."

"It is a consolation but a scant one," Theodore said. "I cannot bear the thought of this criminal Marquis walking free – and he is my own son-in-law! I feel sick at the thought. He was the driver behind all of Taylor's actions. It is on *his* head that all blame must ultimately lie."

Adelia agreed. She was in her nightgown by this point and feeling so tired she could have cried. And what of her, and all that she had done that evening to keep things running? And what of Dido?

But Theodore was fully wrapped up in his own misery, and she understood it, and anyway she was far too exhausted to instigate any kind of righteous argument. She poured herself a very large glass of wine and took it to bed.

28

In spite of her late night, Adelia rose early the next day. She'd only slept fitfully at best. Theodore muttered something unintelligible and rolled over, burrowing under the covers. Smith appeared, as if summoned by a servant's sixth sense, and set about helping Adelia to dress with the absolute minimum of fuss and noise, for which Adelia was very grateful.

"Has anything happened overnight that I ought to know about?" she asked Smith quietly once she was dressed and ready to meet the day.

"No, my lady. One young maid was found asleep in the scullery, under a stone bench, and was shaken so roughly by the cook that she burst into tears and could not be consoled. She was simply overtired. One guest, a certain Mr Hanratty, had far too much to drink, could not find his own room, and consequently tried to sleep at the foot of Lady Montsalle's own bed, which caused some hilarity. He was carried out by two men and dumped in a corridor. Lady Mondial and Lady Mary slept in the same chamber according to Cobbett but I have not heard if they are yet awake."

"Thank you. I hope they are still both sleeping."

"If you don't mind, my lady, I suspect you'll find Lady Mondial awake just as early as you. She was always an early riser and she has attended every morning to the children while we have been staying here."

Of course, thought Adelia; Smith knows everything. She thanked her servant and went off in search of her daughters.

The castle was quiet, but there was activity humming away in the background as the maids and footmen busied about their tasks. Many things had to be completed before the household was up, so that everything appeared to be perfect and clean, as if the hard work had been done by invisible hands – indeed, there was to be no suggestion of work ever having taken place at all.

There was a room on the first floor which had been designated as the family chapel though it was not in any way consecrated for the purpose. Here, she found Dido sitting with her children. The household prayers were not to take place for another hour or so. She smiled at Dido, trying to appear light and normal in front of the two boys.

"You are awfully early; getting a head start before everyone else comes in?" Adelia said, sitting down on a wooden chair.

"Mama says there are to be no prayers today on account of the party," the eldest boy told her with careful enunciation of his words, trying to sound educated. "She said that people would be *generally indisposed* which I think means tired, is that right?" He looked at his mother with anxious eyes.

"You're a good lad," Dido said vaguely without meeting his gaze. "Both of you are. Why don't you run back upstairs now? I wish to talk to grandmamma."

272

"You're sad," said the eldest, standing up with a studied confidence. "But we will take care of you."

That was the point that someone should have said, "No, that's your father's job." The silence swallowed up the unsaid sentence and the boys left.

"Please don't talk," Dido said once they were alone. "Let us just … be. Just for a moment. Let me pretend that I am a girl once more without a care or worry in her head."

Adelia took her hand and they sat in mutual contemplation until it was time for breakfast.

Dido presided over breakfast and this meant the guests were quiet, humble and did not fall into gossiping ways. The servants, though tired, had laid on the very best of spreads, still clearly determined to show the best that Mondial Castle could offer. Footmen scurried from the sideboard to the main table, ferrying mountains of freshly baked French rolls, Vienna rolls, muffins, crumpets, oatcakes and scones. There was the ubiquitous eggs and bacon, the eggs being offered boiled, poached and scrambled. Sausages were piled up, brown all the way around, neatly grilled to show no white line – the tell-tale evidence of an inattentive servant. Baked mushrooms were alongside cold meats such as tongue and ham, and with the bacon and sausages there was also curry of mutton. Endless piles of toast was brought up from the kitchens, and coffee flowed with tea and cocoa too. It was the perfect remedy for a previous night's overindulgence.

Theodore slipped in and sat near to Adelia who nodded, and she flicked her eyes to the door to alert him that Mary and Cecil were coming in. She saw him visibly relax as he studied his daughter closely.

Harriet Hobson came in late and sat at the far end. The Dowager Countess did not appear at all. After breakfast, Adelia went to Dido's side and together they bid their guests goodbye as they straggled out of the castle in pairs and groups, a long and drawn out event that took up the whole morning.

It was not until just before luncheon that Adelia was able to sit down in a quiet room with her daughters both at her side. Harriet appeared soon afterwards, saying that she had just seen the Dowager Countess and she was happily terrorising the gardeners. The four women seemed to settle by inches into the chairs, sighing and closing their eyes and taking a few moments to properly relax.

Adelia didn't want to break the silence. It seemed pointless to say to Dido, "How are you?" when the obvious answer was going to be "Devastated, scared and exhausted."

The uncomfortable peace was broken by a footman tapping on the door. He brought a note to Adelia.

"Oh," she said in surprise. "Who would write to me here? It must be from Mr Postlethwaite," she added, and looked at the envelope in dismay. She felt reluctant to open it and receive more bad news.

Harriet, ever unashamed in her blatant curiosity, shuffled over and said, "No, that is a woman's script."

"Who is it, mamma?" Mary said.

"Mary! Just because you are feeling better, does not mean

that you can poke into someone's private business," Dido scolded her as if she were the older sister.

While the two daughters bickered, Adelia picked the envelope open and glanced first at the name at the bottom. She twisted to show it to Harriet: *Jane Pegsworth*.

Harriet's eyes widened.

Adelia folded the letter back up and shoved it back into the envelope, and then she folded the envelope in half as well. A glance passed between Dido and Mary but neither of them asked anything further; no doubt they'd speculate about it later.

Adelia pursed her lips in annoyance.

As if she didn't have enough to deal with, but her sister-in-law could be as much of a plague as her brother Alfred was.

Theodore hadn't thought he could face breakfast but somehow, the fact that the room was full and everyone was making low conversation on polite topics actually helped. When everything else seemed to be terrible at least one could fall back on etiquette and social manners to steer one's way through the madness.

He desperately wanted to speak to Dido but she was engaged in her role as mistress of the house, though it was an uncertain role now, with Lord Mondial gone. He watched her in the great hall, with his wife alongside her, and felt both proud and sad for the pair of them.

And strangely helpless, too. He'd done what he could to

bring justice to the place, but he had ended up destroying his daughter's security and marriage. Yet what choice did he have?

Gloomily he descended the front steps where he encountered Sir Henry Locksley, on his way back inside. The dew stains halfway up his legs and the mud on his shoes told Theodore the younger man had been taking an early morning walk rather than attending breakfast. "Take care," Sir Henry said. "Everything is quite waterlogged today."

"Thank you. And thank you for ... everything."

Sir Henry looked at him in surprise. "Me? I have done nothing but make things worse. What is going to happen now?"

"Taylor will hang; Mondial has fled."

"No, I mean here. This place. Lady Mondial..."

Theodore looked at the earnest, worried young man. He had broad shoulders and an open expression, reminding Theodore of the old tales of knights dedicated in purity and chastity to the court of King Arthur. He grabbed Sir Henry's hand in an impulsive gesture. "She will need you now more than ever."

"But I cannot bear to compromise her, sir!"

"Then do not. I trust that you won't. But you can be there for her in the coming days and weeks. I beg you."

"I ...?"

Theodore let the man's hand drop and he continued on his way.

He wasn't sure if he was doing the right thing in the eyes of society.

But it was the right thing to do as a human being.

He thought only of Dido as he walked the gardens. He returned to the house just after luncheon had been served but she was not in the dining room with everyone else. Adelia nodded at him from the table. He was pleased to see Mary was there, but he refused the invitation to go in and dine. Instead he went upstairs to Dido's private rooms. He had not spoken to her, yet, of what had happened the previous evening, and though he knew she would have heard the news from others, he wanted to tell her himself.

A chambermaid opened the door and directed him, with barely concealed annoyance, to a private morning room along the corridor. Here he found Dido sitting by the window, wrapped up in a blanket of fine wool, crying gently while her lady's maid fussed around with tea things and toast, trying to tempt her mistress into eating. She retreated as Theodore entered and he ran to his daughter's side.

"You should not be alone! Let me call for someone. Would you like your mother? Or grandmamma?"

"Father – I've sent them away. I spent all morning with them all and they have been lovely but I needed to think. Sorry, sorry," she burbled. "I stayed strong in front of them but... now... I am so sorry."

"You have nothing to be sorry for."

"I don't mean to cry in front of you." She tried to dab away her tears. "I didn't cry before. I didn't cry last night. I didn't cry this morning. I must not cry now but I am so very, very tired;

forgive me. Leave me alone to be a mess."

"Nonsense. If you cannot be yourself here with me, who can you be yourself with?"

"I have never, ever cried in front of John, you know. Yet here I am crying for him. He's gone, hasn't he? He killed Philippa, or as good as did it. I've heard everything and I believe it. It … fits."

Theodore grabbed her hands. "Tobias Taylor did the deed itself and will hang for it. As for Mondial…" He choked on the man's name. "We'll find him."

"You won't. And I don't want you to. I could not bear to ever see him again. Let him go. He knows his name is in tatters. He will never come back. I expect he will go abroad and end his days in shame somewhere. I hope he has a very long life and suffers from constant fever and plague for every single day of it. Boils, everywhere."

The fierce threat seemed to lighten the mood in the strangest of ways. Theodore squeezed her hand in reassurance and began to say, "Unfortunately, most plagues kill rather quickly, so…"

And then he stopped.

It wasn't really what she wanted to hear, was it?

"I hear that in some foreign places, one can get a tick that burrows deep into one's flesh and lives there for years, causing unspeakable agonies," he said, instead.

"Oh, *good*," Dido replied and she squeezed his hand back. Then she said in a more weary voice, "But what will become of me and the children, now? We are quite alone and friendless. The shame will cling to us."

278

"I will see to it that your finances are managed fairly and I have no doubt that Judge Anderson will be an advocate for your case. As for shame – yes, there will be gossip, and you can use it as a way of weeding out the most unworthy people from your circle. Those that remain at your side will be your truest friends. And you *do* have them. I have just seen Sir Henry, you know. Locksley is the most steadfast man you can ask for."

She sighed. "Oh, Sir Henry. He is a saint. But I am married and will always be so, even it is to an absent cad."

"Sir Henry knows that. But he has eyes only for you and a more devoted – and chaste – ally you will never find. It could be enough. Trust him as a friend, at least."

She hung her head, and he hugged her tightly, and that was how Adelia found them, about ten minutes later.

29

"Isn't it interesting how at night, it's the blue and white flowers that come to the centre of one's attention?" Adelia said that evening as they walked in the upper grounds of Mondial Castle. There was a full moon hanging low in the sky, and light grey clouds were riding high in the sky, all small and wispy and looking perfectly fluffy. The ground was still sodden from the rain but the upper garden was well-laid out with paths of gravel which glowed pale in the moonlight. An owl hooted. A spray of lobelia seemed to be brighter than they had ever been during the day.

"That's due to the reflection of the moonlight," Theodore said. "You'll also find they are more aromatic to attract their preferred pollinators."

"I see." She didn't really need the explanation but it was nice to talk of something innocuous for a change.

The whole day had been a blur of activity for her. Things weren't over once the guests had departed. She had trusted the housekeeper to the supervision of the mammoth task of clearing up, and no doubt an awful lot of food and drink would have been pilfered by the servants but that was hardly the current priority.

Now, after a long day, they were walking in the peaceful moonlight and wondering about their own imminent departure from the castle.

"Where did you go this afternoon?" Adelia asked after a while. "I confess I was so busy I did not notice until someone said you had ridden into town."

"I went to call upon Doctor Hardy," he replied.

It was strange that he didn't add anything to the sentence.

"Had he already gone?"

"Yes," he said curtly. There was a thickness in his voice. She turned to look at him but he had angled his head away so that she could not see his face.

So Doctor Hardy was dead, then.

The strain of events on his already weakened heart must have been too much. She wanted to shower empty platitudes on her poor grieving husband: At least you got to see him at last; at least you've brought some kind of justice for his granddaughter. But she held her tongue.

He broke the silence. Speaking in a more normal voice, his jollity forced, he said, "When I got back there was a letter from Mr Postlethwaite."

"Oh?"

"Yes, and it's good news. Heaven knows, we're due something good. He has managed the lawsuit business most efficiently. It has been resolved."

"Oh, good. He is a marvel."

"He is."

"I have more news. While in town, I called in at the Judge's

282

Lodgings, though I was not able to persuade him to reconsider the matter of — the other matter. The trial won't be very long. The man will hang, of course."

"And yet … what of *him*? What will *he* do, then?" She meant Lord Mondial but didn't want to say his name.

Theodore seemed to understand. "I expect he will be booking a passage away from England as we speak."

"Good."

"I will try to find out where he goes. He will not have an easy life of it."

"He had better not. Can we send assassins after him? Probably not. I do feel that our Philippa is avenged to some extent — don't you?"

Theodore hesitated before saying, "I think I can learn to feel that, in time. I will grow used to it. It's hard to accept failure even in part, though."

"I know. You are doing well."

"Pat me on the head too, why don't you?" But he laughed as he said it, and she knew that he was not as insulted at her condescension as he would have her believe. Instead he pulled out a hip flask from an inside pocket, took a swig and then passed it to her.

She gulped down a large part of it and it burned. He had to wrestle it back from her. He said, after consideration, "I do feel proud of myself, you know."

"You should. You did something that no one else could have done, or would have done. You saw the connections and you didn't give up. You pursued truth and justice and you won."

"You, too," he said, nudging her with his elbow. "You saw

the things that I missed. I could not have done it without you. But look; once we have settled Dido and the boys and they have support around them, we must return to our own house. My mother is going to stay here for as long as Dido needs her."

"Dido's written to her sisters, too. I imagine they will organise a rota of people to come and stay with her. Mary and Cecil will need to go home soon but someone else will take their place."

"That's excellent. We have raised an enviable brood of good women, haven't we?"

"We have!" Adelia thought about Lord Mondial and his utter disregard for his own offspring. It was hard to understand his attitude.

"But," Theodore went on, taking another sip, "let us allow them to get on with things. We have our own matters to attend to."

"Yes. About that," Adelia said cautiously. "When we return…"

"There will be no more doctoring," he said firmly. "Mr Postlethwaite was somewhat forceful in his letter. I admit he was rather more adamant than I expected. I suspect he had had to make promises that *I* am the one to make good on."

Relief flooded through her. But there was still a concern in the back of her mind. "I am glad to hear it. However, without the surgery to occupy you, you will be bored."

"I *long* to be bored. This past month has contained quite enough excitement for me."

She took the flask and had another huge gulp. "You cannot bear to be bored. You have thrived here, Theodore. Remember

284

the chase. The use of your logic. The pursuit of justice. Think…"

"You want me to pursue – that man? I cannot be the assassin that you want."

"No. We can't go gadding overseas and we certainly can't become assassins even though I should like to try it – just for *him*. But there are always injustices here around us, and people of our class don't like the police to be involved…"

"Preposterous, Adelia. Listen to yourself."

She passed him the flask. "Have another drink."

He did. "No, it's still a ridiculous idea."

"And yet …?"

They walked on through the gardens. The owl hooted again. Finally Theodore relented. He stopped and took her hands.

"Very well. This is the brandy talking, of course. Once again you might be right, my dear, annoying, confounding, relentless wife – perhaps … perhaps we may seek just a little excitement. But we do this together."

She laughed.

She had never planned on letting him try to do it alone.

The End

Thank you for supporting an independent author! If you enjoyed this book, please do consider leaving a review.

If you really enjoyed this book - there are more to read! Check out my other books online.

Made in the USA
Coppell, TX
26 April 2020

22013539R00169